Bite the Dust

A Low Country Dog Walker Mystery
Book One

by

Jackie Layton

happy reading!
Jackie Layton

B

Bell Bridge Books

This is a work of fiction. Names, characters, places and incidents are either the products of the author's imagination or are used fictitiously. Any resemblance to actual persons (living or dead), events or locations is entirely coincidental.

Bell Bridge Books
PO BOX 300921
Memphis, TN 38130
Print ISBN: 978-1-61194-984-1

Bell Bridge Books is an Imprint of BelleBooks, Inc.

Copyright © 2020 by Jackie Layton

Published in the United States of America.

We at BelleBooks enjoy hearing from readers.
Visit our websites
BelleBooks.com
BellBridgeBooks.com
ImaJinnBooks.com

10 9 8 7 6 5 4 3 2 1

Cover design: Debra Dixon
Interior design: Hank Smith
Photo/Art credits:
Still life (manipulated) © Jm73 | Dreamstime.com
Card (manipulated) © Mmphotos2017 | Dreamstime.com
Bone (manipulated) © Bert Folsom | Dreamstime.com

:Ltaw:01:

Dedication

I dedicate this book to my husband, Tim. You're the love of my life. I'm honored to be your wife and blessed with the many ways you love and support me.

Chapter One

"WHAT'D YOU DO?" A deep tenor questioned me.

I stood over a dead body. Peter Roth's body, to be exact. "I didn't do anything." The stranger glared at me. His expression implied I was to blame for Peter's death. Of all the nerve. I was Peter's friend.

Peter's golden retriever puppy, Chubb, howled where he stood on the imported Persian rug between the dead body and me. Peter had been so excited the day the rug arrived and he often walked around it instead of on it to preserve the beauty. Now he lay dead on the carpet he treasured in the grand living room of his plantation home.

The stranger's eyes widened. "Well?" Then he crossed his arms over his sweaty sky-blue T-shirt, obscuring the words *I like my boat and maybe three people.*

My throat tightened, but I had to defend myself against his accusation. "I just got here. To walk the dog. I'm the dog walker." I pointed at Chubb, as if he could testify to my innocence.

"Why are you holding a paperweight? From here it looks like you might have knocked Peter out with that thing."

"No." I backed away from the body, shaking my head. "I didn't hit him."

The man pulled a cell phone out of the pocket of his athletic shorts. Not the super tiny shorts a lot of runners wore. Long enough to be decent. Short enough for me to notice his long, tanned, muscular legs.

He thumbed the phone's buttons. "Did you call the police?" Despite the harshness of the man's voice, his pale face proved he struggled with Peter's death.

"Not yet. I heard your footsteps and grabbed the paperweight off the coffee table to protect myself. Why are you here? How do I know you're not the killer?" I backed up a few more paces. In that attire, the guy had to be a runner. I probably couldn't outrun him. Maybe I could outwit him.

"We'll let the police sort it out. Maybe you'll get a softie who'll believe you."

"How can you accuse me? Peter is my friend." My eyes drifted down to the still body, and I held in a sob. Through the years I'd gotten used to stuffing down my emotions. Finding Peter's body challenged my ability to hold it together. I perspired, my legs shook, and my stomach churned. "Was my friend."

"You want me to believe you showed up to walk Chubb and found Peter lying on the floor?"

"Yes. It's the truth. I'd never hurt Peter." In one hand, I held an ace of hearts playing card I'd found on the kitchen floor moments before I'd entered the living room. The heavy glass paperweight weighed down the other hand. A colorful Baccarat to be specific. Peter had always been specific when I admired an antique he had displayed in his South Carolina plantation home. He admired beautiful things, and he was a collector. Paperweights were just one of the things he enjoyed. "I know this looks bad. Let me explain."

The man's eyes narrowed, his finger poised inches from his cell phone screen. "You've got sixty seconds before I call the police. What you say will affect what I tell them."

I slipped the slick playing card into the back pocket of my shorts. Telling the truth wouldn't take long. "Peter called me last night to say he had an early meeting in Atlanta this morning. Thursdays he usually works from home but something came up. He asked me to come check on Chubb a couple times today. When I got here, Chubb was barking nonstop. I entered the front door and walked through the foyer and breakfast room straight back to the kitchen. I never entered this room. Chubb's a puppy, and I thought maybe he needed to go out in a hurry. I opened the door to his crate, and he ran in here. All I've done is feel Peter's body for a pulse. His wrist and his neck. There's not one. His body is cold and clammy." The way I rattled on probably made me look guilty. I shivered. Talking too much when nervous was one of my bad habits. "Why are you here?"

His expression tight, he propped his hands on his hips. "I heard a scream while on my morning run along the river. When I got here, the front door was wide open. I came inside and found you standing over Peter with a weapon."

"I don't remember leaving the door open, and I'm not holding a weapon." I looked down at the paperweight in my hand. If this man thought I killed Peter, the sheriff might jump to the same conclusion. Then another thought occurred to me. "Wait, who are you?"

"A neighbor. My land borders Peter's property line to the north.

We've got to report this." He dialed.

I knelt beside Chubb and rubbed his back. Poor thing.

"This is Marc Williams."

I jerked at the sound of his voice, but mystery man's name was no longer a secret. Marc Williams stood a few inches over six feet, judging by the way I tipped my head to see him. I was five foot eight and didn't strain to look up at many people.

Marc paced around the room, never getting too close to the body. "I need to report a death. Possible murder. At Peter Roth's home on River Road."

My legs refused to hold me any longer. I shuffled away and collapsed onto the jacquard wingback chair. Louis XVI in a "muted celadon," according to Peter. Pain pounded through my head. Never again would Peter share his love of antiques with me. I used to stifle yawns at his lengthy descriptions, but now. . . . I'd give anything to have those conversations back. I'd lost too many loved ones in my life.

I'd spent twelve years raising my siblings. When I was eighteen, my parents were killed by a hit-and-run driver in a white sports car. Mom and I had been making plans for my dorm room the week of the accident. Afterward, it was only the three of us kids. No grandparents. Nobody to jump in and offer assistance. The first time I heard the words Social Services, I'd known what I had to do. There really wasn't another choice. I shelved my plans to attend the University of Georgia and remained in Heyward Beach, South Carolina. Then I met Peter. He'd been new to the area at the time. For some inexplicable reason, he'd looked out for me, acted as my mentor and life coach. He never flat-out gave me money, but he'd advised me on finances and encouraged me. Peter had shown extraordinary kindness to a lost young woman when there'd been no reason for him to reach out.

Marc paced from the doorway to the window overlooking the vast front yard. "I'd say we need an ambulance. No, the coroner. And the sheriff." The man spoke to the emergency dispatcher with authority as if used to giving orders and expecting them to be obeyed.

I released the paperweight, and it dropped onto the soft chair. I leaned forward and held out a dog treat to the puppy. A good dog walker always carried some kind of treats, and I was good. "Come here, Chubb."

The puppy raised his head and looked at me. The pain in his brown eyes about broke my heart.

"It's okay, boy. You're safe."

Chubb's ears flopped back before he stood and plodded toward me. His nails clicked on the old pine floor until he stopped and sniffed my hand before biting into the dog bone.

"Good, boy." I rubbed his dark golden sides as he munched on the treat appropriate for forty-pound puppies. "I know how you feel. It's hard to believe somebody would hurt Peter." The puppy whined, and I slid down to the floor so I could wrap my arms around him.

Marc walked our way. "Maybe we should move to the kitchen. Less chance of contaminating the crime scene in there."

I gasped. This was Peter's living room. Not a crime scene. However, my friend's dead body made Marc Williams's words true. This *was* a crime scene. Peter was the murder victim, and it looked like I might be the number one suspect.

My legs barely held me as I stumbled through the foyer and break-fast room on my way to the kitchen. I sat on the first barstool I came to. Chubb plodded to his crate and collapsed onto the soft blankets with a heavy sigh.

Marc opened the refrigerator door and pulled out a can of Coke. He dampened a paper towel and wiped off the top before placing the can in front of me. "You look pale. Have you eaten today?"

"Yeah. I ate a nut bar when I first woke up." I popped the top and drank deeply. The bubbles tickled my throat, and my nose burned at the familiar taste. Cokes and coffee were my two big weaknesses. "It's probably too late to worry, but do you think the cops will mind I'm drinking one of Peter's drinks?"

"I'm sure they'd prefer it over you passing out. You looked like you were about to faint." Marc took another paper towel and ran it over his face.

I finished the drink and checked on Chubb's water and food supply. Both bowls were empty, so I went about the simple task of filling them.

The golden retriever lay in the crate, stretched out with his head resting on his big paws.

I paused beside him. "Poor boy. Do you know who hurt Peter?"

The dog's eyes rolled up, and I scratched him behind the ears.

Marc Williams cleared his throat. "Peter isn't hurt. He's dead."

How could the man be so blunt? I settled on the floor and reached for Chubb. The energetic puppy had lost his spunk. A stranger might not realize Chubb was five months old because he was so large. I managed to wrap him in my arms and rocked sideways in hopes it'd soothe the golden retriever. I also needed soothing, but I'd worry about myself later.

"In case you missed it, I'm Marc Williams. And you are?"

I willed back the tears threatening to erupt from my eyes. "I'm Andi Grace Scott. I was Peter's dog walker and pet sitter for the last twelve years. He was my friend."

"Twelve years?" Marc's eyes narrowed. "That dog's just a puppy."

"I took care of Lincoln for years, but he died back in the winter. Peter adopted Chubb in February, and they were a good fit for each other." Did the man think I was lying? If he didn't believe me about watching the dogs, he probably didn't believe I was innocent of Peter's death. "How well did you know Peter?"

He huffed, strode to the refrigerator again, and opened it. Soon I was holding another cold can of Coke. Marc twisted off the cap of a water bottle and chugged it dry. "Peter and I were neighbors and worked together when a land developer wanted to buy our land to build a hotel and casino. Our properties connect, and we could've made a nice profit, but we weren't interested."

The playing card singed me through the pocket of my denim shorts and I rubbed my thigh. Why had I picked it up? It might be important. Where were the other fifty-one cards? Fifty-three if you counted the jokers. I shrugged off the chill across my neck and refocused on Marc. His calm tone made me want to trust him. "Are you a cop?"

"No."

"Military?"

"No."

In spite of his denials, something about the man screamed authority. "Are you associated with the law in some way? An attorney? A judge?"

He yanked off his hat and ran a hand through his wavy blond hair. It was a couple of shades darker than mine but probably thicker. "Used to be an attorney."

"Aha. So is anything I tell you protected?"

"That only goes for clients. What do you want to tell me?" He tugged his hat back on.

I studied Marc's eyes. Gray, if anything. My gaze switched to coast over his strong chest. He'd quit perspiring, but there was still a damp ring on his T-shirt. The brim of his ball cap had a perfect curve. I should know after all the times I'd watched my brother, Nate, work a curve into the bill of his hats. "I want to hire you."

"Why?"

"What if the sheriff thinks I killed Peter? You thought I did. Maybe I need a lawyer." I blinked, trying to clear my vision from the threatening darkness. Last thing I needed to do was faint.

"I don't officially practice law anymore."

"Kinda young to retire, aren't you?" The rudeness of my tone shocked me but didn't seem to faze Marc. "That was uncalled for. I'm sorry."

He shrugged. "Consider it a career change. I build boats."

"I remember Peter mentioning a boat builder. Any chance you're still licensed to practice law?"

"Yes, but I don't." His jaw tightened.

"I'm hiring you." I'd go with my woman's intuition and trust him. "I found a card." I shouldn't have picked it up, but I did, and now it burned a hole in my pocket. "Specifically, an ace of hearts."

"What are you talking about?"

"On the living room floor." I pulled the card from my pocket, and a tube of lip balm slid out with it and dropped to the floor. "I found this card close to Peter's body. Do you think there's a connection to the casino man? Or could it be the killer's calling card? Maybe we've stumbled across a serial killer."

"Hold it. Serial killers are rare. Why'd you pick it up?"

I shook my head. "I don't know. Peter always liked things neat. I just didn't think."

"Where exactly did you find it?" His fists landed on his hips.

"It wasn't touching the body. I'd say it was close to the end table by the couch. On the dining room side. Not the foyer side of the couch."

"We'll show it to the sheriff."

"It's got my fingerprints on it now." I was too young to go to jail, although truthfully, thirty approached with the speed of a 310-horsepower jet ski. I'd find a way to prove my innocence, because as much as I respected the police, they didn't always catch the bad guy.

"It might also have the killer's fingerprints. Lay it on the counter." He pointed to the golden granite countertop on the white cabinet base.

The slick playing card was cool in my hand. "What if the cops arrest me? Don't forget I've hired you."

"You're not listening. I'm a boat builder now." His spine straightened, making him much taller than me. "Did you kill Peter?"

The faint wail of sirens drifted through the air. We were out in the county, so it'd probably be the sheriff or a deputy. I took a deep breath and released it. "I already told you. I didn't kill Peter."

"Then you've got nothing to worry about." His gaze drifted to the counter where I'd placed the ace of hearts.

"Easy for you to say. You were second on the scene." I reached for my tube of lip balm and rubbed it across my sunburned lips.

"Have you ever been arrested? Do you have a record?"

"No." My answer came out shrill. I was a good girl who followed the rules. I even drove down the appropriate aisles in a parking lot. How had I gotten myself into this fix?

The sirens grew louder, and Chubb howled.

"It's okay, boy. The good guys are coming." I dug through Peter's box of dog supplies and retrieved Chubb's ThunderShirt.

Marc's eyebrows rose and wrinkles waved across his forehead. "What are you doing?"

"Even though there's not a storm, maybe this will calm Chubb down. He's still an excitable puppy, and the sirens and activity may put him on edge." I secured the jacket around his belly and under his neck. "There you go. It's going to be okay."

Although if you considered the puppy was now an orphan, people would soon be stomping in and out of the house, and the coroner would take Chubb's deceased master away, nothing would be okay again.

Marc left us alone in the kitchen and returned moments later. "They're here. I'll meet them at the front door and explain you're back here with Peter's dog."

I nodded. "No, wait. Can I trust you? Or do you plan to rat me out?"

"You're something else, Andi Grace. First you try to hire me, and now you don't trust me." He ran a hand over his face.

"You refused to represent me, but you make a good point." I met his gray-eyed gaze, and something unexplainable flowed through me. "I trust you."

He sighed and left Chubb and I alone in the kitchen until Sheriff Wade Stone appeared. "Andi Grace, I hear you're the one who found Peter's body. I need you to tell me what happened."

Chubb whined before I could reply.

Marc appeared. "Excuse me, how about I take the dog for a walk? Give y'all some privacy."

I attached Chubb's leash and passed it to Marc. "Thanks."

"Yes, ma'am." He disappeared out the back door just off the laundry room.

I faced Wade. "I showed up this morning to walk Chubb and found Peter's body in the living room."

"Did you touch anything?"

"I'm afraid so." The room tilted on me. "Uh, Wade, can we sit down?"

"Sure. Take a seat at the island." He pulled a tall chair out for me, and I sank into it. "Andi Grace, any chance you know why there's only one playing card here?"

I propped my arms on the cool granite countertop. "It's going to have my fingerprints on it. Please don't get mad at me, but I picked it up earlier."

He stiffened. "That wasn't a very smart move. Tell me everything."

I shared my story with him and answered his questions. It took almost an hour, and I was beyond exhausted.

Wade studied me. "Did you kill Peter?"

"No, he was always kind to me. I had no reason to hurt him." A tear rolled down my cheek, and I swiped it away. Nobody cried pretty, but with my blond hair, blue eyes, and freckles I was a legit ugly crier. "Do you believe me?"

"At this point, I'm gathering facts. Walk me through your story from the moment you entered the house."

I followed him to the foyer and retraced my steps for him. Outside the living room window, the sun shone bright. Marc played with Chubb in the shade. I smiled before my thoughts returned to the murder scene.

It seemed like hours before the sheriff finished interrogating me. I plodded out the door, and Marc entered the house. He wasn't allowed to speak to me, and a deputy watched as Marc handed me the leash.

I didn't speak a word until climbing into my Suburban. I'd parked under an old oak tree in front of Peter's home, and it wasn't steaming hot. I sat in the driver's seat, and Chubb lay in the passenger seat.

A breeze drifted up from the river. Combined with the shade, the heat was bearable. I took notes in my journal on everything that came to mind about the crime scene. When I wrote all I could remember, I tapped my pen against the paper. Would the sheriff question Marc as thoroughly as he had me?

I wasn't sure what to think about the handsome, tall, and somewhat brooding attorney. Of course, finding a man dead wasn't the occasion to crack jokes and be the life of the party. I fanned myself with the journal.

Chubb propped his head on the console next to me. His heavy breathing filled the air. Crickets chirped in the surrounding woods. A peaceful day, if not for the fact my friend had been murdered.

What had Peter been wearing? I remembered what Marc wore. If the situation were different, I might be attracted to him. Too bad I'd always think of him as the man who thought I was capable of murder. I wouldn't hurt a mosquito. Okay, that might take it a bit far, but no way would I hurt another person.

"What are you doing?" Marc appeared beside my SUV and propped an elbow on the ledge of my rolled-down window.

I gasped and reached for my heart. "Whoa. You gave me a fright."

"Sorry. Thought you saw me coming."

"How'd your interview go?"

He shrugged his broad shoulders. "Fine."

"Did they mention me?"

"Yes."

"You're a man of few words, aren't you?"

"No need to say a lot when one word will do." He gave me a half-smile.

I'd never get information if he played coy. "Are you sure you're an attorney? I thought y'all had lots to say."

"Might be the reason I quit practicing law."

Arg. He was about to get on my last nerve. "Let's get more precise. Sheriff Stone drilled me on my relationship with Peter and why I was at the house this morning. He asked about my normal dog walking procedures. I'm worried he thinks either I killed Peter or maybe the killer got my key. It's impossible the killer got my key, because I still have it." I held up the key on a ring with a code tag. "Everybody I work for has a key with their own code. Even if somebody had broken into my house to get Peter's key, they'd have to know my coding system of matching keys to homes."

"Sounds like you've thought of everything." He clamped his lips together.

I expelled a long breath and shook my head. "Not even close. I never considered stumbling upon a dead client."

"I'm sure most people don't plan on that."

Un, deux, trois, quatre. "You aren't helping. What'd you tell the sheriff?"

"The truth."

It was going to take more than counting in French to calm me down. I needed to remain cool so Marc didn't think I was a deranged killer. "Did you tell him you accused me of murdering Peter?"

"I confessed that my first thought was you'd hurt Peter."

"You what?" I straightened in my seat. "How could you?"

"Hold on a second. I cleared up the misunderstanding then stuck to the facts."

Relief swooshed through me. "How did Sheriff Stone react?"

"He's got a good poker face."

So did Marc, and I didn't seem to be getting anywhere with him. I gave up. For the moment. "Can we leave now?"

"The deputy has our information and said we're free to go."

I tapped the pen against my purple journal. "Do you remember what Peter was wearing?"

"Braves T-shirt and jeans. Black Converse."

"You're right." I jotted the information down. Why hadn't I remembered?

"Why are you taking notes?"

I avoided meeting his gaze. How could I explain my desire to solve Peter's murder? The police had never found the hit-and-run driver who killed my parents twelve years ago. They called it a cold case. Nobody was perfect, and I'd never blame them for the lack of clues. Still, I realized the sheriff might see me as the most likely suspect and quit looking for the real killer. If I helped find the person responsible for Peter's death, I'd be able to clear my name and get justice for Peter.

Marc rested both arms on the top of my SUV. "Well?"

"What?" Oh, yeah. He'd asked about my notes. "I wanted to be a journalist when I was growing up. Here's a chance to put my investigative skills to the test while trying to get justice for Peter. Any chance you'd tell me the name of the casino developer?" A warm breeze drifted into the truck which gave me a bit of relief from the late afternoon heat.

Marc pushed back and stood straight. "George Reeves. He's not a local."

That much I had figured out on my own. I'd lived in Heyward Beach my entire life, and I knew the locals. To say so would sound bad-mannered. Instead, I nodded and added the name to my list. "Thanks."

"Before you start investigating, do you have a husband or

boyfriend to protect you?"

My shoulders tightened. "Don't you think you're being a little chauvinistic?"

"Not when it comes to murder."

My face warmed. I didn't want to answer, but he'd given me George Reeves's name. "My brother lives in town." No need to explain Nate stayed busy from dawn to dusk with his landscaping business.

"Be careful." He stepped away then turned on his heel and returned. "I know I'm going to regret asking, but why does it matter what Peter's wearing?"

"It was around ten when he called me last night to take care of Chubb. I think the killer came over after our call instead of this morning."

"Why?"

"Peter always wore suits to business meetings. If he'd been killed early today, he would've been dressed up."

"Gotcha. Why do you care so much?"

Anger bubbled up in me. I counted to ten in French before answering. "Why don't you care more?" I shot him the sweetest smile I could summon.

"Touché." He scratched the stubble on his jaw. "I feel terrible for Peter, but we barely knew each other. I know how to research, but I've never tried to track down a killer. Have you actually taken any investigative reporting classes?"

Busted. "No."

"And you don't think the sheriff's department can handle this case?" He crossed his arms and stared at me.

I gripped the steering wheel and could picture the man questioning a witness in a courtroom. "That's my point. To the cops, this is just another case. But it's different for me. Peter was my friend. When I wanted to start my dog walking business so I could have more time with the kids, Peter believed in me. He even helped me create a business plan."

Marc's eyes widened. "You've got kids?"

I opened the door to allow a better breeze into the vehicle. "No. My parents died when I was eighteen, and I raised my brother and sister."

His stance relaxed, and he stepped closer to the Suburban. "I'm sorry." His voice was silky smooth and comforting.

"I miss them every day. I'd registered for college and had a dorm assignment. I couldn't wait to start, and then my parents died. The driver was never caught. The sheriff says it's a cold case. You have no idea what it's like to lose both parents at the same time."

Marc looked down and scuffed the toe of his running shoe in the sandy grass. "Amazingly, I do know. Seems like we've got that in common."

Me and my big mouth. "I'm sorry, Marc. What happened?" I slid my purple journal onto the dash and stepped out of my SUV. I leaned back, hoping to look casual, but I wanted to hear every word he uttered.

He looked me in the eyes. "I was six at the time. It was also a car wreck, but not a hit-and-run. My parents ran off the road and hit a palm tree in the median. An off-duty fireman drove by at the time and rescued me first. He cut me out of my child safety seat and carried me to his truck."

His voice was so quiet, I had to step closer to hear. "And?"

"The car caught fire. The fireman had blocked oncoming traffic with his pickup truck. I guess the traffic on the other side stopped as well. The flames were so intense nobody could reach my parents. They died before anyone could get the fire extinguished." He broke eye contact with me and stared at the ground.

"Oh, no. I can't imagine how terrible it was for you to lose them at such a young age. Do you have any siblings?"

"Only child. I ended up in foster care. Thirteen different homes before I graduated from high school." Marc strode toward an oak tree with Spanish moss draping off its branches. He looked skyward.

I didn't want to intrude on his private moment, especially if he was praying, so I waited.

At last he spun on his heel and walked back to me. "I'll help you."

Chapter Two

DUMBFOUNDED WAS the only word to describe my feeling the moment Marc Williams agreed to help me.

He laughed, a rich, warm, genuine laugh. "You look stunned."

"I am." My voice caught on the words—whether from his comment or his deep tones, I couldn't say. I blinked. "Why the change of heart?"

His lips twitched in a smile. "I should've known you couldn't just accept my offer to help." He looked behind me as if the answers of the universe were in the surrounding oaks. "In all of the years I spent in foster care, I only had one good home placement. Mr. and Mrs. Bobby Joe Wilkes. I moved in with them the summer before I started high school. I was a smart aleck teenage boy mad at the world with a chip the size of a boulder on my shoulder. Bobby Joe changed me."

"How?"

He pulled his gray-eyed gaze back to me. "The short version is for once I had a family who believed in me." The smile he gave me might make some women go weak in the knees.

Who was I kidding? It was a good thing I'd been leaning against my SUV. "I'm still not sure why you changed your mind."

One shoulder hiked up. One very strong, muscular shoulder. "Let's say I'd lost faith in the system. Lost faith in a lot of people as well. The Wilkeses were different. They saw me as more than a paycheck. I was loved and appreciated. I thrived in their home. I know what it's like to fight a battle all by myself, and I understand how much easier it is to have somebody stand beside you. Andi Grace, I get you don't trust the authorities to solve Peter's murder because your parents' death is a cold case. You need help. I understand what it's like to feel like nobody's on your side, and I'm willing to help you."

His words thrilled me. No way he'd have made his offer if he thought I killed Peter. I threw my arms around him and gave him a quick hug. "I'll take you up on your offer. Why don't you put your contact information into my phone?" With a simple swipe and fingerprint,

I'd opened my phone to the contact page. "Here you go."

He tapped in his information while I watched his quick movements. In no time, he pushed save and returned the phone to me. "Text me your information when you have time."

"Any chance you're looking to adopt a dog as well as help me solve Peter's murder?" I texted him my number while I asked.

For the second time, he laughed. A resonant sound I could get used to hearing. "Not likely."

I couldn't explain the connection I felt to Marc at that moment. If he'd offered sympathy or comfort earlier, I might have broken down and gone into hysterics. Instead, he'd questioned my innocence and called the sheriff. His calm and authoritative attitude had forced me to function when the world crumbled around me.

Sheriff Wade Stone stepped out of the house and walked toward us.

"Uh, oh." In high school, I'd watched Wade quarterback on the football field, score and block on the basketball court, and knock home runs on the baseball field. He'd grown more muscular over the years. Thicker. I didn't want to get plowed down by the man he'd grown into.

Wade's nostrils flared. "Thought I told you two to leave."

"Yes, sir." I pushed off my SUV and looked at Marc. "Need a ride?"

"May as well." He strolled around to the passenger side with the grace of an athlete. Shoulders back and head held high.

I slid into the driver's seat. From my days of dating jocks in high school, I'd learned how arrogant some athletes could be. I didn't know about Marc, but I'd give him the benefit of the doubt. Most people were good. That'd been my mantra for years, and I'd continue to believe it. I cranked the SUV. Of course, there were always exceptions to the rule. The person who murdered Peter and the person who left my parents to die were excellent examples of bad people. "Move over, Chubb."

The puppy whined but wiggled to the back.

Marc settled into the passenger seat.

"You can scoot the seat back." I held in a chuckle. His long legs barely squeezed into the allotted space. His knees were scrunched almost against his chest. "My best friend rode over there last. She's much shorter than you. She's also nearsighted and likes to ride with the seat pulled up."

He slid the seat back, allowing his long legs to stretch. "Ah, much better. Thanks."

Chubb hopped onto the console between us, but he was too big to fit. His front paws landed in Marc's lap, and his tail swooshed against me.

I laughed. "So much for staying in the back seat."

With my left hand on the steering wheel, and my right patting Chubb's back, I drove away from Peter's house. It'd probably be the last time, and I took it all in. The view of the river, stately magnolia and oak trees with Spanish moss, grown up rice fields, the manicured lawn and landscaping closer to the main house, and woods bordering the property. "I don't know anything about Peter's family, except he has a sister. They were estranged. Since I've known him, he either spent holidays with us or traveled to some exotic island."

"How'd you meet Peter?" Marc rubbed Chubb's ears between his long tanned fingers.

"After I decided to raise my brother and sister, I knew we needed a smaller house. I went to Seaside Realty, and Peter was there looking for a home in the area. He'd been renting and decided to make it permanent. First time we ever met." I choked up and stopped petting Chubb to reach for a tissue from the box I kept in the glove compartment. I bumped Marc's knee with my wrist. Chills shot up my arm and I yanked my hand back. "Sorry."

With his right hand, he opened the compartment, pulled out some tissues, and handed them to me. "Want me to drive?"

Yes, but I couldn't show weakness to this stranger. I would've liked nothing more than to curl up in bed with my German shepherd, Sunny, my favorite soft, faded quilt, and allow myself to cry. Cry for Peter, whose days were cut short in the prime of his life. Cry for myself. I was going to miss him.

When I didn't answer him, Marc must have sensed my thoughts were gloomy, because he changed the subject. "Tell me about buying a house. You would've been what, nineteen?"

"Eighteen. I didn't think I could keep up with the house payments. Between selling our big house and the life insurance we received, I was able to buy a modest beach home and not have a house payment. Some would call it a cottage. Fine by me. Money was always tight, but I never had to worry about losing our home." I stopped at the end of Peter's driveway. "Peter was always so nice to me. I don't know why, but he looked out for my little family. I had a job as a vet assistant with our local vet, Dr. Hewitt. One day Peter was in with his dog, Lincoln. He needed somebody to watch him and asked me if I could."

"Was that the beginning of your dog walking business?"

I nodded. "I discovered it gave me more flexibility with the kids. Peter helped me create a business plan, and when the bank balked, Peter gave me a loan."

"Impressive."

"It was a loan which I've paid off."

Marc quirked an eyebrow. "Why do you sound so defensive?"

"Not everybody understood Peter's motives. I'm not sure I did, either." I drummed my fingers on the steering wheel. I'd never really figured out what had prompted Peter's generous offer, but I'd been too grateful to question him. I sighed. "Which way do you live?"

"Turn right. You'll see a sign for my business. MAW Wood Boats."

"How'd you come up with that name? Is it a boating word?" I made the turn onto River Road.

"No, it's my initials."

"Oh. Okay." I kept my eyes on the road. Poor Marc. He needed a better name for his business, but he wasn't asking for my opinion.

"Go ahead. You won't be the first to laugh."

My face heated. "I'm not going to tease you about your name, but you might come up with a catchier title for your business. Is there anything else you do besides build boats?"

"Yeah, I refurbish old boats. I can tackle everything from kayaks to whalers to yachts."

I spied the uninspired black and white wood sign nailed to a tree with an arrow pointing to Marc's drive. I turned on my blinker. I'd never been artistic, but I could make a better sign than he had. "Do most of your clients drive here?"

"I also have a dock on the Waccamaw River. Some customers arrive by water."

"Interesting. You have access by water and land."

"Exactly. Do you think I should change the name to Waccamaw Wood Boats?"

I shrugged. "MAW boats and Waccamaw Boats sound similar. It could work."

"You don't look impressed." Marc swiped his face with the sleeve of his shirt. "I'll keep thinking."

I cranked the air conditioning higher. "How long have you been in business?" Even though our paths hadn't crossed before today, I'd heard there was a new boat builder in the area. There were less than eight thousand people who lived here year-round. Spring break and summer vacation were a different story. We were well into June with the usual influx of tourists.

Chubb turned and repositioned himself to sit entirely in Marc's lap.

"Bobby Joe Wilkes—"

"The good foster dad?"

"Yes, the best. He taught me how to work with wood. Building boats was part of it."

"Do you visit the Wilkes often?"

"He died while I was in high school. Heart attack." Marc took off his hat and ran his fingers along the brim. "I learned a lot from him. After he died, I stayed with Momma Wilkes until graduating. Her memory deteriorated, and her sister moved her to a retirement community in Kentucky with memory care."

"Maybe you could name your business for him. Bobby Joe Wilkes's Wood Boats. No, that's too wordy. How about Bobby Joe's Wood Boats?"

"We could shorten it to BJ's Wood Boats."

I smiled. The man was catching on. "I like it."

"Me, too. In answer to your first question, I've only been here a few months."

"What brought you to Heyward Beach?"

"I didn't like the way my law career was heading and decided I needed a change. I love the water, and this property seemed perfect. Hang a right here."

The fork in the sandy drive had caused me to slow. "Toward the river?"

"Yeah. I need to check on something in the shed."

Had the sheriff noticed I was giving Marc a ride? What if he *did* murder Peter? Even worse, what if he planned to make me his next victim? The stupid girls in horror movies often were tortured and murdered in a creepy outbuilding.

With my heart about to beat out of my chest, I gulped down a scream begging for release. Peter had appeared to die from a head wound, and Marc couldn't have concealed a weapon in his running clothes. Yet, with his well-toned body, it wouldn't take much effort for him to hurt me.

"There it is." Marc pointed to a wooden building more the size of a barn than I'd imagined.

"Is that your boat shed?"

"Yes, ma'am." He hopped out. "Thanks for the ride."

Chubb tilted his head and whined until Marc rubbed his head once more.

"Anytime." I didn't literally mean anytime, but the words slipped past my lips. After making a three-point turn, I sped away.

The drive home passed in a blur of questions about Marc. I was surprised when I found myself pulling into my driveway. Never a good thing to be so absorbed you didn't remember driving. I needed to be more careful in the future. "Okay, Chubb. Time for you to meet Sunny."

I leashed the dog because the last thing I needed was for him to run away. Once we settled in the kitchen, I let Sunny out of her crate. "Hi girl. This is Chubb. He's only staying a few days." I loved on the German shepherd and led both dogs through the sliding glass door to the fenced-in backyard.

I pulled out my purple notepad and flipped to a clean page. The time had come for me to start a list of suspects. I wrote down my name and Marc Williams in case the cops thought we were guilty. Who had a motive for killing Peter?

Maybe George Reeves, the man who wanted to buy Peter's land. I wracked my brain but couldn't think of another soul to add to my list of suspects. If it was George Reeves, was Marc in danger? I hoped not. Even though he'd scared me more than once, he'd seemed to care about Peter and Chubb.

Had I left the front door open? Chubb had been frantic, and I'd hurried to help him. It was possible I'd raced in without slamming the door shut.

I'd walked Peter's previous dog on different plantation trails, including the river path. It was the cleanest and most level. Marc claimed he'd been running on it when he heard me scream. If I believed his story, he was innocent. Just like me. I needed more suspects because I had no intention of rotting in prison for Peter's murder.

Chapter Three

AFTER TAKING CARE of the dogs on my Friday morning schedule, I drove to Lovely Locks, with Chubb riding in the back of my SUV. My best friend, Juliet Reed, had bought the local beauty shop a few years ago and brought it into the twenty-first century. Quick-fix facials, total hair design, reconstructing, weaving, color and highlights, and bridal services were all offered. When a tanning booth had gone in next to the salon, Juliet's business grew. Next to the booth was a massage salon, and at the end of the strip of stores was Paula's Pickings, one of my favorite vintage stores.

I gave the puppy a treat and headed for the salon. All the SUV's windows were down, allowing the marsh breeze to keep Chubb cool while I went inside.

The door to the beauty shop opened, and Phyllis Mays walked out. "Andi Grace, how are you doing, honey?"

I did a double take. Phyllis looked amazing with soft rusty color tresses. "I'm fine. Your hair looks pretty. I like the new shade."

"Thanks. I came into a little extra money and decided to splurge." The fifty-something woman touched the straight strands that stopped below her ears. "Juliet is amazing. It doesn't look as brassy, does it? She called it a soft ginger something or other."

"It's a great cut and style for you." Much better than the too-orange color the woman must have done herself for at least the last five years.

Phyllis smiled. "Thanks. I've got to go. Have a good day."

"You too." I slipped into the beauty shop. The usual odors assailed me at the entry. Hair spray, nail polish remover, and some kind of perfume. My nose tickled. I didn't know how Juliet breathed in those smells all day long. They always gave me a dizzy buzz, and I sneezed.

"Bless you." Juliet made eye contact through the mirror at her station and nodded to me as she continued to blow dry a young woman's long dark hair.

"Thanks." I pointed to the back of the shop. "I'm going to help myself to a cup of get-me-to-lunchtime."

"Go ahead." Juliet continued working her magic with the round brush and blow dryer.

The station next to Juliet's was empty, and across the room, her other stylist, Wendy Conn worked on a highlight. I stuck to haircuts only these days, after being Juliet's guinea pig when she was in beauty school.

I scooted to the deserted break room. Since I hadn't slept much last night, I beelined it to the coffee maker. After pouring myself a mug of coffee, I added hazelnut creamer and sugar. Despite the June heat, I needed the comfort only a hot cup of java could provide. A plate of homemade brownies and a bowl of fruit sat on the circular break table. Chocolate and coffee. Who could resist the temptation? Not me. I reached for a brownie. The chewy morsel burst with flavor, and the chocolate chips gave an extra punch of delight. A rare treat for me because I wasn't much of a cook and hardly ever baked. After taking another bite, I closed my eyes and breathed deep. *Mmm, délicieux.*

Leaning back, I sipped my coffee. The tension seeped out of my shoulders. The shakiness in my limbs dissolved. One more brownie couldn't hurt.

"Aha, I caught you. One day all the junk food you eat will catch up with you." Juliet joined me with her ever-present glass of water and reached for a green apple. "You look tired."

"I am. Do you know Marc Williams?"

"Hunky boat builder?"

"That's the one. He heard me scream when I found Peter and came to the house. At first he thought I'd killed Peter."

"How are you holding up? I know how much you cared about Peter."

A bit of brownie stuck in my throat, and I coughed. "I'm hanging in. What's the rumor mill saying about Peter's murder?"

"Most everybody is in shock. Phyllis said Pastor Larry was asked about contacting Peter's family. He doesn't know any family members. What about you?" She crunched into the fruit.

"He has a sister somewhere, but they're on the outs. Have been for years. I used to wonder if Peter considered us his replacement family."

"He was around quite a bit during the years I lived with you all." Juliet used a paper napkin to swipe at the bit of juice dribbling down her chin. "Did you know Peter had been engaged?"

The breath whooshed out of me. A fiancée? I didn't even know he'd seriously dated anybody. Maybe Peter hadn't cared about me as much as I thought if he'd kept his girlfriend a secret. Fiancée. I'd always thought he treated me like a little sister, but a real brother would've mentioned an engagement. "No way. Who was it? I never saw him hanging out with a woman."

"Regina Houp. She's the new owner of Paula's Pickings."

"Oh, is Paula her aunt? I've heard rumors she planned to give the store to her niece." With a shaky hand, I reached for my coffee. It sounded like I wasn't as close to Peter as I'd imagined. I didn't know his family or his fiancée.

"Yes. I'm relieved Regina kept the business. It makes all of our stores stronger to have a full cluster."

"How long have you known about Peter and Regina?" My jaw stiffened as I uttered the words. It was like the time I'd gone to Colorado as a youth group chaperone. The cold had frozen my face while snow skiing, making it hard to speak.

Juliet pushed her thick blond hair behind her ear. "I found out yesterday."

"Wonder why he kept their relationship a secret? What do you think about Regina?" I held tight to the mug.

Juliet's shoulders hiked. "We met briefly last week. She seems nice enough."

I Googled Regina on my phone. "She could be a suspect. I need to meet her."

"What if she doesn't know about Peter's death?" Juliet's eyes widened. "Even worse, what if she does? How tacky for us to show up right now."

Juliet always feared appearing tacky. Maybe because growing up her parents drank and used drugs. In an effort to distance herself from their reputation, Juliet strove to make good choices. "I won't embarrass you. We'll take Chubb with us."

"Why are you so fixated on meeting Regina?"

"I want to help solve Peter's murder."

Her eyes bugged. "Oh, my goodness. You think Regina killed Peter?"

I brushed brownie crumbs off my shirt. "It's possible. Love gone horribly wrong or something." I raised the cup to my lips and sipped the coffee.

Juliet gasped. "Are you out of your cotton-picking mind?"

I set the cup down too hard and it thudded on the stained Formica table. "No. What if Regina *is* the killer?"

Juliet threw her apple core and napkin in the trash and washed her hands. "You don't think she'd go after Peter just because they broke up, do you?"

"She wouldn't be the first jilted lover to kill their ex."

My best friend shook her head, her expression grim. "Girlfriend, I think you need to take a deep breath before you go meet this woman. In fact, you should leave her alone." She wadded the white towel into a ball and slammed it into the hamper.

"Fine. If you won't go with me, Chubb and I'll go by ourselves."

"Why take the puppy with us?"

"Maybe Regina would like to adopt Chubb. I'm only the dog walker. She was the girlfriend. Fiancée. Whatever." The idea that Peter hadn't introduced me to Regina continued to squeeze my heart.

"You're more than a dog walker. Even if he didn't tell you about Regina, Peter was your friend."

Friend? If that was true, I wouldn't have felt like I'd been sucker-punched by the news of his fiancée. I pushed aside the hurt to answer her. "We can go over and offer our condolences to Regina and see how she feels about the puppy." I rinsed out my empty mug and turned to face Juliet.

"I doubt she'll take Chubb off your hands. Regina Houp is beautiful and classy. Citified. If she had a dog, it'd be a little show dog."

I loved all dogs, but give me a big one any day. "One of those itty-bitty things you can stuff in a purse?"

"That'd be my prediction."

I was still struggling to believe Peter had a fiancée. "How come we never met this Regina? And how do you know they were engaged?" By now, a headache had formed behind my eyes.

"Paula told me." Juliet touched my shoulder. "If we're going over, we need to hurry. I've got a perm scheduled in fifteen minutes."

"Really, a perm?"

"One of the choir ladies."

I filled a plastic glass with water. "For Chubb. Come on."

Juliet smirked. "I should've known you didn't plan to drink water."

"Very funny." My Suburban sat in the shade of an oak tree at the back corner of the parking lot. I hurried to the back of my truck and filled a plastic bowl with the water then pushed it into the crate where Chubb lay. "Here you go, boy. Are you thirsty?"

He lapped the water like he was in no hurry.

"Let's go meet Miss Regina before Juliet has to return to work." I opened the gate. Chubb lumbered out, and I helped him to the ground.

"I know you're sad, but we're going to find somebody special for you to live with."

Juliet walked with Chubb and me to the glass door of the gift shop. "I'm going to let you do the talking."

I inhaled. "Me? I don't know what to say. You talk to people all day long. It's part of your job. I deal with animals."

"Yes, but this is your bright idea."

My friend had a way of speaking truth whether I wanted to hear it or not. At the moment, I hadn't wanted to get her opinion, but at least she'd agreed to go with me. "Fine." I took a deep breath and stepped into the store, while keeping the leash tight to my side. The last thing I needed was for Chubb to break something valuable.

Juliet entered after me but walked toward a display of linens, leaving me to meet Peter's fiancée all by myself. I lifted my chin and moved forward.

Country music played softly on a radio behind the checkout counter. Gift wrap and bags were organized on the back wall. A scented candle burned, adding to the warm atmosphere. Cinnamon. Interesting choice, but not really a summer scent. Then again, who was I to judge? I liked natural smells. Nothing artificial.

A redheaded woman moved away from a wicker shelf with a six-inch wooden figurine in her hand. Behind her was a Fourth of July display. "May I help you?"

My pulse spiked. Maybe it'd been a crazy idea, but I was in her store now. "Uh, I'm Andi Grace Scott."

The woman's lips tipped up. Not quite a smile, but not a frown either. "You're Peter's dog walker. I'm Regina Houp. Can I help you find something special today?"

Either the woman was as cold as a snowman in Alaska, or she didn't know the truth. "I, uh, how do you know about me?"

"Peter mentioned you many times."

Juliet appeared. "Hi, Regina."

As Regina turned from me to Juliet to say hello, my chest tightened. So Peter had told Regina about me, but never mentioned this woman or their relationship during all the time we spent together. A deep pain settled deep in my heart. I shook myself from the sadness and heard Juliet talking.

"If you'd like me to hand out flyers or coupons promoting your store, let me know. I could set some in the salon."

I needed to focus on something besides my loss, so I studied Regina.

She wore adorable turquoise wedge sandals with a zipper on top. "Thanks. Social media works wonders. It's my primary means of advertising. I'll keep your offer in mind, though."

I couldn't take my gaze from her sandals. "Your shoes are super cute. Where'd you find them?" The heel must be close to four inches, and I had no idea how she worked in the things, but I loved those shoes. Maybe we could bond over them.

"I bought them at the Charleston City Market. I liked them so much I also bought another pair in hot pink."

"Nice." Chubb tugged on the leash, but I kept a tight hold. I bolstered myself and drew in a deep breath. "Have you known Peter long?"

"A few years. Why?" The woman looked curious.

My throat tightened.

Juliet approached Regina and touched her arm. "We actually came to talk to you about Peter. Maybe you should sit down."

Chubb barked. I didn't give him an inch to budge in the fancy shop. "Sorry. We won't stay long. We just need to tell you something."

Regina glanced at the puppy. "I don't normally allow dogs in my store. Even if it belongs to Peter. There are way too many breakables. As for your news, I usually find it's best to yank off the bandage." One well-shaped eyebrow raised, daring me to spit out whatever I had to say.

"Jump right into the water, no matter how cold? I get it." I took a deep breath. "I went to Peter's place to walk Chubb yesterday, and I found Peter. I'm so sorry to tell you this. He passed."

Her eyebrows shot up. "Passed? Passed what?"

I gulped. "He's dead."

Regina's face crumpled. "What? How? He's one of the healthiest men I know. He eats right and runs for exercise. He's only forty, for crying out loud. You must be mistaken."

I wouldn't argue with the woman, although I felt like a creep for blurting out the news. "Uh, actually . . . he may have been murdered."

Regina sucked in a breath and swayed. Her eyes widened.

"The sheriff is looking for relatives to notify. Maybe you can help. Do you know Peter's family?"

The woman regrouped quickly. "He told me a little about them, but we never met."

Juliet grabbed some tissues from the box by the register. "Here.

Can I get you something? A glass of cold water? Would you like me to call your aunt?"

"No. It's such a shock. I've been in and out of town this week to sales and auctions, so Peter and I didn't talk much the last few days. Are you sure he's dead?" Her eyes didn't water and not a tear flowed down her face, despite her forlorn expression.

I nodded. "I'm really sorry."

Regina took a tissue from Juliet and wiped at her dry eyes before sitting on an antique velvet love seat. "Thank you for telling me. I would hate to read about his death in the paper or overhear the news in the coffee shop."

I inched closer. "I just heard y'all were engaged but Peter called off the engagement. Is it true?"

Regina's nostrils flared, and if fire could've blazed out of a person's eyes, it might have happened in the little shop. "It was a mutual decision, and we remained friends. One day we might've gotten back together."

Not trusting the antique seat to hold both of us, I knelt beside Regina. "How can we help? Do you want to keep Peter's puppy?"

Chubb stayed at my side.

Her spine stiffened. "I need to be alone right now." She pulled another tissue out of the box and then another, even though not a single tear had spilled from her eyes. She shot a glance at Chubb. "Please take Chubb with you. I'm not a dog person. Too many allergies."

Juliet tapped my shoulder and made a motion to go. "Regina, we'll leave you alone, but if you need anything, I'm right down the block."

I pulled a business card from the pocket of my shorts. "And you can call me at this number. I need to find a home for Chubb. If you think of anybody who might like him, please give me a call. Or if you need a friend, call me. I cared about Peter. He was always good to me. We didn't have the relationship y'all did, but I cared about him."

Regina stood and placed her hands on our backs. She exerted pressure and herded us to the front door. "He cared about you like a little sister. Thanks again for letting me know."

As soon as our feet hit the sidewalk, the door's bolt clicked.

After a taking a few steps, I turned to Juliet. "Did you notice her words didn't match her actions? I can't believe she didn't cry."

"Maybe she's in shock." Juliet checked her watch. "I've got to go. Are you okay?"

"Not really, but thanks for going with me to meet Regina. You don't think her reaction was weird?"

We started walking toward her shop. "I don't know. We all grieve in different ways. I'll call you later."

I hugged Juliet. "Thanks again."

"Hey, what are friends for?" Juliet slipped through the door.

I opened the back of my vehicle and helped Chubb hop up. "Did you hear or see Peter's death? What about Regina? Is she Peter's killer? Although you were calm around her. Wait, you were in your crate when I found you." I was getting nowhere fast. It was doubtful Chubb would've watched his master get murdered then obey the killer and go into the crate. Dogs were loyal creatures. Chubb would've tried to defend Peter. I'd keep Regina on my suspect list.

I rubbed Chubb behind the ears. "Was the breakup mutual like Regina claimed? Or if she couldn't marry Peter, was she going to make sure nobody did?"

"Are you looking for a motive?"

My heart near about jumped out of my ribcage, and I screamed.

Marc backed away and held up a hand. "Whoa, Andi Grace. It's me."

Chubb barked once then moved and sniffed Marc's outstretched hand.

I dropped my hands from some kind of defensive move I'd made up years ago. Not karate or judo, but I used to pretend I could defend myself with it. "Marc Williams, you liked to have scared me to death." I wasn't just saying the words. My heart beat so fast it was a wonder I didn't have a coronary event right there in the parking lot.

"Sorry. I thought you saw me coming."

"You're two for two."

"What?"

"You've snuck up on me two days in a row. What do you want?" A deep sigh eased from my chest and my shoulders sagged. I shouldn't take my worries out on this man. "Sorry, I didn't mean to sound rude."

He held up a paper bag with a twinkle in his gray eyes. "I was at the coffee shop across the street when I spotted you. Have you eaten?"

My stomach growled loud enough for Marc to hear. "I'm starved."

"Do you have time to eat with me?"

"Yep. I'll be right back." I hurried into the beauty shop and told Juliet I planned to eat with Marc. I wanted to trust him, but hey, you couldn't be too careful with a killer on the loose. In case Marc hadn't bought drinks, I grabbed water bottles from the fridge and left a couple of dollars in the money jar before running outside. "How about Huntington? It's probably a five-minute drive from here."

"Sounds good."

"Would you mind driving my SUV so I can take notes on the case?" I dangled the keys in my hand.

"No problem." Marc reached for my South Carolina flag needlepoint key chain with his free hand and jumped into the driver's seat.

I secured Chubb in the very back, settled into the passenger seat, and pulled my notepad out of my oversized purse.

It didn't take long to reach Huntington Beach State Park, but I had time to record my thoughts on Regina.

I looked up when Marc parked. "There's an empty picnic table under the tree over there."

"Looks good to me. I'll get Chubb. Do you have a leash?"

I couldn't help but laugh. "I'm a dog walker. I always have a leash. It's in the clear plastic box beside the crate."

I carried our food, water, and my notepad. "I think you'd make a good dog owner. You should adopt Chubb."

"I'm pretty sure I already told you it's not gonna happen." He joined me at the concrete table and kept one hand on the leash. "Your choices are ham and cheese or vegetarian."

"A veggie sandwich?"

He shrugged. "I didn't know what you'd eat. Some people are picky."

"I'm easy to please. Why don't we take half of each?" I unwrapped the sandwiches and divvied them up on the wax paper wrappers. "Do you care if I say a blessing?"

"Uh, go ahead."

"Father, thank you for this food and this beautiful day. Help us to find Peter's killer, protect us, and please don't let Wade arrest me. Amen."

Marc opened a small bag of potato chips. "You afraid of getting arrested?"

My appetite disappeared. "Honestly, I'm worried they're looking at me as the number one suspect. Are you prepared to defend me if they do haul me to jail?"

"Yes, but I don't see that happening. You have a good reputation around town."

His words surprised me. "Really? How do you know?"

"I investigated you this morning."

An inexplicable flutter batted in my chest. "What'd you discover?"

"So far everything you told me is true. You raised your siblings, and except for the pizza man finding your brother drunk on the beach late one night, you've done a good job as a parent."

I broke eye contact with Marc. "On the fifth anniversary of our parents' death, Nate had had too much to drink. He was of legal age, but if the cops had found him, he'd probably have gotten arrested for public intoxication. Tony brought him home, and to my knowledge, Nate hasn't had another drunken episode."

had some major bumps in the road through the years."

"It couldn't have been easy. How do you handle stress?"

"My vices all begin with the letter C. Coffee, Coke, and chocolate. Give me a pint of Rocky Road, and I'm good."

"Su-weet." He smiled.

I eyed his sandwich. "We should eat. I'm sure you've got a boat to build or repair in that big shed of yours."

"That's true, but nobody's going to fire me if I take a long lunch break." He bit into the veggie half first. "What were you writing on the way over?"

"I was trying to come up with a list of suspects." I lifted the bread of the vegetarian sandwich. Spinach, sprouts, tomatoes, shredded carrots, cucumber slices, mushrooms, red bell pepper, avocado slices, and mustard. I bit into and the flavorful and hearty sandwich. "This is delicious. I feel healthier already, and thanks for adding mustard."

"You've gotta have mustard. It's too hot around here for mayo." He crunched into another chip. "Suspects? I figured as much. Who's on your list?"

"Turns out I don't know as much about Peter as I thought. So far, I don't have many suspects. Regina Houp made my list this morning. She's Peter's ex-fiancée. You and George Reeves, the land developer you told me about. Do you know any of Peter's friends?"

Marc choked on his water. "Me?"

I shrugged. "It didn't take you long to arrive."

"I told you I was running by the river. Why isn't your name on the list?"

"It was at first, but I scratched it off because I'm innocent."

"You can cross me off, because I'm also innocent." His frown evolved into a smile.

I drew a line through Marc's name and showed him. "Happy?"

"Much better." He pulled the bottom crust off his sandwich before taking another bite.

"You didn't answer my question about Peter's friends." I slipped a chewy bone to Chubb who sat beside me.

It took Marc a minute to finish his bite before he answered. Maybe he was thinking. "He introduced me to Thomas King, the contractor in charge of the room Peter was adding to the back of his house. Thomas's son, Dylan, was around helping with the addition. Not that I think either of them are suspects. They're only some men who knew Peter."

"I know both of them." I wiped my mouth and scribbled their names onto my list. My excitement grew. "Thomas is an on-again and off-again local. He grew up in the area, and his son, Dylan, is the same age as my little sister, Lacey Jane. Dylan was the typical high school bad boy." Oops. I shouldn't be blurting out those ugly thoughts. I needed to get a grip. "Sorry."

"For what?" He twisted the top off a water bottle. "For being honest?"

"No, but it's not nice to say mean things about people. It's possible he changed recently."

"Hmm." His eyebrows rose. "You know I'm not accusing anybody. Right?"

"Yeah, but I've got to start somewhere."

"Finding Peter's killer won't bring him back."

I slapped the pen down on the pad and reached for my sandwich. The man could infuriate me. "I know, but when he's caught, he can't hurt anybody else."

He sighed. "Andi Grace, you don't have training to catch a killer. I wish you'd let Sheriff Stone do his job."

I tipped my nose in the air. "He's got a lot of crimes to solve. I'll share my research with him."

"Finding answers can be dangerous. Especially if you're not experienced."

A sand dune stood between us and the ocean. Waves crashed on the beach in the distance, and the air held the salty tang of the sea. I set my hands on my hips. "I need to question Thomas."

Marc shook his head. "Not a great idea. If he's guilty, he's already killed once. Peter was bigger and stronger than you, yet the killer got the best of him. How will you protect yourself?"

"I'll be subtle." I turned toward the ocean and avoided looking at Marc. "You know, maybe I should look into home improvements."

"Please, don't." He reached down and patted Chubb. The best

way to connect with me was being kind to my family or an animal.

I relaxed my posture. "It'll give me an opportunity to get to know Thomas better."

"I'm serious. Don't invite him into your home. Between you and me, I think he has a mean streak."

I agreed with Marc's assessment, but nobody was going to stop me from trying to find the killer. "Then how do you suggest I get closer to him?"

Marc looked at Chubb. Seconds ticked by. At last his gaze met mine. "I'll ask him to come to my place. It needs work. You can be there during the interview process."

I latched onto his hand. "Marc, thanks. You won't regret helping me."

"Too late. I already regret my offer." He smiled, and my heart cartwheeled. "I won't back out, though. You'll discover I'm a man of my word." He studied me some more. "And I need a promise from you."

"What?"

"Keep me in the loop, and don't meet with Thomas by yourself."

I tightened my lips and felt a grunt form in my throat. "Why? Because I'm a woman?" I released his hand.

He drummed the table with two fingers. "No, because there's safety in numbers."

My brows shot up. "Are you saying if I tell you everything I do then you'll help me question Thomas?"

"Not everything." His shoulders relaxed. "Just everything related to your so-called investigation."

I could agree to that. "Deal." I held out my hand and shook his. The tingles zipping up my arm must be related to making progress on my investigation. Not from any attraction to the oh-so-handsome man sitting across from me.

Chapter Four

AFTER STRIKING A deal with Marc, I left Chubb at my house with Sunny and walked the dogs on my schedule. I'd even met an elderly couple struggling with their Bernese mountain dog. I gave them my business card, and they guaranteed they'd be calling me.

By six o'clock, my work was complete. I stood in my backyard, watching Sunny play with Chubb. Despite her advanced years, Sunny kept up with the puppy as they ran from one end of the yard to the other and wrestled over dog toys. They got along fine, but Chubb needed a home of his own. I spent so much time caring for dogs that didn't belong to me, I enjoyed giving Sunny special attention when I was home.

"Hello. Andi Grace?" Juliet's voice rang out from inside the house.

"I'm in the backyard." As far as beach homes went in my price range, it was a big yard. Plenty of room for the dogs to run around, and good space for entertaining. I'd fenced it in after my first year of dog walking for the times I needed to bring other dogs home with me.

Juliet appeared, wearing running shorts and a hot pink T-shirt with the Lovely Locks logo emblazoned across the front in large silver letters. "Hey there. I picked up pizza for us. You hungry?"

"Starved." I pushed the farmhouse table into the shade and angled the chairs to face the yard. "Let's eat on the deck where I can keep an eye on the dogs. It'd be my luck Chubb would dig his way under the fence and try to run home. Do you want a Coke?"

"You can't eat pizza without Coke."

I laughed on my way inside. Juliet and I'd been friends since high school, and there'd been plenty of lean years for both of us when eating out had been a splurge. We used to joke we couldn't wait for the day when we could always eat pizza with our favorite soft drink.

My kitchen was a mess. I needed to wash dishes but managed to find two clean sweat-proof tumblers in the back of the cabinet. Perfect. I filled them with ice and grabbed a two-liter bottle from the refrigerator. Paper napkins and a couple of clean plates completed my supplies. I hurried back out before the pizza cooled.

Outside, Juliet ran her hand over the farmhouse table. "This is really nice. When did you get it?"

"Nate made the entire table by himself for my birthday." I placed the dishes on the table and poured our drinks. "The stain he used is supposed to help it hold up outdoors. I love the light color."

"It's beautiful, but your birthday is next month."

"He couldn't wait to give it to me."

"Nate never could keep a secret." Juliet opened the pizza box. "Your brother and sister are amazing."

"Yes, they are." I reached for a slice of Hawaiian style. The spicy aroma drifted up. "This smells delicious."

"Umm. Wait until you have a taste."

Salty bacon, ham, sweet pineapple, and green peppers tickled my taste buds. "This has a ton of cheese. Did you ask for extra?"

"Tony is trying a new recipe with two types of cheese. I got it for half-price."

I nodded. "I'm not sure I would've survived raising Nate and Lacey Jane without pizza coupons and Tony's kindness."

Juliet eyed me over the slice of pizza going into her mouth. "You made a lot of sacrifices to keep your family together."

"But?" How had this evening taken a serious turn so fast?

Juliet smiled. "God brought people into your life to help you through the rough times."

"Your faith has always been stronger than mine. But you're right. Tony, Peter, and you always looked out for me. If you hadn't moved in with us during the first few years after graduation, I'm not sure I would've survived. You paid me rent and helped with household chores. Most important, you supported me emotionally." I gulped my Coke, and tears sprang to my eyes.

Peter was gone. Forever. He'd taught me business basics, but I didn't feel prepared to stand on my own. Who'd advise me on work decisions? "Now I've only got you and Tony."

"Nate and Lacey Jane are adults, and what about Marc Williams? I'm sure he'd help if you asked. Tall, dark, and handsome. You could do worse."

I laughed. For years Juliet and I had joked about meeting the right guy. He must love God, love us, and be oh, so handsome. Marc had stepped in when I needed a friend the day before, even though it would've been easier for him to walk away. I ignored my slice of pizza and sipped my Coke. Juliet was right about God sending people my way when I needed them most. Time after time. And Juliet was one of the many friends He had sent my way. "You're right."

"Helpful or handsome?" Juliet's eyes twinkled.

"Both." My face grew warm. Time to change the subject. "Hey, isn't it about time for you to get a dog?"

"Ask me when I get my car paid off. Until then, no." Juliet took a second slice of pizza and closed the box. "Don't look at me like that. I've got to keep up mortgage payments on the salon, pay rent for my apartment, and there's no room in the budget for a pet."

"The salon seems to be a success."

Juliet watched the dogs and ignored her pizza. At last she turned her gaze to me. "It's okay."

"What's wrong?" I studied my friend. "You may as well tell me now, because I can be like a dog with a bone."

A smile curled her lips. She knew me too well. "You won't let it go."

"Exactly. So spill it."

Her shoulders drooped. "The salon is fine, but it's just not how I imagined my life. There's no adventure. I see the same people day after day. Nothing new ever happens."

I reached for my glass and swirled the ice cubes around. "What would you rather do?"

"I'm not sure. I only know there's got to be more to life." She pounded her fist on the table. "I need to be intellectually stimulated. I want a challenge. It sounds crazy when I say it out loud, but there's little joy in my life."

My friend needed some encouragement—a boost. "People are happy when they know they look nice. You help women look their best."

"Maybe you're right." Juliet slumped in her chair. She didn't look convinced. "Have you heard any updates on Peter's murder this afternoon?"

"Not a word. What about you?" I refilled my glass and got comfortable. The dogs continued to run back and forth across the yard. Both seemed happy. Did I need another dog to keep Sunny company? *No.* I had plenty of dogs spend the night from time to time. If I owned another dog, it'd add to the chaos. But Chubb was so cute . . .

Juliet sat straighter. "Mrs. Merritt was my last customer of the day, and she loves to talk. She mentioned overhearing an argument between Regina and Peter a few weeks ago."

"Dottie Merritt." At Juliet's nod, I continued, "What about?"

"Mrs. Merritt and Paula had come home from a junking trip. Regina's living with her aunt for now." Juliet twisted her napkin. "Even though Paula's retired and gave the business to Regina, she still likes to hit the garage sales, flea markets, and estate sales."

"Gotcha. The fight?" I shot a quick glance toward the dogs before zoning my focus back on the conversation.

"Oh, yeah. So Mrs. Merritt said they got out of the van and heard loud voices. Paula claimed it must be a lovers' spat and suggested they go out for coffee because she didn't want to interfere. When the ladies returned later, the house was empty."

"Interesting."

"I haven't told you the best part. Mrs. Merritt is sure Peter dumped Regina. Evidently, Regina complained she wouldn't have moved to Heyward Beach if she'd realized he was afraid of commitment. She sold her home and gave up a good job to take over Paula's business. She was ticked."

"How did Mrs. Merritt learn this?" I leaned closer to hear every word.

"The windows were open, and she claims they heard plenty before they took off. At least they heard Regina better than Peter."

"Hold on." I glanced toward the dogs to make sure they weren't playing in the flowers Nate had planted for me. Both lay in a shady spot under a pine tree. I ran inside and grabbed my notepad off the kitchen counter and hurried back out. I flipped to a clean page and looked at Juliet. "Anything else?"

"This is pure gossip and speculation now. Mrs. Merritt thinks Regina wanted to plan the interior decorating for Peter's new room, but he had different ideas. When he bought his place, it came furnished with a lot of period pieces."

I nodded. "That's true. He admired so many things in his house and always wanted to make sure I appreciated them. It excited him when he found a new piece to fit the time period of the house. Maybe he met Regina looking for antiques."

"Could be. What's the house like?"

"It's like a museum and not a home. I think Peter spent a lot of time in the kitchen because it had the most comfortable furniture. The little nook and easy chair, ottoman, and side table, and made it his favorite place to watch TV. Even though the television set was small enough to be placed on the counter."

Juliet chuckled. "I thought all men liked to watch shows on the biggest possible screens."

"There's a fifty-inch flat screen in the main room, but the furniture is hard and old. There's no way to really relax in there. So it'd make sense to fill the new addition with comfortable furniture instead of making it another room to show off. It'd be a place to relax and not worry about Chubb destroying priceless antiques." My hands almost shook as I added this new information to my notes. More motive for Regina to have killed Peter.

Juliet tapped my hand. "Don't forget. This is pure speculation."

A squirrel jumped from the neighbor's magnolia tree to my crape myrtle. Chubb barked and ran in circles.

I met Juliet's gaze. "I hear you, but Regina has two possible motives. Jilted lover and disappointment over not getting to decorate Peter's new room." I clicked the pen. "We need to find out if Regina's got an alibi for the night of the murder."

Juliet's eyes widened. "Do you really think she could have killed her fiancé?"

"Maybe she didn't go over to see Peter with the intention of hurting him. They could've gotten into another argument. It escalated. It's possible she threw something at him."

Juliet snapped her fingers. "Or she could've hit him with a hard object."

Cold chills zipped up my back. "Like a paperweight. I picked one up in the living room to protect myself when I heard Marc's footsteps. It's heavy."

"Heavy enough to kill Peter?"

"Maybe. Except he's taller than Regina." A few were taller than I was when I wore tennis shoes or sandals.

"What if she wore high heels? Like the cute ones she wore in the shop yesterday. The extra inches might have been all she needed to be able to smash his head with a heavy object." Juliet reached for my notepad and sketched the wedges Regina wore earlier.

Both dogs growled and tugged on a toy.

I stood. "Sunny. Chubb. Come here."

Sunny dropped her end of the toy and trotted to me with her head held high. Maybe I should rename her Queen Sunny. Chubb's tail dropped. "You're not in trouble, boy. Come here." I loved on both dogs and filled the water bowl.

Sunny drank from it first, and Chubb nudged his way in. When they had lapped up all of the water, the dogs dropped onto a shady spot on the deck.

I returned to my seat. "I love the long days of summer."

"Me, too." Juliet twisted her thick blond hair up and fanned the back of her neck. "Do you suppose Regina and Peter could've fought over an object? Each one pulled on it. Regina lost her hold, and it hit Peter in the head. He falls and dies. She runs off because she's scared."

"It's a theory."

"But what?"

I doodled on my notes. "Who knows? I'm still struggling with the thought of Peter arguing loud enough to be heard outside. I can't imagine him fighting over an object. He was too dignified."

Juliet touched my hand. "Sweetie, you've got to be realistic. I think you see Peter as a hero who can do no wrong. You won't figure this out unless you adjust your perception of the man."

"He was always so good to me." I often considered myself strong and self-sufficient. Was it because I knew Peter would be around to catch me if I fell? A shiver shook me. God was my strength. Not Peter. "Do you remember the Bible verse about God giving strength to the weary?"

"He gives strength to the weary and increases the power of the weak is from Isaiah, but don't ask me the chapter and verse."

"That's the one. Do you think I shouldn't have depended so much on Peter?" My words came out whisper soft.

She squeezed my hand. "I'm sure I would've done the same thing. Keep in mind, he wasn't perfect. He was just a man. Human like us. He made mistakes."

"Yeah, but a mistake worth killing over? I find it hard to believe."

"I know, sweetie. But if you think you're going to help find his killer, you need to exchange those rose-colored glasses and see this crime with twenty-twenty vision."

"Very funny. I figure out what needs to be done and do it. Sometimes Peter showed me the right steps to take and I took them. He was smart about business. I know my limitations. I'm a realist." Was it time for me to be more realistic in my opinion of Peter?

"Except where Peter's concerned." Juliet squeezed my hand and stood. "Your bangs need a trim. Come to the shop tomorrow, and I'll take care of them for you."

"I'm trying to let them grow out." I fingered the hair hanging in my eyes and pushed it back.

"That never works for you. You're always too impatient."

"No, I'm not. I'll make it this time." The problem wasn't patience. I was never sure growing my bangs out would be my best look.

"Okay, but stop by the shop, and I'll trim the rest of your hair. See you tomorrow." My friend left me sitting with two dogs for company.

I reached for my notebook and started a to-do list. I needed to find out Regina's alibi for the time of the murder. Also, I needed to figure out if Peter might have any other enemies. Before the murder, I would've said no way.

Life had made an abrupt turn. One minute Peter was alive, and before you knew it, he was dead. I'd been living a normal life, and now I was trying to catch a killer. Like the topsy-turvy carnival rides, I struggled to know which way was up.

Chapter Five

THE DAY'S STRESS had gotten to me and I turned in early. So early it was embarrassing. I flipped the page of a business magazine quietly in order not to wake my dog. Sunny lay beside me in bed. Her gentle snore gave me a sense of normalness. I was home with my dog. What could be better?

Chubb hadn't been able to settle down in my bedroom. We tried my closet in case he wanted a small space and my family room to see if he wanted more space. At last, he crept into Sunny's crate in the kitchen and fell asleep.

I loved the four-bedroom cottage I'd bought to raise the kids in. It was a couple of blocks from the ocean, and we could hear the waves when the windows were open. The rooms were small, but each person had their own private space. It'd been perfect for them, with no sad memories to overcome.

Never in my wildest dreams had I ever imagined at eighteen I'd be figuring out health insurance, life insurance, utilities, and all the issues most parents faced. With only a high school education, I hadn't been able to manage many extras for the kids. When it came time for Nate and Lacey Jane to drive, they'd had to get jobs to pay for car insurance. Mom and Dad would've encouraged them to focus on good grades and extra-curricular activities like they'd done with me. My parents' early death had affected us emotionally and financially.

God had provided for us. Tony had given Nate his old Chevy pick-up truck, and the church organist sold Lacey Jane her ancient Camry. Each owned a vehicle by the time they had a driver's license. In addition to Nate's work truck, he still had the old Chevy. For Christmas, Lacey Jane upgraded to a late model economy car.

Moving out of our parents' home had been a necessity. The excess furniture that wouldn't fit in our new little house had been stored in the garage. When Nate and Lacey Jane grew older and moved to their own apartments, we had plenty of furniture for them to divide up.

Juliet moving in with us had provided a bit of extra money and moral support. On the flip side, we'd given her a place to live where there were no drugs, drinking, or fighting. Her parents had been arrested more than once for domestic violence. My home had become Juliet's safe haven, and she'd lived with me for a decade. As we approached turning thirty, we decided to live on our own.

So last year, Juliet moved into her own apartment, and I turned the fourth bedroom into an office for my pet-walking business. Customers rarely came to my house, but having a dedicated room allowed me to keep work separate from my home life.

My phone buzzed and the bright screen lit up my bedroom. Marc's name blazed across the glass. "Hi, Marc. What's up?"

"Has Sheriff Stone called you?"

"No. It's almost nine o'clock at night." My heart raced. "Does he have more questions for me? At this hour? I told him everything I know. Do you think he'll arrest me for Peter's murder?"

"Calm down. He's only trying to get the timeline fixed in his mind. He caught me out in the shed working on a kayak."

I'd put on a pajama T-shirt and flannel shorts. "You think he's heading this way?"

"Yep. Thought I should warn you."

"You're sure he's not going to arrest me?" I didn't want to get hauled off to prison wearing pajamas.

"Pretty sure. Do you want me to drive over?"

"Pretty sure" didn't exactly instill me with confidence, but I couldn't let Marc Williams think I was a wuss. "No." I wouldn't ask him to come hold my hand. I was a big girl used to fighting my own battles. "I'll be fine."

"Let me know when he leaves. If I don't hear from you, I'll call the sheriff later to make sure I don't need to bail you out."

"Ha. Gee, thanks." But his request for me to call him tickled the hairs on my neck.

"It's what any good lawyer would do, but I don't think you're a suspect. Take deep breaths and relax. If you're too uptight, he may take a harder look at you."

"Deep breaths. Right." I kicked off the sheet and ripped open a dresser drawer. "Any chance you had time to contact Thomas about a remodel?"

"Not yet. I'll call him in the morning."

"Let me know what he says." I pulled out something more decent than my sleeping clothes.

"Will do. Bye."

I tossed the phone onto the bed and changed clothes before moving into the living room. There was never much traffic on my street, and I turned on the porch light. Most people were probably celebrating Friday night at the Marsh Walk. Lots of bands would be playing at restaurants and bars.

Sunny barked which led to Chubb barking.

"It's okay, girl. We need to check on Chubb." As I walked through the family room, a vehicle pulled into the driveway. "You always hear things before I do."

I peeked out the window. Sure enough, the sheriff's SUV sat in my drive. Good thing Marc had warned me so I could be prepared. What would Wade Stone think if I'd come to the door in flannel pj's? My hands trembled. I'd known the man most of my life. He had to know I wouldn't hurt Peter. It didn't make sense to be nervous.

The doorbell pealed, and Chubb barked from his spot in the kitchen.

Sunny stayed on my heels as I walked over and opened the door. "Wade, looks like you're keeping late hours." He wore his uniform, but it was wrinkled. His mussed hair and five o'clock shadow made me think he hadn't gotten much rest.

He nodded. "It's been a long two days. May I come inside for a minute?"

"Sure, but I need to check on Peter's dog. I brought him home with me since I was responsible for his care. Is that okay?"

"Not a problem."

"Have a seat. This won't take long." In the kitchen, I opened the crate door and let both dogs into the backyard and turned on the outside lights.

Wade was sitting in a slip-covered armchair with a small computer in his lap.

"Did you find the killer?"

"Not yet. I need to clear up a few details. You say you were at Peter's home to walk his dog." He positioned his hands over a little keyboard.

"Yes. Peter was supposed to leave town on Thursday morning for a business trip in Atlanta. It was a last-minute thing. Wednesday night, he texted to see if I was awake and available. When I replied I was still up, he called me. It was about ten." I reached for my phone and showed him the message.

He read it then typed on his computer.

I eyed the computer he had resting on his knees. It didn't look like any other laptops I'd ever seen. "Is that a laptop?"

"Toughbook."

"Okay." Never heard of one, but it seemed like an appropriate phrase for a sheriff. "I thought law enforcement guys took notes on little pads of paper."

"Sometimes we do. Do you know Regina Houp?"

"I heard she was Peter's fiancée. She's the new owner of Paula's Pickings."

Wade quirked a thick eyebrow. "I'm aware." He pressed his lips together.

"Wait, I want to be completely honest." Perspiration broke out along my hairline. "I went to meet Regina earlier today. At her shop."

"Ms. Scott, you better not interfere with my investigation." He pounded the keys on his Toughbook before piercing me with his gaze. "What time did you get to Mr. Roth's place yesterday morning?"

Okay, so formality was the word of the evening. I adjusted my demeanor. "Middle of the morning."

"Can you be more specific?"

"Maybe ten-thirty or eleven. I spend at least thirty minutes per house, and I started my day at seven. Owen Ray has a new litter of puppies, and I stayed there over an hour. He lives in Litchfield. Did you know Peter broke up with Regina? I heard she wasn't too happy about it."

"Ms. Scott, I'm conducting an official investigation."

"Come on, Wade. You know me. It's okay to call me Andi Grace."

"It's been a long time since we've seen each other. Just trying to keep the conversation official." He tapped more on his Toughbook. "I hope you're not going around town gossiping about Mr. Roth's death."

"I respected Peter too much to spread rumors."

"Yet, you're telling me he broke up with his fiancée."

"That's different. You're the sheriff. I needed to tell you." I pushed myself to the edge of the couch. The man needed to understand Regina had more than one motive. "I want to make sure you question her. Don't they say the spouse, or lover, is usually the killer?"

He studied me with eyebrows raised.

I plowed on. "She had a second motivation. She wanted to be the designer for the addition to Peter's house. He wanted to handle it on his own. He didn't want to marry her, and he refused to let her decorate his home."

"Again. I'm in charge of the investigation." He stood. At over six feet, the man filled my room. Although he wasn't as tall as Marc. Not as handsome either. "Are we clear?"

"Yes, sir." I walked him to the door. "Did you learn anything about the ace of hearts playing card? Were there fingerprints on it?"

He took a deep breath that puffed out his broad chest. "I can't tell you."

"I voted for you as senior class president, and I voted for you to be sheriff. You're doing a good job, Wade."

He shook his head. "Don't play me."

"I'm not. You look tired, and I wanted to encourage you."

"Thanks, Andi Grace." With all of his sports accolades, females flocked around him. I'd been on the newspaper staff. Not part of his world. "You used to wear glasses and worked on the *Red and Black.*"

Of course he'd remember *that*. I sighed. "Right. So if there's anything I can do to help, please let me know. Peter was a friend."

"He was a good man. Where were you Wednesday night after the phone conversation?"

"Here. At home." I grew dizzy and held onto the nearest chair for support.

His eyes narrowed. "Was anybody with you?"

"Just Sunny." My dog's ears perked up.

"How well do you know Marc Williams?"

"I just met him yesterday morning at Peter's house. After the murder. I'd heard of him, but yesterday was the first time we met. Why?"

He shrugged. "I'm putting the puzzle pieces together."

I paused, considering my predicament. "Do I need a lawyer?"

"No, but I need you to stay out of the investigation."

"You believe I'm innocent, right?"

"You were standing over the body, holding a paperweight. Peter died from a blow to his head." He tilted his head and lifted his free hand palm up.

I tightened my grip on the back of the chair. This was too much. "I can't believe you think I'd kill Peter."

His lips parted, and he stared at me without blinking. "There are multiple reasons for you to stay out of my way. Got it?"

"Yes. But I don't think you realize how connected I am to Heyward

Beach. I know people all over the county, and they confide in me. You'd be amazed what I learn walking dogs. I'm in homes, and I know when people are out of town. It'd be so easy for me to help."

Wade frowned to the point a deep line formed over the bridge of his nose. "Stay away from my investigation. Next time I won't be so nice." He stepped onto my front porch. "Lock up."

I shut the door and turned the lock.

He jogged to his truck.

I watched him maneuver the official vehicle from my drive then sent a brief text message to Marc.

He didn't arrest me.

I traipsed back into the house, my belly swirling. I couldn't sit back and wait for the authorities to solve the case. They were overworked and understaffed. The same as twelve years earlier when my parents had been killed. Nothing would stop me from moving forward, but I'd have to be extra careful not to get caught by Sheriff Wade Stone.

Or the killer.

Chapter Six

SATURDAY MORNING, I walked out of Lovely Locks with a fresh cut just below my shoulders. Juliet had teased me again about letting my bangs grow out, but I was determined to try one more time. My friend had taken extra time to style loose curls into my hair and sprayed it with a new hairspray that might hold up to the beach humidity. "Might" being the key word.

The open sign at Paula's Pickings flashed on with an orange glow.

I took a deep breath and headed over. The door rang as I entered the cheery space.

Regina stood at the counter, taping plain, brown paper around a box. "Good morning." She spoke before making eye contact. When she spotted me, her brows furrowed, but she recovered in record time. "How are you today?"

"Good. I was wondering if you sell items on the internet." I smiled because there was no reason to treat her as the enemy until I learned more.

"I sell through a couple of websites. How can I help you?"

I'd already planned for this. "I need a gift for my sister. She recently got accepted into a program to become a paralegal."

"What'd you have in mind?" Her lips turned up in a frozen Botox-like smile.

"A gavel or scales of justice? Feather pen?"

The woman didn't crack a true smile when I attempted to lighten the atmosphere.

I pushed on. There had to be some way to reach this woman. "What do you suggest?"

"A nice scarf or leather briefcase would be fitting for a career in law."

The briefcase was probably out of my price range. "She's young, and I'm not sure a scarf is her style."

"Look around. Maybe something will appeal to you. In the back corner is a table of antique jewelry."

"Okay. Thanks." Her lack of customer service startled me, but I wasn't giving up. I allowed my gaze to roam over the store before heading to an area that seemed more like Lacey Jane's style. A white candelabra hung over a distressed pink desk.

"You're in my French chic area. Have you ever been to France?" Her snobby tone confused me. How did Peter ever fall for her? He was kind to everybody, and Regina seemed to have a burr under her saddle.

I counted to ten in French while forming a polite answer instead of spewing an ugly response. "I've never had the opportunity to travel. My sister and I would love to visit Paris one day."

Regina picked up an old piece of crockery. "I found quite a few antique crocks on my last trip to France."

It would've been a nice gift if Lacey Jane wanted to become a chef. "Your pieces are beautiful but not quite right for Lacey Jane. Were you going to decorate Peter's new room with French antiques?"

She sighed. "I would have loved filling the space with antiques from France and England. Peter insisted he wanted a man cave, though."

"It would've been your house, too, after you married. Did he consider your opinions?" Why wasn't she telling me how much she loved Peter?

"Not when it came to his precious room." Regina set down the crock and pointed to a gold and cream something. "What about the vintage Florentine letter holder?"

Ah, the *thing* was a *Florentine* divider. My sister could use it to organize all of her papers. "It looks perfect, especially if she puts it on my mother's desk. It's got some age on it, and it's not a fancy antique, but it's got potential. I'll get my brother to help paint the old desk, and I know the perfect lamp I can give her. Thanks, Regina. I'll take it."

"Would you like me to wrap it for you?"

"Yes, please." I continued to mosey around the jam-packed store. "I'm impressed with how much stuff you have, and it's all displayed so nicely."

"Thanks." Regina was going to have to get a whole lot chattier if she planned for her business to survive. Her aunt had often told stories and questioned people until they found the perfect gift. It'd be a shame if Regina's attitude ruined the business Paula had started.

I paused beside a poker table. The ace of hearts. Had Wade done anything with the playing card I'd found at Peter's house on Thursday?

Was it significant? The time had come to fish for answers. "Do you sell many of these tables?"

"I've sold three since taking over the store. Don't you think that's weird?" Regina propped a hand on her hip and the woman's eyes showed real interest in learning my opinion.

I licked my dry lips. "Yeah. I don't think it's legal to host private gambling events. Did Peter play poker?"

"No. He believed he worked too hard to wager his money." She reached for the tape dispenser and paused. "Did Peter talk to you much about me?"

My face warmed. "We mostly talked about dogs and my business. What about Spades or Bridge or some other kind of card game?"

"No." She shook her head then cocked it to one side and peered at me. "You mean he never discussed our relationship with you? I heard all kind of stories about you and your family."

"I'm sorry, Regina." I stepped closer to her. "Peter never talked much about his personal relationships with me. Maybe he didn't mind telling you about my family because. . . . " Because we didn't matter as much as I thought? I blinked back a forming tear.

"Oh, now I'm sorry. I know he cared about you. He was proud of all you accomplished. He bragged about you like a proud papa." She squeezed my hand. "I had a feeling we were going to break up before we did."

Wow, I hadn't expected her to share something so personal. Maybe we were bonding. "Oh, Regina. Maybe he was just getting cold feet. I bet you could've figured something out."

"Yeah, maybe."

Her posture didn't convince me she believed that. I moved on. "Did Peter talk about anybody in his family besides his sister?"

"No. She's married and has a son. They live in South Carolina, but I don't know where."

I propped an elbow on the checkout counter. "Do you know what happened between Peter and his sister?"

"I think it had to do with money. They argued, and they didn't communicate after that. He wasn't a fighter." Regina played with a strand of turquoise ribbon. "He never wanted to hurt anybody's feelings, and he didn't have a poker face. Between us, I knew something was off, but he wouldn't talk to me about it."

"Off with your relationship, or off with his life?" I held my breath while waiting for her answer.

She shrugged. "I guess both. I hadn't talked to him in days."

"Was it unusual not to talk?" When the love of my life, Danny Nichols, dumped me, I didn't talk to him unless we physically ran into each other at a store or church.

"Yeah. We'd agreed to remain friends, and a part of me hoped we'd eventually get back together."

Regina was messing with my theory of her being a suspect. Time to switch gears. "They say a lot of good marriages start as solid friendships."

She puffed out a stilted chuckle. More of a grunt. "I guess we'll never know now." Her shoulders drooped.

I needed to pull the conversation away from this topic. "Do you remember who you sold the poker tables to?"

She gave me a questioning look. "Why? Are you a gambler?"

"No. Just curious." I adjusted my purse strap from sliding off my shoulder.

"Hey, I was curious as well. It was a young man who claims it's illegal to gamble in South Carolina. He wanted the tables for friends who live out of state." Regina tied the bow on the package and rang up the purchase. "Your total is one hundred and thirty-five dollars."

I almost fainted. Why hadn't I asked the price first? Steep prices and her haughty attitude might not keep Regina in business long. Maybe the woman was hoping for a different clientele. I pulled out my credit card. "The sheriff came by my place again last night asking about Peter's death."

"Why?" Regina's eyes widened.

"I guess because I found the body. They're working on the timeline. Where were you Thursday night?"

Regina's nostrils flared. "Aunt Paula and I were at an auction in Hemingway. Not that it's any of your business."

My face grew warm. "I'm sorry. I was only wondering about the last person to speak to Peter. I hope it was somebody friendly."

Regina shook her finger at me. "You might want to curb your curiosity. I'd hate for you to end up like Peter."

I shivered at her icy tone. It didn't sound like we'd be bosom buddies anytime soon. The only word she hadn't uttered was *dead*. In the future, I'd be super alert around Peter's ex-fiancée. But her threat wasn't going to stop me from my search for the killer.

Chapter Seven

I TURNED OFF RIVER Road at the small brown sign pointing the direction to get to MAW Wood Boats. "A little more signage wouldn't hurt Marc's business. Bright nautical colors would attract the eye as well, and a catchier name would be a bonus."

Chubb barked as if agreeing. Then Sunny yapped like an older sibling correcting a younger child, and both dogs grew quiet, except for panting.

The rutted driveway turned smoother as I neared Marc's house. He'd told me to follow the private residence sign and continue to the front of his home. At the split, I veered left instead of turning toward the shed like we'd done on Thursday. It didn't take long for a blue cottage to appear. I parked under a sprawling oak to prevent the Suburban from heating up on the inside. Marc's house was simple and masculine. Like the man himself.

I leashed both dogs, and we walked up the five wooden stairs to Marc's front porch. There was one solitary white wooden rocker. Not two. It seemed lonely sitting by itself slowly moving in the breeze. I rang the doorbell.

Peter's larger, more elaborate home would soon be on the market. Would the casino developer scoop it up and be one step closer to creating his resort on the river? George Reeves was the only suspect on my list with a motive to transform the property into a business.

Footsteps sounded from inside, and Marc opened the door. "Hey, Andi Grace. Thomas isn't here yet."

"He may not be happy to see me."

"Tough. Come on inside."

I pointed out the dogs. "Them too?"

"This isn't a show place. Dogs are welcome."

"I like your attitude." I followed him inside to a great room. Couch, recliner, coffee table, and a big screen TV. "Nice open concept. Way more modern than Peter's place."

"Don't forget, at one time Peter's house belonged to the owner of the plantation, Hewitt Kennady. It remained in the family for years until the Kennadys ran out of money. Parcels were sold, and the new owners either built their own smaller homes or converted other buildings into houses. My home was built with repurposed materials from barns that'd been torn down on this parcel of land. Before it was trendy to repurpose, it was practical. The previous owner was practical." He backed up a step. "I was told the floors came from the original carriage house. Peter still has a carriage house on his property built closer to the time automobiles were made."

I knelt down and rubbed my hand along the surface of the wood. "Not slick like a new floor, but it's smooth and beautiful."

Marc nodded. "Thanks. Would you like some juice or water?"

"Water is good." I followed him through the open dining room to the kitchen, passing by a powder room on the way. "What's back there?"

"My bedroom. I have two guest rooms upstairs. I don't really use the space up there much, but I bought this place for other reasons." He filled two glasses from a filtered water pitcher.

"Such as?" I accepted the drink and sipped it.

"The building by the river is perfect for a boat business. The dock is the icing on the cake." Marc's eyes sparkled. "I'd have pitched a tent if necessary in order to get this land. The house was just an added bonus."

"What are you going to ask Thomas to do for you?"

Marc shrugged. "I'm not sure. Do you think I should ask him for a bid to update the kitchen?"

I laughed. "You're really content with your house the way it is, aren't you?"

He looked around the space and smiled. "Yeah, I am. I just didn't want Thomas to go to your house. So am I asking him to remodel the kitchen?"

"It couldn't hurt. I mean, you're only asking for a bid. Right? There's no commitment involved. What will you give him for a budget?"

"That's the point. He's supposed to give me an estimate."

Chubb tugged on the leash. I released the clasp, and he headed straight to Marc. "I think he likes you. Are you sure you don't want to adopt him?"

"I don't have time to train him properly."

I had to give Marc credit for wanting to be a responsible dog owner. Sunny remained at my side like the good dog she was. "It takes a lot of work to have an obedient dog. I kinda thought you might have more time since you work from home."

His nostrils flared. "Building boats is hard work. Many days I'm in the barn from dawn to dusk. It's honest time-consuming work."

"I didn't mean to insinuate you were goofing off. Sorry." I made a mental note to not question Marc's work. Ever again.

His shoulders straightened. "I'm running a business. Same as you. How would you feel if people thought you were playing all day because you walk dogs?"

"You're right. I really am sorry. Of all people, I should've understood."

The rigid set of his shoulders deflated like a popped balloon. "I'm sorry, too, for being oversensitive. I took a lot of criticism when I quit my job to build boats."

"Don't worry about it. We'll pretend like we kissed and made up." My face grew warm at my own audacity.

He smiled before pointing out the window. "Thomas's truck is heading up the drive. King Contractors."

White dust billowed behind the vehicle as it sped up the narrow drive.

I pulled my thoughts together. "I like how you can see through your house. Your kitchen has a nice farmhouse feel."

"Thanks." He reached for a kitchen towel and swiped at the counter where our glasses sat sweating. "I hope you're ready, because it's showtime. Thomas is walking toward us now."

My eye twitched, and I rubbed it. "So we're going with kitchen remodel?"

Marc nodded, stepped to the door, and opened it for the man approaching. "Hi. You must be Thomas. I'm Marc Williams. Thanks for stopping by. Come on inside."

"No problem. I'm working on Peter Roth's house, so I was in the area."

"Even though he died?"

"Yes, sir. The estate will finish paying my bill. I always require some upfront money. Along the way, if we make any changes in the initial contract, you can pay then. Otherwise, you'll finish paying when the project is complete." Thomas caught sight of me. His eyes narrowed. "Didn't expect to see you here."

I shrugged. "I'm trying to talk Marc into adopting Peter's dog."

Marc laughed. "Not sure that'll happen. Let's sit at the kitchen table."

Thomas didn't move. "What are you looking to change?"

"The kitchen could use some work." Marc did an amazing job of improvising.

Thomas walked through the space in slow motion. He seemed to study every nook and even looked under the sink before sitting at the table. "Whatcha got in mind?"

"First, can you explain what kind of changes you referred to requiring up-front money?"

"Sure can. Today, you'll tell me what you want done. I'll make notes and draw up a plan tonight. I'll calculate expenses and send you an estimate. After we sign a contract, you might decide you want lights in your cabinets and glass doors. Say that costs an extra thousand dollars. I'll need a check for the additional changes because they won't be included in the original contract."

"Okay, then. Good to know."

"Are you wanting something shiny and new?" He took notes on a tablet.

"I don't want the kitchen to outshine the rest of my house, but it needs updates."

I eyed the room. "Are you thinking retro?"

"I doubt it." Marc reached down and rubbed Chubb between the ears. "Not even sure what a retro kitchen would look like."

Thomas snorted. "It's a female thing. I'm sure you're looking for something manly. Stainless steel appliances with concrete countertops. Or we could go dark. Black farmhouse would be a masculine look. Black cabinets with some floating shelves would keep it from getting oppressive. Stay away from retro unless you're planning to set up housekeeping with a woman." His beady gaze drifted to me.

I took a deep breath and silently started my counting. Thomas wouldn't upset me with his rude insinuation. Or at least I wouldn't let him know he did.

Marc stood and moved to the kitchen counter. He ran his hands over the Formica top. "Concrete and granite seem too cold and hard for my taste. I'd rather have wood countertops. Lighter colored cabinets. Not necessarily painted white, but naturally light. Tall counters and a double sink."

Thomas sat at the table and took notes on a little worn spiral pad. "Not a farmhouse sink? They're popular these days."

"Nope. I like to soak my dishes before I wash them. Two sections." He tapped his hand on the counter twice as if to emphasize his words.

"Gas or electric?" He continued to write.

"I've got electric now. No need to change to gas."

Thomas leaned back and scratched his belly. "You're not going with popular trends. It'll make it harder to sell in the future."

"I don't plan to move." He rejoined us at the old oak table. "Why? Is that what you thought this was about?"

I studied Thomas and waited for a response.

His shoulders hiked in disinterest. "I assumed with Roth's death, you thought it was too dangerous to live on the river. Lots of people remodel before trying to sell their homes."

Marc's calloused fingers drummed on the table. His hands were strong, probably from the work he did, but they were clean. "I've been taking care of myself for over thirty years. I'm not worried about Peter's killer coming after me."

I couldn't stop myself, realizing it could be my best shot. I leaned forward and propped my elbows on the table. "Thomas, who do you think killed Peter?"

"No idea." His eyes narrowed. He pushed his chair back on two legs. "Maybe some homeless person looking for food or money. Roth had a nice place. Lots of good stuff worth stealing over there."

"Nothing was stolen." I raised my palms.

Thomas shrugged. "Then I guess it was personal. You were his friend, right? Maybe it was you."

Sunny growled.

"It was not me." Pressure built in my head until I thought it might explode.

Marc stood. "I didn't ask you here to insult my guest. I think it's time for you to leave, Mr. King."

"I meant no offense." Thomas gathered his papers and stalked through the great room to the front door. He turned and faced us across the room. "But you know what they say. It's usually somebody close to the victim who committed the murder."

I gasped. "I'd never hurt Peter."

Thomas laughed as he walked away.

Marc turned the lock and dead bolt but remained in the same spot, watching out the door's window.

The sound of Thomas's vehicle driving away filtered through the windows, and I sighed.

Marc stepped away from the door. "Hey, don't let him get to you."

"He's a mean man. Always has been." My hands shook. I stood and planned to pace to work off the anger, but my legs shook too much. I ended up leaning against the counter.

"Always?" His gaze met mine.

"I'll share my story another day."

Marc crossed the room and took a seat at the kitchen table. "I'd like to hear it when you're ready to share. I agree that he's dangerous, which is exactly why you need to be careful around him."

"No wonder Dylan is so ornery." I needed to stop talking before I said something truly ugly.

Sunny and Chubb stood on either side of me. Then Chubb rubbed his head against Marc's leg. Marc petted the dog's side, and the two of them made eye contact for several seconds. A smile broke out on Marc's face. He rubbed his hands together the way some people did before making a big announcement. "Maybe I should give Chubb a trial run."

Tears filled my eyes, and I collapsed into the chair next to him. "That's the nicest thing you could've said to me."

"You do understand it's only a trial run. Right?" He handed me a paper napkin.

"Yes. But I believe you'll fall in love with him. It won't take long." I wiped the tears falling from my eyes.

Chubb deserved a good home, and I appreciated Marc giving it a shot. "He'll be good company for you. Both here and at the boat shed. Or whatever you call your work building."

"Boat shed is as good a name as anything." He leaned his sinewy forearms on his thighs and petted Chubb. "Besides the obvious, did you learn anything from Thomas?"

I blew my nose then sniffed. *Deep breaths.* Marc didn't strike me as the kind of man who put up with sniveling females. "I thought the money angle was interesting. What about you?"

"I understood his process in one way, but as a customer, I'd want a detailed list of receipts. Especially if I was paying extra after signing the contract. Actually, I'd want an additional contract for each change order."

"How do you write contracts for your customers?" Sunny plopped her head on my lap. What a good dog. She always could sense my moods, and I ran my hands over her head and neck.

"We go over a design and discuss finances. If the customer wants something different later on, I write up a change order, and we both sign it. The buyer agrees to pay the additional charge when the boat is finished."

"So the exact opposite of Thomas. Which is the best way?"

"As long as Thomas uses the additional money for the home-owner's project, it's fine." His eyes narrowed ever so slightly.

"But?" I leaned forward, not wanting to miss a word of his answer.

"What if he's using the money for another project? He could be able get away with those shenanigans with most clients."

I tapped the table with my pointer finger. "Peter was an account-ant. He'd be likely to figure out what was happening."

"Yes, but is the situation so bad Thomas would murder Peter? How much money is involved? Hundreds, thousands, or even tens of thou-sands of dollars? Are there liens Peter discovered he'd be responsible for in addition to what he agreed to pay Thomas? The more money, the bigger the motive."

A chill shot through me and I shuddered. "I'm sure you're right. Money is a legitimate motive. On the other hand, what if it's not about money? It could be a jilted lover. I questioned Regina earlier."

"And?" Marc's eyebrows lifted.

The air whooshed out of my lungs. "She has an alibi. Or so she says."

Marc laughed. "You asked her? How'd she handle your questions?"

"She pretty much told me to mind my business. As in curiosity killed the cat."

Marc's hands flattened on the oak table. "Maybe you should listen to her warning and let Sheriff Stone do his job. Without any help from you."

My throat spasmed. "Marc, maybe it was a legit warning. But it doesn't make any sense. If Regina has an alibi, why would she tell me to mind my own business?"

"I don't know—I'm not a detective. Sheriff Stone is trained and equipped with a gun to handle the investigation. Trust him to do his job."

True. Wade was a good sheriff, but he had lots of cases to deal with, pulling him in different directions. I only had one case. Peter Roth's murder. No need to convince Marc to help me find the killer. Maybe it was crazy, but it wouldn't be the first crazy thing I'd ever done. Besides, I didn't need Marc bossing me around. My face grew hot, and I took a deep breath. "Thanks for taking care of Chubb and for helping me. I've got to get going, but I'll get some puppy supplies for you. See you later."

Chapter Eight

"STONE HERE." WADE answered my call.

My palms grew damp. "Hi, Wade. This is Andi Grace. How's the investigation going?"

"It's going. What can I do for you?"

I swallowed hard. "I've been taking care of Peter's dog, which hasn't been a problem because I have different kinds of dog food at my place. I've found a home for Chubb, though, and I wanted to go into Peter's house to get Chubb's supplies for the new owner." At least a temporary owner.

"I don't have time to let you inside."

"I've still got my key." My heart dropped. Would having a key make me look guiltier? "You recall I have a key, right?"

Wade sighed. "Hadn't given it much thought."

"As a dog walker, I have keys to lots of people's homes. I'm very organized with a system of identifying keys for me but not revealing the homeowners to strangers."

"I remember."

Relief washed over me. "So is it okay for me to enter the house?"

"I'll say yes for the sake of the dog. When do you plan to go?"

"Today."

There was a pause in conversation. I held my tongue because I'd already talked too much.

At last Wade said, "That's fine. We've finished up our investigation inside the house."

"If I notice anything unusual, I'll let you know."

"You're not there to help with the investigation. I'm on top of it. Pick up the dog supplies and leave." He paused and his tone turned gruff. "Got it?"

"Yes."

"You might want to take a friend. Nobody can accuse you of doing something if you have a witness."

"Thanks, Wade." Did he still consider me a suspect? Or was he being helpful?

"Andi Grace, be smart."

That stopped me dead. So to speak. "What do you mean?"

"I mean, don't do anything to make yourself look more suspicious."

More suspicious? I didn't care for the sound of that. "Please tell me you're looking for other suspects. I can share my list with you. George Reeves is at the top."

"I can't share anything with you about an active investigation. Just stay out of it, and let me do my job." Wade hung up.

But was he doing his job? I tugged my lower lip with my thumb and finger. Had he done anything with the paperweight or ace of hearts? Did he have any other suspects besides me? I'd cleared Marc's name off my list, but what about Wade's list of suspects? Did he have George Reeves on it? And what about Regina and Thomas? I considered both of them suspects.

Wade did make a good point. I needed to be smart so the killer didn't come after me. I texted Marc to see if he'd go with me, and he agreed. We decided to meet early in the evening.

Later, while I drove to Marc's place, I reflected on my feelings for the man. We'd known each other for less than a week. I didn't know if the stress of dealing with Peter's death had helped us bond faster than normal. Maybe our aloneness drew us together. Marc had no family. I only had two siblings. One set of grandparents had died when we were young, and my dad's parents lived in Ireland. They'd written off my family the day Dad and Mom married. Mom was a South Carolina Protestant. My dad's parents wanted their son to marry a good Irish Catholic girl.

Nate inherited my father's red hair and green eyes. I had blond hair and blue eyes like my mother, and Lacey Jane's dark hair and dark eyes always confused me. The three of us had grown close after my parents passed, and I couldn't imagine anything coming between us. What kind of conflict had come between Peter and his family?

I pulled in front of the boat shed and parked. Despite evening shadows, I spotted Chubb lying on the floor beside where Marc stood sanding wood by hand. Slow and methodical. Kinda like the man himself. I rolled down my window.

Marc was talking to Chubb, and his voice carried to me. "I should've kept my mouth shut, boy. You know it and I know it. I've only just met Andi Grace, but she seems a little prickly when it comes to me."

Prickly? Not me. I tooted the horn to get his attention before he said anything else to hurt my feelings. Eavesdropping was rude, but I hadn't done it on purpose.

Marc wiped his hands on a white rag while he walked up to me. "Sorry. I lost track of time."

"Can you still go?" I dreaded doing this by myself, and I sure didn't want to run into Thomas alone if he was working on the addition.

"Yep. Can you give me a few minutes to clean up a bit?"

"Absolutely. There's no hurry." I hopped out of my SUV. "I'll play with Chubb."

"I'll hurry." Marc got into the red Chevy pickup and drove away with one wrist on the steering wheel. Did the man ever get in a hurry? Seemed funny for a runner to take life slow and easy.

Chubb bumped my leg with his nose.

"All right. Let's play fetch." I found a stick under an oak tree and tossed it across the yard. "Go get it, boy."

The puppy showed spunk for the first time since we'd found Peter. He chased the stick and brought it back to me, dropping it at my feet. We played until Marc returned with damp hair, wearing a plain gray T-shirt and khaki shorts.

"You must've set some kind of record for cleaning up." It looked like the man wasn't slow at everything.

He shrugged. "I didn't want to keep you waiting. Want me to drive?"

"I like driving. Bring Chubb along."

I hopped in the Suburban, turned to a country station, and hummed along with a Darius Rucker song.

Marc opened the passenger door. "In a hurry?"

"Not really." I'd needed to get my equilibrium. Marc was so handsome, and I was clueless as to why he helped me. And why he thought I was prickly.

"Where do you want the pup?"

"It doesn't matter. I've got a kennel in back, or he can sit in your lap."

Marc nodded and slid in with the puppy. "You got any tips on dog training?"

Nice. I could do dog talk. "Be consistent. Whether rewards or discipline, be consistent. If Chubb's confused, he's less likely to obey. Also, boredom leads to behavior problems. Peter had plenty of dog toys and treats to keep Chubb entertained. We'll grab those while we're at his house." I prattled on while I drove down the road.

"What else?"

"Dogs want to please their owners. Instead of saying no all the time, tell Chubb what you want him to do."

"Isn't that a lot of words for a dog to understand?"

I laughed. "Spoken like a man. Say you don't want Chubb to run after cars. When you're walking him and a car comes by, he may bark and try to chase after the vehicle. Tell him no. Then tell him to sit. In time he'll stop trying to chase after cars, and you can reward him for his good behavior. Once he understands how you want him to act, he'll repeat the action."

Marc nodded. "I'd love to be one of those dog owners who walks with a dog that's unleashed and obedient."

"Not impossible, but rare." I turned onto the drive leading to Peter's house, never dreaming how hard it'd be to return knowing I wouldn't see Peter. The King Contractors truck was parked next to the back porch. "Oh, man. Thomas twice in one day. How lucky can a girl get?"

"Do you want to come back later so you don't have to deal with Thomas?"

I shut off the engine. "No. I don't want him to spot me driving away. He'll think I'm afraid of him."

Marc chuckled. "I don't imagine there's much that scares you, but Chubb and I will be your bodyguards."

"I'm glad you came along." The relief surprised me.

"Is this a good time to share your history with Thomas?"

I ran my hands along the steering wheel. "When Lacey Jane was in high school, she had a date with Thomas's son, Dylan. The kid had un-nerved me, and I was worried about Lacey Jane's safety. I could be a momma bear when necessary." I needed to change the topic. "Thanks for coming."

"Anytime." Marc and Chubb followed me up the back stairs. "You seem to lead an exciting life. No time for boredom."

I laughed. "It's usually calmer than these last few days."

Thomas met us on the back porch. "I just finished for the day. I'll get that estimate to you soon, Mr. Williams."

"Please, call me Marc, and I'm not in a hurry."

"Marc, it is." Thomas turned his sights on me. "Be sure to lock up when you leave. I don't want the family holding me responsible if any-thing disappears."

I threw my shoulders back and chin up. No way I'd let Thomas think he intimidated me. "Sheriff Stone knows we're here to pick up dog supplies for Chubb. Don't be surprised if the kennel and dog food are gone when you come back. Are you in touch with Peter's family?"

"None of your business." Thomas cocked his head to the side.

Chubb growled.

Marc spoke before I uttered words I'd probably regret. "If the family wants Chubb, give them my number."

"Will do." Thomas walked away.

After he drove off, I grabbed Marc's arm. "Do you know Peter's family?"

"We talked sports and politics. I barely knew Peter, and I sure don't know his family."

I released his arm. "I asked Wade for permission to enter the house. Do you think Thomas did the same?"

"I doubt it." Marc moved to the door closest to the laundry room.

"While we're inside, let's look at his pictures. Maybe we'll get a clue."

"I thought we were here to pick up Chubb's belongings." His familiar frown appeared.

"Yeah, but it can't hurt to look around."

Marc rolled his shoulders. "We can't help catch the killer if we get thrown in jail."

"Ha ha. I worked too hard to make sure my siblings stayed out of trouble. I don't plan to get arrested for a murder I didn't commit."

Once inside, I filled the dog bowls. One with puppy chow and the other with water.

Chubb lapped the water but ignored the food.

"It's going to get better, boy." I hugged the big puppy before I began my search. Nothing in the kitchen or dining room gave me a hint about Peter's family. I entered the living room and inspected the floor-to-ceiling bookshelves. Books, antiques, and artwork. No family pictures in any of the public spaces. "I'm going upstairs. He probably kept sentimental photos in his bedroom."

Marc shook his head.

"Come on. Two sets of eyes are better than one."

"Will it do any good to try to talk you out of this plan?"

"Don't waste your breath." I started up the grand staircase.

"I thought as much." He followed at a slower pace, and Chubb remained downstairs, sniffing around.

The fifth step squeaked, and I jumped. "Oh, that scared me."

"Probably your guilty conscious." He touched my back. "You okay?"

"Never better." I wouldn't admit it to anybody, especially not Marc, but it'd be creepy to explore Peter's house all by myself. "I always thought this place would be a great museum. I was glad Peter was adding on a room where he could relax. Too bad Regina wanted the new room to be as uppity as the rest of the house."

"I'll take my little house any day. Of course, I often come in from the boat shed covered in sawdust and sweat. I need a place where I don't have to worry about tracking in dirt."

"Your house seemed clean to me."

We paused at the top of the stairs and gazed at each other in the dim light of the landing's candelabra. "It is. As a foster child, I learned to be a neat freak. One less reason to get rejected. I really meant I want to be comfortable and not worry if my shoes are dusty."

Having raised my brother and sister, I got that. "I gave up worrying about a picture-perfect home years ago. Like around the time we moved into the bungalow. My home may have been disorganized, but I did the best I could."

The landing was almost as big as my home office. There were built-in bookshelves, a sturdy chair, a table and dresser each with a lamp, a long wool rug over the dark planked floor, and pictures covered the remaining wall space. Five doors led to rooms off the landing. I turned on the cranberry glass lamp and turned in a circle. "Which room do you think was Peter's?"

Marc chuckled. "May as well look in every room. You're dying to anyway."

"Not sure I appreciate your choice of words there." I turned left and opened the door over the dining room.

"Dying? I'm sure the sheriff doesn't want anybody else getting hurt or murdered. Maybe you should back off."

"No way. Peter was my friend."

Marc held up his hands. "I know. You've told me before. What about the sheriff? Do you think he's capable of solving the murder?"

"He does a good job, but he's overworked with a small staff." I entered a room. "This looks straight out of a museum display. I wonder if Peter let people sleep in this bed?"

"What's the point in having a guest room if you don't have people spend the night? Tell me about Sheriff Stone."

I studied three silver-framed photographs on the dresser. "Wade and I graduated together, but we ran in different circles." Might as well spit it all out. "He was in the cool crowd. I wasn't."

"I can see that."

"Really?" His words pinched.

He shrugged. "Yeah. You're intense, and usually the cool kids are more interested in having a good time. I bet you're the same way today. I doubt you go barhopping to pick up guys."

"Of course I don't go barhopping. And what do you mean by 'intense?'"

His eyebrows rose, and one side of his mouth lifted.

I laughed. "Okay, maybe I'm a tad intense."

"You took my assessment well."

Not as much as he thought. "Thanks. But back to high school. Do you think we would've been friends, or were you a cool kid only focused on fun?" My voice cracked, and my face grew warm. Why would I ask him that?

"I was a loner focused on survival. If we weren't friends back then, it would've been my fault. And my loss."

His words warmed my heart, but what had he meant mean about survival? "Were you bullied?"

"Not by other kids, but I didn't always land with the best families. I wasn't the warm and fuzzy kind of kid. One family even referred to me as damaged. So my plan became to study and do everything possible to get a college scholarship and accomplish some good with my life."

"Looks like your plan worked or you wouldn't have a law degree, and you wouldn't have me for a client." I grinned at him.

"Very funny." His eyes sparkled.

"Any chance you're a defense attorney?" I rested my elbow on the dresser.

"Afraid not. I worked for a big law firm in Charleston."

"You can't blame me for hoping." I shifted my focus back to the pictures. "These look old. Maybe they're Peter's parents or grandparents."

Marc stood behind me and looked over my shoulder. "Parents could still be alive."

"True. I guess Wade looked into them. Regina thinks Peter fell out with his sister over money."

Marc scratched his chin. "Interesting for an accountant to cut himself off from family because of finances."

I moved from the dresser to the bedside table. "Or they severed ties with him."

"It's hard to imagine not being able to get along with family. To willingly cut yourself off from people who love you blows my mind." He stepped into the hall, muttering.

I followed him. "Marc, are you okay?"

"Yeah. I'm fine." He paced back and forth on the wool rug. "We both lost our parents at early ages. I think it's a terrible waste to walk away from family. If I'd known Peter better, I would've said the same thing to his face." Marc avoided looking at me and opened the door to the room behind the master. "Another guest room."

The floor creaked as we circled the feminine space. Wallpaper with roses, pink ruffles on the bed, white eyelet curtains, and a wicker vanity set. "No man designed this space."

Marc whistled. "I'm not even sure a man would be comfortable sleeping in here."

"Let's try another room." I paused in the hall and listened for Chubb. His nails clicked on the wood floor as if taking slow steps. I debated checking on him but wanted to hurry. The sooner I finished my search, the sooner we'd get Chubb settled into his new home. A huge bathroom with both a shower and claw-foot tub was located at the far end of the hall. The room to the right of the bathroom contained a king-size bed placed in the middle of the far wall with a navy bedspread. "This must be the master."

"Thank goodness. I was starting to feel sorry for Peter." Marc stopped behind me, and his warm breath tickled the back of my neck.

"I know he loved history, but this place is over the top." I moved to a nook with an easy chair, side table with a lamp, and a big screen TV, which was overkill for the small sitting area. Two pictures were on the table. One photograph was of Peter and a little boy. "Wonder who this is?"

Marc picked up the framed picture. "Peter looks much younger there. His hair is longer, and I don't see any wrinkles."

I stepped closer. A sense of déjà vu or recognition hit me. "The boy seems familiar."

"Do you think you know him?"

My nerves prickled. "No. At least not at the age he is in the picture. Maybe it's the similarity to Peter."

"They don't look anything alike." Marc handed the picture to me.

"I feel like I've met him, but I guess you're right. It's probably my imagination." I pulled my phone out of my pocket and took a picture of the photo. I wasn't sure I agreed with Marc this time. I would run a print later and study the image.

"Is it possible Peter was married and divorced? This could be a son or step-son."

I shrugged. "At this point, I don't feel like I knew Peter. Whoever this child is must have been very special to Peter."

"Why?"

"Because it's one of the few pictures of a person in this entire house." I returned the picture to the table.

"Hey, you've got a lead. Who is the boy, and what is his relationship to Peter?"

"If we can figure out who the child is, we might discover more about Peter. I never dreamed he was a man with so many secrets."

"We've all got secrets." Marc walked to the master closet.

"You care to expand?" My curiosity piqued.

He leaned against the door. "Nope. I'm not ashamed to admit I've got plenty of secrets."

"Are you challenging me to find out more about you?"

"Ha. I'm not from Georgetown County. You won't find out anything I don't tell you myself."

Challenge accepted. Although I'd keep my research a secret.

"Don't waste your time trying to figure me out. We need to finish up here and get Chubb back to my house."

"You're right." I surveyed the room. A book and clock on the bedside table. An ornate mirror hung over the dresser with an antique cherry frame. A brass lamp and a sweetgrass basket with keys and a wallet.

"Do you see this?" I held up the basket.

"What do you think it means?"

"The keys and wallet make me surer than ever Peter was murdered in the evening."

"Because he'd have these on him if he was about to leave?"

"Right." I looked around the sparsely furnished room. "In some ways he was a minimalist."

Marc disappeared into the walk-in closet. "Maybe not a minimalist. The word might be non-sentimentalist. If that's even a word. Check out this closet."

I glanced into the huge master bathroom on my way to the closet. A tub with jets sat under a tinted window. It was the showpiece of the en suite, which included a double-sink vanity, toilet, bidet, and shower.

Marc whistled. "He's got a rotating tie rack. I've never seen so many ties."

Inside the closet, Marc held a remote-control device and watched neckwear circle around. "Jealous?"

"Of the gadgets? Sure. Of having to wear a tie to work all the time? No way." He sighed. "Those days are behind me."

"Walking dogs doesn't require a dressy wardrobe either." The closet was as big as a room. "This is huge."

"I bet he took a small bedroom and turned it into the closet and bathroom. I know for a fact these old houses didn't have closets as big as this one."

"The wood is beautiful."

"Red mahogany. Check this out. A sound system." Marc pointed to another remote.

"How much money do you think Peter had?" I'd known he was wealthy, but this closet was ridiculous. There had to be around twenty suits in various shades of gray, black, and navy. Polished business shoes and different sorts of running shoes filled slanted shelves. The room-sized space even held a chest of drawers.

Marc's expression became thoughtful. "I wonder who he left all this to in his will?"

My mouth grew dry. "I don't know, but do you think it could be a motive for murder?"

"People have been killed for less money than Peter seems to have had."

I flipped through the suspect list in my mind. "We've got the ex-fiancée, the construction worker, and the land developer. When we hear who's listed in the will, we may have a third suspect."

"I thought you told me Regina had an alibi."

Crumb. Marc was right. I wrinkled my nose. "Yeah. She claims she was at an auction in Hemingway. So we're down to two suspects."

Chubb barked.

A quick glance at my watch showed we'd been here much longer than I'd planned. "We better check on your dog."

Marc held up his hands in a surrender motion. "Trial basis only."

"You're going to love him. I just know it." I exited the closet. "We missed the other front room."

Chubb's barking grew intense.

"You're right." I turned on my toe and hustled to see what we'd overlooked.

Marc beat me to the last room. "This looks like Peter's office."

A two-drawer chest sat between two windows. One drawer stood partway open. "Look at that. Everything in the house is in perfect order except for the open drawer. Doesn't it seem weird?"

"Yeah. What are you thinking?" Marc propped fists on his hips. His eyebrows rose, and a softening in his eyes encouraged me to continue.

"Did somebody in the sheriff's department leave it open? Or has this area been inspected?" I walked past the five-foot-wide writing desk in the center of the room. A laptop sat open in the middle of the desk. The black-leather office chair was turned toward the cabinet. A glance down revealed the drawer was full of files hanging in neat folders. "Did the deputies only focus on the crime scene?"

Marc shook his head. "Seems like the sheriff would go through the entire house."

I tried to imagine Peter in this office space. "Suppose Peter was sitting here working on his computer. He needs something in a file. Turns around without getting up. Rolls over while sitting in his chair, opens the drawer, and pulls out the material he needs. Maybe he didn't shut the drawer because—"

"Because he was interrupted. Somebody comes to the house. Let's say Peter carries the file to the door for some reason."

"Or he may never have pulled the file out. He was brilliant but absentminded sometimes." There'd been many times he didn't remember we'd made plans to meet.

"Okay. Let's say it's the killer at the door. A person he knows. Peter invites him inside."

"Or her."

Marc paced. "Yep, it could be a woman. Peter invites his killer inside. They have a discussion. Hold on. It'd be a whopping big coincidence for the file to be connected to the person at the door. Let's back up."

"Right." I slid lip balm onto my lips. "Our theory has to make sense."

"What if Peter was working on a side project—he finds an accounting discrepancy. He calls the person he thinks did something wrong. The guilty party comes up with a story for why Peter's conclusions can't be right. They hang up, but Peter can't let it go. He works a little longer trying to solve the problem."

"Meanwhile, the killer drives here. He or she wants to see Peter's face to decide if he's bought their story. They argue. The killer hits

Peter in the head. Maybe Peter didn't have a file with him when he opened the door. The killer searches for evidence and finds the file up here in the office. The killer swipes the file and deletes whatever is on the laptop." I dropped to my knees and looked through the files.

"What are you looking for?"

"A file telling me who the killer is. If only it was so simple. I don't guess you know how to get into his laptop."

"Computer guru is not on my resume." Marc took the desk chair and tapped buttons on the computer. "If his password is as simple as 123ABC, we'll be in business."

I pulled out some files then my phone.

After a few minutes Marc asked, "What'd you find?"

"Here's a contract between Peter and Thomas King. There's a file on Richard Rice Plantation. It's a nonprofit and Peter is, er, was on the board." I had to stop thinking of my friend in the present tense. There would be no more "is" for Peter Roth. I took pictures of the pages in the file. "How are you coming with the computer?"

"I'm trying different password possibilities. Feel free to take over here if you want." Irritation laced his words.

"Nope. I'm good with these files. You're doing great. I wish Peter had kept a copy of his will."

"If he has one, it's probably in a fireproof box or with his attorney."

"Why wouldn't he have one?"

Marc's shoulders hiked as he continued to tap on the laptop. "You said he was estranged from his sister. Maybe he didn't have anyone to leave the money to."

"That could be, I guess. But would an accountant not have a will?" A squeal caught my attention, and my heart leapt. "What's that sound?"

"A car. It might have a loose belt." He snapped the laptop shut. "Let's get out of here."

"We're at the front of the house. Whoever's driving must've seen the light on up here. How am I going to explain?"

Marc headed for the office door. "Say Chubb ran up here and you came to find him. Hurry."

"I can't lie." My voice vibrated, and my knees shook.

Marc sighed and darted out of the office.

"Hey, where are you going? Do you plan to leave me all by myself?" *Please, God, let it be a deputy and not the killer.*

How could Marc run off and leave me to fend for myself? Had

years of living in foster care made him a coward? Deep down was the man scared of law enforcement?

Whatever his reason to desert me, I was alone to face possibly the killer or a deputy. Wade had given me permission to pick up dog supplies. If the driver was a deputy, I had an excuse. Although how would I explain my presence upstairs?

My belly did a flip. If I got arrested for snooping, at least I wouldn't have to worry about my siblings. They were old enough to take care of themselves.

Chapter Nine

MARC APPEARED AT the office doorway with Chubb in his arms. "Now you don't have to lie. The dog is here. You're here. Let's go."

My heart softened. He hadn't deserted me. "Come here, Chubb."

The puppy hopped out of Marc's hold and hurried to my side. "Good boy."

A knock sounded on the front door, followed by the doorbell. Marc left the room. "You better be right behind me."

I wasn't sure his bossy side was attractive, but the man was helping me and I couldn't really complain. I turned off the office light and walked down the stairs with Chubb by my side.

Marc opened the front door. "Hi, deputy."

I tried my best to act normal. "Hi, sir." The man stood at least six feet tall and wore a brown deputy uniform. I'd seen him before on the news and hoped nothing tonight would make a TV crew race out here.

Marc opened the door wider. "Would you like to come in?"

"I'd like to know why you two are in Peter Roth's house." He spread his legs and held one hand near his gun. The man's name tag read B.R. Hanks.

Chubb barked.

My head spun, and it became hard to breathe. "Sheriff Stone gave us permission to come get the dog's belongings. I'm Andi Grace Scott and this is Marc . . ." My face grew warm. Marc what? How could I forget his name at a time like this?

Marc inched forward and held out his hand. "Marc Williams. Would you like us to step outside while you confirm?"

The officer ignored Marc's outstretched hand, his eyes narrowing as if trying to figure out the two of us.

The grandfather clock marked off uncomfortable seconds. *Tic. Toc. Tic. Toc. Tic. Toc.*

My heart beat double time to the clock's tempo. Why didn't the officer say something? I bit my lip to stop myself from babbling. If I started running my mouth, I'd look guilty. Which I was. But only of snooping. Not murder.

At last the deputy pointed and spoke. "Let's move to the front hall while I call my boss."

We stepped back and allowed the officer to enter.

Chubb whined.

"It's okay, boy. This is a nice man." I hoped.

The deputy removed his hat and revealed a completely bald head. "You say you're here for dog supplies? Where are they?"

I gulped. "In the kitchen."

"Why was the upstairs light on? I saw it when I came out of the woods and into the clearing in front of the house."

"Chubb ran upstairs. He's the puppy." I shut my mouth, willing myself to not divulge more than necessary.

The deputy's nostrils flared. "Why was he upstairs if his supplies were in the kitchen?"

I giggled. My nerves were shot, and I hoped like all get-out the officer didn't notice. "You know how puppies are. He took off. I was Peter's dog walker and took care of Chubb when Peter was out of town. I'm still training him."

Marc said, "One minute we were in the kitchen, and the next we were upstairs in Peter's office."

"Don't go anywhere." He punched a button on the phone. Guess he had the sheriff on speed dial.

I nodded and picked up the whining puppy. Great. So far, no lies. Lots of gray area, though. I adjusted the forty-pound puppy in my arms.

Marc motioned with his head to move toward the stairs.

When the deputy spoke into his phone, I looked at Marc. "What?"

He whispered, "Did you put away the files?"

"Yes. At least I think so. I meant to when I shut the drawer."

The deputy cleared his throat. "Sheriff Stone confirmed he gave you permission to get the dog's things. Gather them up while I inspect the rest of the house."

I pivoted and headed to the kitchen. The run-in with the deputy had been a close call. One I'd rather not repeat.

Marc remained with the officer. "Thomas King was here before we were. He's the contractor working on the addition."

His eyes shot daggers at us. "This is a virtual three-ring circus." The deputy's gravelly voice gave me goose bumps. "I'll check the house then lock it up."

I made it to the kitchen without uttering another word. I set Chubb on the floor and gathered his toys, blanket, pillows, and very expensive food. Nothing but the best for Chubb, in Peter's opinion. Would Marc be able to afford this special brand? Did it really matter at this point? Chubb needed love and attention more than expensive chow.

Marc appeared and rubbed Chubb between his ears. "I'll carry the kennel to your Suburban."

"Thanks." I attached the leash to Chubb's harness and followed Marc outside. After we got him loaded, I gave the puppy a treat. "Good boy."

A gentle breeze floated up from the river providing a bit of relief from the evening's humidity.

Marc stuffed his hands in his worn shorts pockets. "What do you think?"

An owl hooted in the distance. The sound added to my nervousness.

"I think we're lucky he didn't catch us in Peter's office going through the laptop and files. As long as he doesn't check my phone and find the pictures I took, we should be safe."

Marc got Chubb settled into the back of the Suburban but left the door open.

"I'd say it was a close call. You ready to head out?"

I choked. "Leave without permission from the deputy? No way. Plus I need to get Chubb's toys and doggy bed."

"I've already figured out you don't always follow the rules."

The accusation crawled up my spine. "What do you mean? I'm not a lawbreaker."

Marc laughed. "It'd surprise me if we didn't break some kind of law in there. I only need to figure out which one."

I turned on my toe and headed for the kitchen. "Well, I've never heard of such."

Marc matched my stride. "Then, Miss Scott, I suggest you brush up on the law before you find yourself sitting in a jail cell."

I entered the kitchen with Marc on my heels. A jail cell was the last thing I needed, but I couldn't give up looking for the person who murdered my friend. "The authorities should be thankful for any help I provide. Do you know a lot of murders are never solved? They're called cold cases."

"Really?" Sarcasm laced his voice.

"I looked it up on the internet. Witnesses aren't comfortable talking to cops. Without a witness, the bad guys don't get arrested. Have you noticed how easy it is to talk to me? I'm not big and scary. I don't carry a gun. I've lived here all of my life. Talking to me is easy-peasy." I continued to ramble on. "I've never gotten over the fact the driver of the white sports car who hit my parents was never caught. Was the driver drunk? Distracted? Talking on his cell phone or changing a radio station? We may never know. I wasn't able to do anything to help the cops then. Peter needs justice. He was my friend, and I owe it to him to help find the killer."

Marc grabbed my arm. I ceased speaking and faced him. Time stood still.

Marc's lips moved. His tone had softened. "It won't bring Peter back, and it won't bring back your parents."

"I know, but at least I'll have tried." I inhaled deeply. "One of the regrets in my life is I didn't even try to find the hit-and-run driver twelve years earlier. The evil person ran over my parents, sideswiped a parked car, and drove away to live happily ever after. Has the driver ever considered the devastation he inflicted on my family?"

"I don't know." Marc shook his head. "I'm so sorry for your loss."

His kindness unglued me. Tears streamed down my face.

"Andi Grace, don't cry." He wrapped his arms around me, and I clung to him.

Deputy Hanks appeared in the kitchen. "You two should leave now."

I pulled away from Marc. "Yes, sir."

We left and walked to my SUV. Chubb barked, and I started to check on him, but Marc beat me to it.

"Yeah, boy. I don't know how I got roped into caring for you, but we'll give it a try. I know how hard it is to lose someone and search for a place to fit in."

"What did you say?" I stared at him, unable to move.

"Just talking to the pup."

Why hadn't I kept my big mouth shut? I might have learned more, but it seemed wrong to listen to a conversation between a man and his dog. Marc didn't give the impression of the kind of person who shared intimate details of his life. It appeared he needed a dog to confide in. I nodded and moved to the driver's seat.

Marc closed the back and hopped into the passenger seat.

I remained quiet on the drive to Marc's house. I parked but couldn't decide whether to help unload or leave the man alone.

"Something wrong?"

"I need to tell you something." I trained my eyes on Marc's shirt— I couldn't bring myself to look him in the eye.

"I can handle whatever you want to say. Spit it out." His stoic tone didn't reassure me.

"I left Chubb's special food in the kitchen."

"On purpose?"

I nodded.

"Why? What am I going to feed him?" He clenched his fists.

"I wanted to get back in the house, and it seemed like a good excuse."

"We're not going back tonight." Marc sighed. "I don't guess he can eat people food."

"Lots of dog owners feed their pets real food, but Chubb's been on a special diet. A quick shift might upset his stomach. Don't worry, though. I've always got supplies in the back of the Suburban."

His mouth twisted. "Okay, but don't go back to Peter's place alone. Come get me if you can't find somebody else."

"Listen here, I've taken care of myself for twelve years. I don't need you to watch over me." Why did I let Marc get to me?

He unclenched his fists and reached for my hand. His was warm and calloused. "I respect how you've handled adversity, and I'm sure I only know the tip of the iceberg that's your life. However, have you dealt with murder before?"

"No." My shoulders dropped. "Unless you consider hit and run murder."

"If it was premeditated and intentional, it's vehicular manslaughter or negligent homicide." He turned in the seat and faced me. "Andi Grace, let me rephrase my request. Please don't go back without protection. I want to help if you need me."

"Thanks." I opened my door. I needed air. "Let's get you and Chubb set up."

"Don't forget. This is a trial basis."

"Gotcha." I shot him a smile. "For the record, I think you make a great dog owner. He needs you." Also, for the record, I thought Marc needed Chubb as much, if not more. The man sometimes got under my skin, but I sensed a vulnerability and loneliness in him. I needed to cut him some slack next time he irritated me.

He grunted. "Don't get your hopes up."

Instead of responding, I hopped from the SUV and helped Chubb out of the back.

Marc reached for the leash but he didn't move. "Are you going to agree to call me instead of going back to Peter's place alone?"

I studied his face.

He smiled. It looked forced, but I'd give him credit for trying.

"I'll call you."

The smile became more sincere. "Thanks. If you insist on looking into Peter's death, we need to keep our eyes open."

"We?"

"Yes. Like swimming, we'll use the buddy system until Peter's murderer is caught. Don't take any unnecessary risks."

"Trust me. I'll be careful."

He rolled his eyes and took the dog inside the house.

Chapter Ten

A FEW HOURS LATER, I finally stretched out on my bed with Sunny at my side. Relief seeped into my bones as I lay on the firm mattress. Despite the heat of the day, the warmth of Sunny's body next to mine comforted me. As much as I needed rest, lying there wasn't solving Peter's murder.

I sat up, fluffed the pillows, grabbed my laptop, and opened the file dealing with Peter's murder. I added some of my scribbled notes.

Regina's alibi took her off the suspect list provided she'd told me the truth, which left Thomas King and George Reeves. Both men were in some kind of construction or land development.

Were two suspects enough? I guessed if you were dead, one suspect was more than enough. If it was the guilty party. A shiver shook me, and I scooted closer to Sunny.

With a swipe of my finger, I opened my phone and forwarded the pictures I'd taken at Peter's place to my laptop. The larger image allowed me to get a better view of the papers.

The Richard Rice Plantation was first. I searched the internet for information on the plantation. John Paul Young was the past CEO and current CFO of the nonprofit. The list of board members included Peter. The plantation was in the middle of a fundraising campaign. The first phase included a café and gift shop, which would bring in extra funds to help keep the plantation in business. Also on the list of board members was Corey Lane. He'd married a friend of mine, Erin.

She had been my friend since high school. Corey met Erin in college at Clemson and swept her off her feet. Erin had dropped out of college when she inherited her grandmother's money. Not long after, Corey showed up in Heyward Beach and proposed to Erin, and they'd eloped to the shock of friends and family. Erin seemed very happy, though, so I wouldn't judge. I copied and pasted the information to my murder file.

Next I added Corey Lane and Mr. Young to my list of suspects. Why not?

If the plantation was in the middle of a huge fundraiser, money was a possible motive for Peter's death. If there were any unscrupulous money issues, Peter would have caused a stink. He'd taught me to always keep a clear record of my finances in case my business was ever audited. If anything seemed shady to Peter, he would have been all over it.

My eyes drooped then popped open. What a day. Almost midnight according to my phone. No wonder I struggled to stay awake. With my notes and laptop in hand, I shuffled to my office and glanced at my schedule. Tomorrow would be another early morning. Two regular customers were heading out of town for vacation. The families were friends and were flying out early for a trip to France.

Both families had requested I bring the dogs home with me for a few days. There'd be a lot of excitement around my house, but it'd be worth it.

Paris. One day I planned to find a way to visit the city of lights. I pulled my secret money jar from behind a stack of travel books on France. I dumped out the cash and counted. Fifty-eight dollars and thirty-seven cents. Well, I wouldn't be going anytime soon.

My phone buzzed. "Hey, Juliet. What are you doing up so late?"

"I thought you'd want to know. Peter's visitation is tomorrow from four to seven. The funeral is Monday morning at ten."

Her words sucker-punched me. With shaky legs, I sat in the desk chair. "It's real."

"Sweetie, you found the body. You know he's gone."

"I know, but it's still hard to accept anybody would be angry enough to kill him."

"Do you want to go to the visitation together?"

Juliet's voice and offer soothed my jangled nerves. "That'd be great."

"I'll pick you up around four."

Another thought crept into my mind. "Do you know if they found any family?"

"No. The reason I know the funeral plans is because sometimes I fix hair for the deceased. The funeral home keeps me posted on services whether I'm needed or not."

Yuck. Would Juliet have handled finding Peter's body better than I did? I'd never touched a dead body before Peter. Not even my parents. I always wanted to remember them as warm and alive. Not cold and clammy. Plus, the minister had advised seeing their mangled bodies could distort our memories. We'd held a closed-casket funeral with their wedding portrait in front of the caskets.

Juliet said, "Do you want me to spend the night with you? Are you okay?"

I shook off the memory. "I'll be fine. Sunny's here."

A small voice nudged me. Even better than my dog, God would see me through tonight and the days ahead. No matter how awful.

Chapter Eleven

TRANSFERRING TWO dogs from their homes to mine caused me to run late for church on Sunday morning. The additional income from keeping the dogs at my place would be nice, but the timing wasn't great.

I slipped into the back pew as the congregation sang praise songs. The church was full with many of my friends. Good friends. People of different ages who'd been kind to me over the years. Both before and especially after my parents passed.

A familiar dark head caught my attention. My breathing stopped. No. It couldn't be him. Same wavy dark hair but shorter. The man's height appeared no different than before, but his shoulders filled out the white collared shirt he wore.

Lack of sleep and stress must have played with my imagination.

The praise band changed songs, and the man turned his head ever so slightly to the center of the church.

My legs trembled. It was Danny Nichols. My Danny. Here in church. My sanctuary. Not his.

Okay, it was God's house and open to both of us. How many times had we sat together in high school listening to sermons and singing praise songs?

I took a deep breath. What was Danny doing in town? His parents still lived in the area, but they didn't socialize with the locals much.

The worship leader prayed while strumming a guitar.

I closed my eyes. Peace rained down on me. Another deep breath. I could handle this. First, I'd focus on the sermon. Then I'd slip outside during the last song and dodge an encounter with Danny.

Pastor Mays preached. Despite supreme effort on my part to con-centrate, I failed. The musicians appeared and started the last song which was my cue to leave. I escaped without running into Danny. Praise God.

At home, I changed clothes and sat on my back deck with Sunny. I dove into a burger and fries I'd picked up at the burger joint. A warm breeze fanned my ponytail. "How about a walk on the beach today, girl?"

Sunny's ears perked up. The German shepherd eyed me as if understanding.

The dogs I was watching played in the backyard. The two pups had come from the same litter of West Highland terriers. Their owners adopted them at the same time, and the dogs had a special relationship. Sunny seemed content to ignore them and stick by me. Good. It was what I needed today.

My phone buzzed, and I snatched it off the table. "Hey, Juliet. What's up?"

"I saw you slip out of church early. Did you spot you-know-who?"

"Yeah. What's Danny doing in town?" I was over the man. He'd dumped me at the lowest point in my life, and I'd survived.

"No idea. Do you need company?"

I needed to move. "How about a walk on the beach? I can pick you up in a bit."

"I had something a little cooler in mind. Like ice cream at Market Commons."

"Good thing I'm not dieting." I lifted the burger to my mouth.

"You never need to diet with your job."

"They say thirty is when gaining weight catches up with you, but I'm up for ice cream. Maybe we can eat, walk on the beach, and clean up for Peter's visitation."

"I don't guess Danny's in town for the funeral."

"I'm not sure those two even knew each other." Did they? "Although I didn't know Peter was engaged."

"When did you meet Peter?"

I rolled my shoulders. "At the real estate office after my parents died."

"Danny was in college then."

"Yep. It's the reason he broke up with me."

"I guess it's possible Danny knew Peter. They could've met one summer."

My stomach heaved, and I pushed the takeout container to the side. "Yeah, it's possible."

"It would explain why he showed up this weekend." Juliet always had a soothing voice over the phone. Scratch that, Juliet had a soothing voice. Period.

"I never really understood why Peter took such a kind interest in me. I got to know him better through the veterinary clinic. Then he started asking me to take care of his first dog when he left town for business. He preferred me to care for him than boarding him."

"I remember." Juliet cleared her throat. "I'll pick you up instead. Be ready in ten minutes."

"Yes, ma'am." I giggled at Juliet's bossiness but moved inside to brush my teeth.

The beautiful afternoon was exactly what I'd needed to restore my equilibrium. I always felt closer to God at the beach. Between the ice cream and taking a walk with my best friend, I felt ready to attend visitation.

When we arrived at the visitation, very few vehicles filled the parking area around the church.

"Where do you suppose everybody is?"

Juliet parked the car. "According to the rumor mill, Peter knew lots of people but didn't have many close friends."

"He traveled a lot for work. Still, I thought the crowd would be bigger." I followed my friend into the church and toward the front of the sanctuary, where the casket rested by the altar.

Juliet stopped so fast I bumped into her. She spun on her toe and faced me. Wide-eyed, she pointed with her thumb like a hyper hitchhiker. "Danny's up there."

"Like going through the line shaking hands with family members?"

"No," she hissed. "Like he's part of the family."

My heart dropped. "How can they be related?"

"I guess we're about to find out."

"Hey, Sis. I thought we'd see you here." Lacey Jane slipped an arm around my shoulders, and Nate touched my elbow.

Tears welled up in my eyes. "Peter's advice helped the three of us survive. I'm glad you came to pay your respects."

Juliet moved ahead.

Nate said, "Wait up, Jules. We'll stick together."

I smiled. Nate always had a soft spot for Juliet. He often joked he'd inherited a third sister the day Juliet moved into our house. "Let's go."

Nate motioned for Lacey Jane to move ahead next to Juliet. He leaned back and bent his head close to mine. "What's Danny Nichols doing here?"

"Good question." My feet felt like concrete blocks as I inched forward. The line wasn't long, but the people ahead of us seemed to have a lot to say to the family.

Danny stood to the side of the closed casket, beside his parents.

I lifted my chin and stuck out a hand to greet Danny. "Hi. I didn't know you and Peter were friends."

"He was my uncle."

Uncle? How was that possible? I'd never heard Danny or Peter mention the other. Danny had grown up in the area. Peter moved here about the time my parents died. Questions ping-ponged across my brain. There were too many to voice only one. I nodded. "I'm sorry for your loss. Will you be in town for the funeral?"

His gaze connected with mine. "I'm back to join my dad's law practice."

Danny was back. In South Carolina. Not Georgia. A lawyer. Just like he'd strategized. He'd made a life plan and stuck to it. No disasters or interruptions in his journey. No girlfriend tied down a state away raising her siblings.

I swallowed. "Congratulations on the job."

Nate squeezed my elbow. "Sis, let's keep moving. No need to hold up the line."

"Right." I walked beside my big, strong brother and fought the weakness in my knees. I needed Nate's strength tonight. So sue me. A bubble of hysteria hit. Sue me. Yeah. My ex-boyfriend could file a lawsuit against me with a snap of his fingers. That was what attorneys did. Right?

"You okay?" Nate held open the front door of Little Community Church.

"Never better." With a spurt of speed, I rushed out and bumped smack into Marc.

"Whoa there, Andi Grace. Where's the fire?" Marc's hands reached out to my shoulders and steadied me enough not to fall off my new block heel mule shoes. He bent his knees and we gazed at each other.

I regained both physical and emotional balance. "Hi, Marc. Have you met my brother, Nate?"

Marc turned his attention to Nate. "Hi. I'm Marc Williams. Peter's neighbor. Good to meet you."

"Hey, there." With narrowed eyes, Nate shook Marc's hand, and I knew there'd be questions to answer later.

I kept my focus on Marc. "How's Chubb?"

"That dog loves to chew on pine cones. I guess it's a good thing I've got plenty in my yard to keep him entertained. How do they fit into his diet?"

I shook my head. "Sorry. I forgot to get the food."

"Don't go back to Peter's by yourself. Call me."

Nate circled my arm with his rough fingers. "What's going on, Andi Grace?"

Marc's dimple appeared. "I'd best get inside. See you around."

I looked around the parking lot for Juliet and Lacey Jane.

Nate tightened his grip on my arm. "You may be the oldest, but I'm the man of the family. It's my job to look out for you and Lacey Jane. It's time you tell me what's going on."

"Let's walk." I told him the whole story. Everything except my concern about being on Wade's suspect list. "It looks like Danny is Peter's nephew."

Nate scratched his fresh-shaved chin. "Didn't see that coming."

"Me, either. You look nice, by the way." I rubbed his shoulder.

"Even without a tie?"

"Yep. Don't let anybody say you don't clean up well. Your usual scruff and dusty landscaping attire might confuse people."

He shrugged. "Landscaping is what I enjoy."

"I know. And you're good at it."

"Hey, are you trying to distract me from the real issue?"

I bit back a smile. "What? Me?"

"Cut the innocent act. Let's go buy the special dog food you need for that guy."

"Marc Williams. Problem is you can only buy it at the vet clinic, and Doc Hewitt is closed on Sundays."

"Figures." He pulled his keys from the pocket of his khakis. "I'll drive you to Peter's place, then we'll deliver this hoity toity dog food."

"Thanks. I need to let Juliet know I'm leaving with you."

Nate pulled out his phone. "I met Lacey Jane here, so she can drive herself home. I'll text her because I sure don't see her anywhere around."

"Her car is still in the parking lot. There's no telling who she's talking to. Our little sister doesn't know a stranger." I slipped away and bumped into Juliet under a shade tree in front of the church. "Nate's going to take me home. Thanks again for spending the day with me. I appreciate you."

Juliet gave me a firm hug. "Hang in there, girlfriend. I wish I could come to the funeral with you tomorrow, but I'm booked solid."

"I'll be fine." I'd done tougher things than attend the funeral of a friend. Even if Peter had kept his relationship to Danny, the love of my life, a secret all these years. Later, I'd ponder the reason why. Of course, I'd never spoken to Peter about my love life, so maybe there wasn't a reason to bring it up.

Juliet walked beside me to the parking lot and stopped beside Nate. "I hear you're stealing my friend away."

Nate ran a hand through his red hair. "Little brother reporting for bodyguard duty."

I shook my head. "Let's go, Nate."

"Yes, ma'am." He winked at Juliet. "You know she goes easier on me when I use good manners."

"I hear ya. See you later." Juliet slipped a band off her wrist and pulled back her long blond hair.

"Like always, Jules, it's been a pleasure." Nate opened the passenger door for me and jogged around to the other side.

I waited for a wall of hot, sticky air to escape the truck's cab and looked out the window at Juliet. "He's incorrigible."

"Part of his charm. I wouldn't change a thing." Juliet's dress puffed out as she turned and strolled to her car.

Weird. Had Juliet blushed? Nate was a little over two years younger than we were. Not too young for them to develop an interest in each other. Although Nate had always treated Juliet like a sister. Never had there been any hint of romance.

Maybe instead of looking into Peter's murder, I should open my eyes to what was happening between my brother and best friend.

Chapter Twelve

NATE WALKED TO Marc's front door with me. I rang the doorbell. The sound of the TV lowered, and the door swung open.

Marc's eyes widened when they connected with mine. He smiled enough for his dimple to appear. Chubb appeared at Marc's side and barked a greeting to us. "Hi there."

My heart fluttered. "Hi. Sorry to bother you. Nate and I've got your dog food. I mean Chubb's dog food. This is what Peter had left. When you run out, you can buy more from Doc Hewitt or gradually change him over to something more affordable."

His smile melted my heart. "Hey. Thanks. Did you manage to gather any more clues while you were at the house?"

I laughed. "My brother's not as adventurous as you."

Nate frowned. "I'm not going to get arrested for any reason. We went in for dog food. Nothing else."

Marc reached for the bag. "Sheriff Stone didn't give you permission to search the premises?"

Nate handed the food to Marc. "I'm more worried about Deputy Hanks. I went steady with his daughter in high school. He's the kind of dad who cleans his gun while his daughter is on a date. Believe me, we didn't date for long, and we never missed curfew. He's not the kind of man you want to get sideways with."

"I hear you. Would y'all like to come inside?"

I spoke up before Nate took over. "No. I wanted to make sure you had the right food for Chubb. How's it going?"

"We're getting used to each other, but it's still a trial basis." He smiled again. "You going to the funeral tomorrow?"

"Yes. What about you?"

"I guess it's the neighborly thing to do."

I stepped closer and whispered, "Maybe we can get a lead on the killer. How about we compare notes after?"

"Sounds like a plan. May as well go together."

Nate cleared his throat. "Let's go, Sis. I've got a backyard to design after I take you home."

My face grew hot. Why was Nate being so rude? "Bye, Marc."

"Hey, Andi Grace. Would you like me to pick you up?" Marc put the bag of dog food on the porch and stepped toward me.

Chubb circled Marc and sniffed the bag.

"That'd be nice." I clutched Nate's arm and led him away. I didn't need my brother analyzing my relationship with Marc when I didn't understand it myself.

"See you tomorrow." Marc chuckled. "Come on, Chubb. Let's get you some dinner."

I'D SPENT A RESTLESS night at home and was up before the alarm went off Monday morning. I took care of all the dogs, and before long, I sat next to Marc in his red Chevy Silverado.

I ignored my damp hands as Marc pulled into the church parking lot. Not a huge crowd, but it was a Monday. "When my parents died, cars filled the parking lots, the church's side lawn, and parked along a few nearby streets. I guess it's different though because my parents were such a big part of Heyward Beach."

Marc drove to the end of a line of cars in the grass and stopped under a large southern magnolia. Shade filled the cab's interior. "Monday morning might not be the easiest time to get off for a funeral."

My black-framed sunglasses slipped down, and I pushed them back in place. "You're going to keep your eyes open for anybody acting suspicious?"

"Yes, ma'am."

"Nice manners." A bit of tension eased from my shoulders. "I think it'll be less obvious if you watch Regina and her aunt since I'm already on her radar in a bad way."

"What about Peter's family? I met his sister, brother-in-law, and nephew at yesterday's viewing. Do you want me to watch them?"

My face heated. "On second thought, you watch them, and I'll watch Regina."

A Mercedes coupe pulled into the empty spot next to us. A man in his sixties, wearing a black suit and black cowboy hat, got out in a smooth move. The lady in the passenger seat looked as if she'd just stepped from the pages of a celebrity magazine. Her brown hair was pulled back in a neat chignon, with nary a hair out of place. I didn't buy expensive clothes, and my guess was the woman's black dress cost as much as I made in a month.

I ran my hand over my simple sleeveless black dress and took a deep breath. "Any chance you know them?"

"George Reeves, and I guess his wife."

I angled my phone to the rearview mirror and snapped pictures of the two walking into the church. "Had Peter and George become friends?"

"Not to my knowledge. If money was the motive for Peter's death, George would be a good one to watch."

"Gotcha. This afternoon I plan to take the dogs to Richard Rice Plantation for a walk. I'd love to see Peter's file on the place."

Marc opened his door. "It's too hot to keep sitting here, even in the shade. Let me do a little research on the plantation before you head over."

"You do your own research?"

"Hey, I'm more than just a pretty face. I learned the fine art of investigating while in law school and when I worked at the firm. I don't have any juniors to help me these days, so I can do it myself." He flashed me the biggest smile I'd ever seen on him. Then his gray eyes turned serious. "Give me a day."

"I hate to keep taking up your time."

"Please. One day. What can it hurt?"

I nodded. I couldn't refuse his simple request when he looked at me so intently. "Okay. Thanks."

He slid out of the truck, and before I could swing my legs out, he stood beside me with an outstretched hand waiting to help me exit.

"Your mother must be so proud of your good manners." I stepped onto the blacktopped surface and remembered his parents had died.

A pained expression passed across Marc's face.

His look bushwhacked me. "Oh, Marc. I'm so sorry. Did Mr. Wilkes teach you how to be a gentleman?"

"Yes, he was a great role model." The tendon in his jaw twitched hard enough it pushed out.

It was obvious the man didn't want to discuss his background. Fine. I'd give him his privacy. Despite losing my parents, I'd at least had them for eighteen years. Plus, I still had Nate and Lacey Jane. Marc had nobody.

We walked through the narthex and signed the guest book before entering the sanctuary.

Ms. Sally Mae Zorn played soft soothing music appropriate for a funeral. Danny sat in the front row with his mom and dad. It still seemed unreal that Peter's sister was Danny's mom.

Peter had shown me special pieces in his home that he'd collected on his travels during his twenties while he built his business and made a name for himself. He'd been twenty-eight when I met him and had decided to make Heyward Beach his permanent home. Why had I never asked where he grew up? I should've asked more about his family, but he'd always shut me down when I tried. Unwilling to severe ties with him, I never pushed for answers.

I slid into one of the back pews. Far enough away to avoid contact with Danny and his family but not so far as to be too obvious.

Marc took the empty spot next to me. His presence gave me a measure of comfort. It'd be a lie to say I wasn't pleased to have such a good-looking man at my side. Marc was the kind who turned heads. The entire town knew Danny had dumped me. Not the other way around. Showing up with Marc wouldn't make me look so pathetic.

Had Peter known about my relationship with Danny when he met me? No. The first day we met at the real estate office, I'd still been dating Danny. The fact that Danny hadn't been supportive during the first weeks after my parents passed should've been a clue we weren't going to make it.

Marc passed a funeral program to me without saying a word.

Peter Wayne Roth. Dead at forty.

My throat constricted. I was here to pay my respects to a good and decent man. My friend. I wasn't here to prove anything to an old boyfriend.

I blinked and tried to focus on the printed words. Danny was Peter's nephew. Danny's mom had come to Heyward Beach when she married Mr. Nichols. Peter had been highly recruited out of college and spent years traveling for his job. I'd known that much, but the program listed some of the worldwide charities he contributed to, thanks to his travels. The family requested donations to the groups instead of flowers.

Wait. There was no mention of Richard Rice Plantation. I elbowed Marc and whispered, "Look."

He squinted at the words then met my gaze. "What about it?"

"Does it seem weird he's on the board of Richard Rice Plantation and it's not one of the charities listed?"

Marc's eyebrows shot up. "Yes." He ran a hand down his clean-shaven jaw. "Unless the family thought Peter had invested enough personal resources at the plantation. Money does weird things to families."

A memory hit me. "True. Money was the divisive factor between Peter and his family. As long as I knew him, he didn't celebrate any holidays or birthdays with his family. They lived in the same county, but to hear Peter talk, they may as well have lived in Alaska."

At the front of the church, Pastor Larry led Danny's family to a designated pew.

I couldn't help but study the man I'd imagined spending my life with years ago. He was tall and a bit more muscular than he'd been in high school. He still had amazing black hair. Oh, how he'd broken my heart twelve years ago. I'd heard he worked for a big law firm in Atlanta, but I hadn't heard anything about Danny getting married. Of course, it didn't mean he wasn't involved with a woman in Georgia.

Danny's parents never reached out to me after our breakup. After all the years Danny and I had dated, it'd hurt. In a few short months, my parents had died, Danny dumped me, and his parents purged me from their lives too. They'd even quit attending my church. Danny's mother had never been warm to me, but his dad had always been friendly.

Pastor Larry tapped the microphone before speaking. He talked about a man who loved his friends and *family*. If Peter was so devoted to his kin, I'd have known he was Danny's uncle. The more the preacher talked, the less I recognized the man he spoke about. I couldn't stand to listen to the generic words. Yet, I was there to pay my respects.

I wouldn't say the family lied to the pastor, but he was speaking words about a man I didn't know. I'd visit his gravesite later by myself and mourn. For now, I'd study the others attending the funeral. I angled my body to view the people on the other side of the aisle.

George Reeves and his beautiful wife sat two pews behind the family. A couple who looked to be in their thirties sat in a center pew. Next to them was a distinguished man with a deep tan and shocking white hair. All three people looked familiar. Had they been in the news for some reason? When we reached the cemetery, I'd take pictures with my phone of as many people as possible.

Whoa, there was Lacey Jane. She sat close to the church ladies. Why would my sister skip work to come to Peter's funeral? She'd attended the visitation. Had she felt closer to Peter than I realized? If she'd wanted to be here, why hadn't she come with me?

Later I'd figure out how much Peter's death was affecting my sister. The age gap of seventeen years between Peter and Lacey Jane was big enough for a father-daughter relationship. Although the two never spent much time together. I'd get to the bottom of their relationship. If Lacey Jane needed my support, I'd be available. My sister's well-being was more important than catching a killer. Besides, Marc had asked me to hold off one day before going to the plantation.

Today I'd focus on Lacey Jane. Tomorrow, the killer.

After the funeral, Marc followed the other cars down the cemetery lane and parked. Cool air blew from the truck's vents. "Is there something going on with you and Peter's family?"

My sigh came out more like a moan. "I used to date his nephew."

"I didn't think you knew Peter's family."

"Turns out I know them. I just didn't know they were related." My stomach roiled.

"I don't understand."

"Me, either." I rubbed my temples and hoped the forming headache would disappear. "Danny and I dated in high school. He's two years older than I am and went to college first. We continued to date until the summer after I graduated from high school. I'd planned to join him at the University of Georgia. He was pre-law with plans to get into Georgia's law school, and I wanted to be a journalist."

Marc turned the air conditioner blower down a notch. "What happened?"

"That was the summer my parents were killed. When I didn't go to college, Danny broke up with me."

"Because your parents were killed?"

"Well, kinda. More like because I decided to stay home for my brother and sister."

"What a jerk." The flare of Marc's nostrils comforted me.

"He was young, with his whole life ahead of him. I understand he didn't want to date somebody raising her siblings."

"He should've been proud of you. It took a lot of guts—no, integrity—to put your life on hold for your siblings. You kept them out of foster care. Older kids get overlooked and shuffled around." People walked past the truck, and Marc sighed. "I guess we should join them."

I nodded and hopped out before he could shut off the engine. Marc really understood my predicament. Too bad he hadn't been my boyfriend all those years ago.

Marc joined me on the fringe of the crowd. I crossed my arms as if they could protect me from more pain. Danny was responsible for the hurt he'd inflicted in the past. Peter's death led to a different kind of pain. It'd be crazy to blame the man for dying, but I found it hard to understand the secrets in his life. His ex-fiancée and the fact his family lived here in Heyward Beach were two major parts of Peter's life I'd been clueless about.

Marc stuck close to me, and I appreciated his attention.

A funeral home employee walked among the people and passed out red roses. I took one and looked at the casket. White spots danced before my eyes. The flower slipped from my fingers, and I swayed.

Marc slipped his arm around my shoulders.

I leaned into him.

His fingers curved around my upper arm.

I closed my eyes at the sight of Peter's casket. I'd never see him again. It'd been twelve years since my parents had died. I'd had to be the strong one back then and lift up my siblings. Marc supported me for Peter's funeral. I should've at least pretended to be strong before falling apart. Yet, I wasn't able to summon enough willpower to push away from Marc.

"Amen." Pastor Larry ended the prayer.

I heard people moving, and soft voices murmured. I opened my eyes. Funeral home employees directed us to approach the casket and lay our roses on top. Some people stopped and laid their hands on the casket before moving away. Others kissed the rose they held before adding theirs to the spread. Many spoke to Peter's family.

Marc bent and picked up the red rose I'd dropped in the sandy grass.

I couldn't cause a scene, but the desire to run away hit me hard.

Marc took my icy hand in his warm one. He led me forward.

It might sound cliché, but I held on to Marc for dear life. We walked to the casket. We paused. Added our roses to the others. Walked away. Through the entire process, I held back tears but never released my grip on Marc's hand. We stopped at his Silverado, and I leaned against it in hopes of catching my breath.

A group of people stood off to the side in a circle.

"I'm calling an emergency board meeting for tomorrow morning." John Paul Young, the past CEO of Richard Rice Plantation, spoke to the others. Most nodded in agreement.

Marc removed his jacket and tossed it in the cab of his truck. He leaned against the vehicle and nudged me with his elbow. "Do you know who that is?"

I identified the man and explained his role to Marc. "Is it normal to call an emergency board meeting when a member dies? It seems like the board would vote in a replacement at the next scheduled meeting. What's the rush? Plus, Corey is the present CEO. How much authority does Mr. Young have as the past CEO? Or do you think because he's the current CFO, he has authority?"

"Maybe, with all of the expansion plans, it makes sense to fill Peter's spot as soon as possible. Although it seems strange for Mr. Young to be the one to call it. Maybe he doesn't have faith in Corey."

"I wonder how Corey managed to replace him?"

"It could be one of those boards where you can only be CEO for a certain time period before rotating off the position. The board may have been forced to rotate Young from CEO to CFO. Both are huge positions." He paused a second. "Hey, you did good today."

I reached for his hand. "You're a liar, but thanks. At least it's over."

"Looks like the first couple of cars are moving on. You ready to go?"

"Absolutely." I climbed into the passenger seat and lay my head back. I'd talk to Lacey Jane later.

"Hey, Marc." A deep voice called out.

I looked through the windshield. George Reeves approached. With my cell phone, I clicked his picture. Too bad I hadn't taken any other pictures when we stood for the graveside service. Some investigator I'd turned out to be.

Marc walked around the front of his Silverado. "Mr. Reeves."

The man held out a business card. "I think we should talk."

"Nothing to discuss. I don't plan to sell my land."

"You may change your mind. Give me a call. I think you'll like what I have to say."

Marc stuffed the card in his pocket. "Have a good day, sir." He hopped into the truck.

"I overheard your conversation."

"I have no intention of calling the man or selling my property." He started the vehicle and turned on the air conditioner.

We left our windows down until the fresh coolness overtook the hot stale air. Soon we were moving with the rest of the cars out of the cemetery, past Peter's grave, and onto the road home.

I sat straighter. "Do you think Mr. Reeves is the killer? It's possible you'll be in danger if you don't agree to sell. If Mr. Reeves killed Peter to get the land for his casino and resort, you could be next on his hit list." My volume grew with each word until I forced myself to stop speaking before I sounded hysterical.

Marc white-knuckled the steering wheel. "I left practicing law in order to be a simple boat builder. How is it now I'm wondering if I'm next on a killer's hit list?"

Chapter Thirteen

TUESDAY MORNING I pulled into the visitor parking lot of Richard Rice Plantation. All dogs had been fed, played with, and walked. The summer heat was already cooking, and you could burn your feet on the asphalt parking lot. Problem was, the note I'd found earlier left a chill in my soul.

After I'd taken care of a vacationing family's hamsters, gerbils, and fish, I'd returned to my SUV to find a threatening note on my windshield. "Back off or else." There'd also been a photograph of Lacey Jane. My baby sister had been threatened, most likely by the person who'd murdered Peter.

I counted in French and took deep breaths. Both actions calmed me enough to think straight. I found it interesting the note appeared at the one house where I didn't take a dog outside to walk. My hands trembled. The killer must know Heyward Beach well enough to realize which job would keep me occupied inside. How could I continue to investigate Peter's death? I couldn't put Lacey Jane in danger.

Marc pulled next to my Suburban, with Chubb riding shotgun. Marc could deny wanting to adopt Chubb all day long, but the two needed each other.

I met him in front of his truck. "Good morning."

"Morning." He leashed Chubb. "I thought bringing him would help his socialization skills."

"Did you research how to be a good dog owner?"

His complexion reddened. "After I studied the plantation and board members, I read tips on puppy training. How old is he?"

"Five months. Peter had taken him to obedience classes, and I'm happy you're continuing to work with Chubb. Do you remember that I told you I'll help train him?"

"Believe me, if I keep the pup, I'll take you up on your offer." Marc chuckled.

"What did you find out about this place?" Even if I planned to drop my investigation, it couldn't hurt to hear what Marc had discovered.

"Let's go that way." He pointed toward a path and began walking. "The board is raising money for a café and gift shop. The theory is if those are the first stage of the building campaign, they can bring in additional funds. If they work on the stable first, it's just part of the cost of admission. But visitors will hopefully spend extra money at the café and gift shop."

"Seems like a smart plan. I'd think Peter would be in favor of it."

Marc slowed his pace and veered toward the rice mill. "I tried to come up with reasons of concern for Peter. He's an accountant. I assume they took bids for the project. What if there was a suspicious bid? He might have known there was no way to build the café for the projected money. Or what if they raised the funds, and when it was time to start building, the money was gone. Peter's would have been suspicious and questioned the board."

"Do you have a list of board members? Maybe one of them can shed light on the situation."

Marc pulled his phone from his pocket and opened a file for me. "The only name I recognize is John Paul Young."

"Plantation CFO. The same man who called the emergency meeting for today."

"Right. Do you know anybody else?"

My eyes traveled down the list. "Paula Houp is Regina's aunt. I'm sure she's a real asset for keeping the integrity of the time period. We've discussed Corey Lane, who married my friend Erin."

"He's the current CEO." Marc relaxed his hold on the leash allowing Chubb to sniff around.

I paused at the name of Asher Cummings.

"Somebody else catch your eye?"

"Yeah."

A wagon full of tourists rambled down a grass-worn path through a field of lavender toward the old slave cabins.

Chubb barked.

"Quiet." Marc knelt beside the dog and stroked his back. "Good boy."

When the wagon got far enough away, I looked over the list again. "I think I saw Asher Cummings at Peter's place one day. Peter didn't introduce us, but I heard him use the name Ash."

"Were they arguing?"

I thought back to the night in question. I'd been at Peter's house taking care of Chubb. Peter had gotten home earlier than expected from a trip to New York City. He'd been exhausted and had asked me to finish caring for the rambunctious puppy. "It was a couple of weeks ago. I'd taken Chubb for a run to wear him out. When we came back from the river, Peter had company. There was a red Porsche parked in front of the house. So I took Chubb inside through the kitchen door. I didn't want to disturb whoever was meeting with Peter."

"Did you hear the conversation?"

"A little. I stayed long enough for Chubb to drink water and for me to brush his hair. The men were upset but not at each other. Actually, the other man did most of the talking and thanked Peter for looking into his concerns."

"What else?"

"I finished with Chubb and left. As I drove off, I saw a tall man with a white cowboy hat walk out to the car. I remember wondering why a great big man would want to scrunch up in such a little vehicle. He even had to take off the hat in order to fit."

Marc chuckled. "It's not about comfort. Otherwise people might buy a Buick or Cadillac. The Porsche is a high-performance sports car. It's an exhilarating ride. You buy it for speed and handling. Owning a Porsche is also prestigious."

I held up my hands. "Okay. I'm getting the picture."

Marc reached for his phone. "Let's see if we can find Asher Cummings on social media. Then we'll know for sure if it's who you saw."

I searched for the man by name. His picture popped up. White cowboy hat, moustache, and in his fifties. "It's him. Asher Cummings. See?"

Marc touched my hand holding the phone and moved it closer to his face. He squinted as he studied the picture. At his touch, chills raced up my arm.

"Do you need glasses?"

"Maybe." Chubb pulled on the leash, but Marc kept a firm hold. "Where do you think the board will meet today?"

"The main house. The Rice family enclosed a sunporch years ago and turned it into a meeting room. They say the views are spectacular from there." I pulled my arm back to my side. Time for me to be strong and stand on my own two feet. This wasn't the time to get giddy over some man. True, Marc Williams was très handsome and kind, but the timing seemed off. I was trying to find a killer, and Marc was starting a business.

"Let's head there. Maybe we can talk to somebody."

"I don't think we know any board members well enough for them to share with us."

Marc whipped off his sunglasses. "I thought you were all gung-ho to catch Peter's killer. What's going on?"

"It won't bring Peter back."

"What about justice and protecting others?" He didn't look mad. More confused than anything. "Andi Grace, talk to me."

Birds chirped in the trees. In the distance a horn honked. Perspiration beaded my hairline. Could I trust Marc? For so long, I'd made my own decisions. Nate, Lacey Jane, and me. We stuck together. We had each other's backs. No matter what.

"Andi Grace."

I met his gaze and gulped. "I'm scared."

"You're not trained to catch a killer. It makes sense to be afraid. We'll stop our informal investigation." He touched my elbow and guided Chubb and me toward a bench on the path.

I sat down. "It's more than catching a killer."

Marc sat beside me, placing his arm along the back of the bench. His fingers grazed my shoulder. "What's going on? Did somebody threaten you?"

Chubb lay at our feet.

I pulled the paper from my pocket and handed it to Marc. "It's worse than that. They threatened to hurt Lacey Jane. I've loved and watched over my baby sister since the day she was born. I'm six years older and was ecstatic the day I got a baby sister. How can I ignore this?"

"Where'd it come from?"

I shivered. "My windshield. It was the last stop of the morning. I played and cared for all of the indoor pets of a family in town. When I finished and walked out to my Suburban, the note was on the windshield, waiting for me. I snatched it off, thinking—actually, I thought it might be a flyer like you get in shopping center parking lots. I started my SUV, and while waiting for the air conditioner to cool me off, I opened the envelope. First, a picture of Lacey Jane fell out, then I read the note."

Marc sighed. "Why'd you decide to meet me?"

"It was the next thing on my list. I drove straight here."

"You didn't call the sheriff?"

"No."

He pulled out his phone. "Sheriff Stone needs to see this. Maybe he can get fingerprints."

"What if the killer finds out we called the sheriff? He might hurt Lacey Jane."

"The more the sheriff knows, the better he can protect y'all. Why don't you call your sister? She should know about the potential danger."

My gut clenched. I needed to take care of Lacey Jane. It was one thing to think I could catch a killer and another thing to imagine I could protect my sister. For the moment, I pushed all that aside to call Wade.

The sheriff had been less than pleased to discover I hadn't reported the note right away. He lectured me for a long time. Blah, blah, blah. Bottom line, take care of dogs and let him catch the killer.

As soon as Wade finished bawling me out, I texted Lacey Jane and told her not to leave the coffee shop until I could talk to her.

On the walk back to our vehicles, I shared with Marc everything Wade had said.

When I finished, Marc opened the door for me. "I'm going to follow you."

"Thanks, but you really don't need to. I'll be fine."

"I insist. Let's go." Marc followed me to town, and we parked across the street from Daily Java. I waited on the sidewalk while he attached the leash to Chubb's harness. "I want you to be a good boy so they don't kick us out."

When Marc and Chubb were ready, I hoofed it to the coffee shop and opened the door. It took them a while to catch up with me. "Why are y'all so slow?"

He surveyed the area. "No sign of Thomas's truck. No suspicious characters lurking in the shadows of trees or buildings."

Heat warmed my face. While my impatience reared its ugly head, Marc had scoped out the area. "Oh, thanks."

Two retirement-age women sat at one of the bistro tables in front of the coffee shop. Their heads were bent together, and they were in a big conversation about politics.

Marc might be more help to me if he knew more people in town, but he'd been kind to volunteer his assistance in my quest to catch Peter's killer. A quest I needed to put aside for the sake of my sister.

A black Lexus entered the parking lot driving faster than I considered safe. The car parked, and Danny Nichols jumped out and breezed toward Daily Java. At the last moment, he whipped out a cell phone from his pants pocket and answered a call before entering the shop.

My heart jolted.

"Don't look now, but your old boyfriend is staring at us." Marc slid his arm around my back and drew me to his side. "Keep your eye on the ball."

"What ball?" Had Chubb dropped a dog toy?

"Focus. We're here to warn Lacey Jane. Ignore your ex. It's possible he's the killer, and we don't want to let him know we're on to him."

"Right. I called Lacey Jane on my way over. She has a break in ten minutes. I'll wait on the patio, but you don't have to stay and babysit me."

"I'm not leaving. We need to come up with a plan." He nodded toward the sitting area on the shaded patio. "Why don't I order while you take Chubb out there?"

Taking Chubb's leash, I walked to the patio door but didn't exit yet.

"Hey, sis." Lacey Jane waved. "Hi, Marc. What can I get you?"

Marc's tenor could be heard over the murmurings of other people. "I'd like a green smoothie and whatever your sister's favorite drink is."

"Do you want her budget friendly coffee or a specialty?"

"She's had a hard day. Fix whatever will lift her spirits."

My heart melted at his kindness. The man wore a bright blue T-shirt proclaiming, *My boat. My rules.* However, once I'd gotten to know Marc, he was much kinder than I'd first imagined. Maybe I should buy him some shirts with nice sentiments instead of words to put people off.

"Because it's already hot today, I'm going to fix a cinnamon roll iced coffee."

"Sounds good. What about a couple of elephant ears?"

"Perfect combination. Some people would have chosen cinnamon rolls, but it would've been overkill. I'll bring this out to you directly."

"Thanks."

I hurried out to the patio while he paid. No need for him to suspect I was eavesdropping.

Before long, Marc plopped down in the iron chair across the table from me. "Does your sister own this place?"

"No. My friend Erin Lane owns it. She inherited money from her grandmother, dropped out of college, and opened this coffee shop and bakery."

"Corey's wife. Right?"

"Yes. Good memory." The hair on the back of my neck stood to attention. I'd chosen a chair where I wouldn't have to watch Danny, but somehow my radar had warned me of his closeness.

Marc's eyes widened.

"What's going on?"

He shook his head. "Nothing."

"You're a terrible liar."

"Pretty sure you've told me that before."

"I peeked over my shoulder. Inside the coffee shop, Lacey Jane had come around the counter and hugged Danny. Heat suffused my body. It looked like more than a friendly hug. He leaned in more than made me comfortable.

My throat constricted, and my face burned hotter than coals. What in the world? "Is he putting the moves on my baby sister?"

Marc's fingers wrapped around my hand. "I wouldn't make too much out of it."

I nodded but didn't remove my hand from his. "Right. Danny was always hanging around the house. I mean, we dated for years. Five years to be exact. I bet Lacey Jane thinks of him like another brother." Now who was a liar?

"I'm sure the hug is only sympathy for an old friend."

"I wonder where our order is." I turned my focus to our hands. I couldn't watch the scene unfolding inside the coffee shop any longer.

"It's probably my fault. I ordered a smoothie."

My body shook the way it did when I forget to eat. Good thing I was sitting down, but could Marc tell?

His fingers tightened around mine. "You're a remarkable woman, and I'm impressed with your mental toughness. You've got a lot going on. Peter's death, your old boyfriend is back in town, and now your sister has been threatened by the killer. Yet, you're holding it together."

Danny walked through the doorway and stopped by our table. He held a cup of coffee in a to-go cup. "Andi Grace."

"Danny." My face was so hot it must have been pomegranate red, but maybe nobody would notice in the patio's shadows. "Have you met Marc Williams?"

Marc stood and stretched out his hand. "We met at the visitation. Again, I'm sorry for your loss. Peter was a good man."

"Thanks. Do you mind if I speak to Andi Grace for a minute?" Danny's smile dimmed when Marc didn't move. "Alone."

Marc's nostrils flared. "We're kinda in the middle of something."

Surprise flitted across Danny's face. "It won't take long. Then you two can get back to your business."

I looked at each one. "Why don't you both sit down? Danny, anything you need to say to me, you can say in front of Marc."

Marc slid his seat closer to me, while Danny snatched an empty chair from another table.

I debated asking what Danny wanted to talk about versus letting him speak first. The tension got to me, though. "What's on your mind?"

His gaze bounced from Marc to me. "I'm joining my dad's law practice, and we'll probably see each other around town. I'm renting a condo on Heyward Beach until I can decide where I want to settle. I'd hate for things to be awkward between us."

"Awkward?" My voice squeaked, and I took a deep breath. "Why didn't you ever tell me Peter was your uncle?"

He shrugged. "It never seemed important. He moved here after I left for college."

"Why was he on the outs with your family?"

"Money, thanks to my grandpa's will. Uncle Peter was good to me, though." Danny crossed his legs. Left ankle over right knee. Dress shoes and no socks. "I didn't stop to talk about my family. I want us to be friends."

"Why? You haven't reached out to me in over ten years."

"It's different now. We're both living in Heyward Beach, and it's a small town. We can't avoid each other."

I nodded. "Fine. When was the last time you saw Peter?"

Danny took a sip of his coffee. "It's been a while."

"Ballpark? Years? Weeks? Months?"

Danny frowned. "Last year we went to a Braves game when he was in town."

Lacey Jane walked out carrying a brown tray with our drinks. "I've got your order, and it's time for my break." She placed the tray on the little table intended for two people.

Danny stood. "It's good seeing y'all. I've got to get back to the office."

Lacey Jane's smile dimmed. "It was nice to see you, Danny. Stop by anytime."

Marc reached for his smoothie and slurped a drink.

After Danny left, I turned to my sister. "Are you and Danny friends?"

Lacey Jane sat in the chair Danny vacated. "I guess. When he broke up with you, it left another gap in our family. I missed him."

"I never thought of it that way. How are you doing with Peter's death? Are you holding up okay?"

"Yeah. I'm fine. You know he always intimidated me a little."

"Really? You never said anything."

My sister shrugged. "You thought Peter hung the moon. What could I say?"

"Did he ever hurt you or say anything inappropriate?"

"No. Oh, gross. You and Mom taught me about good touch and bad touch. I would've screamed bloody murder if he'd tried anything inappropriate. Peter was so smart and intense. His strong personality intimidated me."

"Okay, good to know." I felt weak with relief. If Peter had hurt my sister, I might have attacked him myself. I reached for my drink. "What's this?"

"Cinnamon roll iced coffee."

I took a sip. Sweetness with a hint of spicy cinnamon. Nice. Soothing and refreshing. "I like it."

"Good. It's new. Hey, I've only got a few minutes. What'd you want to talk about?"

"This morning I received a threat."

Lacey Jane leaned forward. "Oh, Andi Grace. You've got to quit trying to catch the killer. I don't know what I'd do if you got hurt."

I inhaled. "It's not me they're after. The note said if I don't quit, they're going to hurt you."

"Me? What'd I do?" Her eyes widened.

Marc said, "Nothing. They're trying to get to Andi Grace by threatening you."

Lacey Jane clutched my arm. Her nails bit into my skin. "You've got to quit, Andi Grace. What's to stop them from killing me? Then you or Nate could be next. And Danny might get in the way and be the next one in danger."

Weird she was concerned about Danny. I patted her shoulder. "Calm down. I'm not going to do anything else. I promise."

"You better not. All of our lives could depend on your next move."

"Is anything going on with you and Danny? More than friendship?"

Her mouth dropped open. "What? No. He's your old boyfriend and my friend. Nothing else." Lacey Jane stood with enough force to cause the chair to crash to the ground. She set it up and glared at me. "I've got to get back to work."

After she left us alone on the patio, I looked at Marc. "What do you think? Is there something between them?"

At that moment, his gaze bounced around before he met my eyes. "One thing you need to know about me is I always tell the truth."

"Good. I can handle it." Could I really handle it if my little sister dated Danny?

"I think there might be some sparks between those two. I'd hate to think they'd act on it, though."

"Because you think it'd devastate me? I got over Danny Nichols a long time ago." Would Marc believe my bold declaration? Did I believe myself?

"You're a strong woman, but a sister should be loyal."

Had I babied Lacey Jane too much after our parents died? Or had I been too strict? I agreed a sister should be loyal, and, despite Marc's pep talk, I wasn't sure how I would handle it if she began to date Danny.

I stirred the paper straw through my iced coffee and took a drink.

Loyalty.

Danny.

Money.

Family.

"What are you thinking?" Marc passed me a pastry.

"We need to find out who Peter left his estate to. According to Danny, Peter and his sister split because of their grandfather's will. Is it possible the family reconciled? If so, would the sister inherit the bulk of the estate? Or Danny? I think whoever inherits Peter's estate should go on the suspect list."

"Your theory has potential, but there's a big problem."

"What?"

"You're supposed to leave the murder alone if you want to protect your sister."

"You're right." Air whooshed out of my lungs. Of course Marc was right, but could I count on him to find the killer on his own if I was arrested?

Chapter Fourteen

AFTER WE TURNED the note and photograph over to Sheriff Stone, I parted ways with Marc and Chubb. I ran home and tackled the dreaded paperwork. Once it was completed, I treated myself to a walk with Sunny before making my afternoon rounds. I took Sunny with me because her presence made me braver. She was always loyal, and I continued to believe Lacey Jane would be loyal to me. I didn't want her to be rude to Danny, but I didn't want her to date him either.

My phone was in my hand, and I was about to order Chinese takeout when Marc texted me.

Thomas King is on the way over with an estimate. Can you join us?

Since my work was done for the day, I sent a reply and headed his way.

The wind blew through the windows, causing strands of hair to escape my ponytail. Sunny sat in the passenger seat with her head propped on the console and one front paw in the cup holder.

"Poor thing. You needed some special time with me, didn't you? I know you enjoy having other dogs around, but you'll always be my baby."

I let up on the gas at the sight of a black cargo van going under the speed limit. Tinted windows and no advertisements, in addition to mud on the back bumper and license plate, made the vehicle about as nondescript as possible. I followed at a safe distance along River Road. The lower speed might even be good for my blood pressure.

Sunny perked her ears and stared at me as if wondering why I was driving so slow.

I laughed. "You're a good girl. Faithful to a fault."

Marc's words drifted back to me. Did he think Lacey Jane wasn't a loyal sister? Why was she so friendly to Danny? If it came to choosing, Lacey Jane would side with me. Right? Not that there'd be any choosing. I'd play nice. Heyward Beach was big enough for Danny and me.

I ran my hand over Sunny's head.

My jaw twitched. Did Lacey Jane not remember how devastated I'd been when Danny dumped me? I'd suffered one blow after another the summer before I was supposed to start college. Had she been so wrapped up in her own grief that she missed what a jerk Danny had become? Ancient history. Still, I should warn her Danny was a heart-breaker and she'd be smart to avoid the man.

The black van slowed, and the right blinker flashed.

I snatched my phone from the cup holder and placed my finger on the circle to bring it to life. I drove slow enough to find the camera app and take pictures of the other vehicle before it disappeared.

The van turned onto the lane leading to Peter's house. There wasn't a subdivision or other homes on the lane the black van had chosen. It was all Peter's property.

I tightened my grip on the steering wheel. Would taking pictures of a strange van endanger Lacey Jane? As much as I wanted to follow it, the action might put my sister in peril.

I stepped on the gas and raced to Marc's turnoff.

Sunny barked.

"It's okay, girl. At least I think it is." I slowed for the turn then took the bumpy road faster than I should. Soon I screeched to a halt in front of the house and jumped out. "Marc!"

Please, God, let him be here and not at the boat shed.

The front door flung open. Marc wore jeans and held a shirt wadded in his hand. Water glistened in his hair. "Andi Grace, what's wrong?"

The first thing I noticed were his abs. The man's muscles took my breath away.

Marc tugged the shirt over his head. "Andi Grace. Look at me."

My face grew warm. I had been looking at him. He probably meant look him in the eyes. So I did. "Marc, a van just went to Peter's place." I explained what I'd seen and handed him my phone. "Look at this picture."

He took the phone, held it close to his face, tromboned out, then close again. "I think there's too much shade to get a clear idea what it looks like."

"See what I mean? The driver made it look as unimaginative as possible. Dull. Bland. Unidentifiable. You get what I mean. The van was conspicuous because it tried to be so inconspicuous. They also drove slow, and you know how people like to speed on River Road."

"Yeah. You're right about that. But I thought you were backing off the murder."

"Hey, this is me backing off."

Sunny moseyed over to stand beside me.

Marc shook his head. "If you hadn't been warned, what would you have done about the van?"

I looked at the ground. Marc wore a pair of brown leather flip-flops. Rainbows. A shade darker than mine. His were well worn as if one of his favorite pairs of shoes. I moved my gaze back to his face. "I might have followed the van to Peter's house if I wasn't scared of Lacey Jane getting hurt."

"Then I'm glad you got the warning note this morning." He looked in the distance.

The sound of tires rolling over Marc's sandy drive could be heard.

"I bet it's Thomas coming over. How do you feel about being my girlfriend?"

My heart leapt. "What? We've never even been on a date. Unless you count the funeral, and that'd be a terrible first date."

Marc held up his hand. "You're right. Going to a funeral together is not first-date material. I know you don't lie, but Thomas will wonder why you care what I choose for my remodel. So will you be my girlfriend? At least for today?"

"Yes." Had he guessed I had feelings for him? It'd been so long since I'd dated anybody, I wasn't sure I could pull off being a pretend girlfriend.

Thomas pulled next to my Suburban and paused a minute before hopping out of his truck.

Marc reached for my hand.

I held mine out to him. When our fingers intertwined, chills shot up my arm, then up my neck, and down my spine. *Whoa.* Goose bumps? Before I embarrassed myself, I better get my *true* emotions under control.

Thomas joined us with a rolled-up paper under one arm and a soft-sided briefcase in the other hand. "Afternoon, folks. How y'all doing?"

Marc nodded. "Good. Looking forward to seeing what you've got."

I said, "Hello, Thomas."

His gaze drifted to me and returned to Marc. "I stayed up most of the night creating this plan just for you. It'll be an original, one-of-a-kind kitchen renovation. A Thomas King innovative design like nothing you've ever seen before."

Well, I had to give the man credit for promoting his work.

"Let's head inside." Marc opened the door and allowed me to enter first. Thomas came next.

I took Sunny to the kitchen and let her out in the fenced backyard. Chubb barked a greeting, and I returned and sat on Marc's denim couch.

Marc took the spot next to me and moved the TV controllers and boating magazines off the simple cherry coffee table. He placed the items on the recliner. "Thomas, what'd you come up with?"

Thomas rolled the plan out on the coffee table. He anchored each corner with tile samples he'd pulled from his briefcase. "I focused on two M's. Modern and manly."

Marc looked at the plan. Thomas talked on and on. And on. Thomas was so enamored with his proposal, he didn't seem aware Marc seemed less than enthusiastic. It was like Thomas hadn't taken any of Marc's wishes into consideration from the previous meeting. At last the man paused and looked toward Marc and me with expectation.

Marc rubbed his hands together. "I need to know the cost before we proceed."

"It depends on which tiles you choose, backsplash, countertops, and appliances. When you decide, I'll give you a final cost. This is the base price." Thomas slid a contract across the table to him. "You can sign this today and pay for the extras as we go."

I leaned close, even though I could tell Marc didn't like the plan.

Marc cracked his knuckles. "Is this the same thing you did with Peter? Pay as you go?"

Thomas frowned. "Each client has different preferences."

Marc reached for the contract and read it. "This dollar amount seems too low. I'd rather make some choices to add to the contracted price. I only plan to go to the bank once for a loan."

"It'll slow down your project to make decisions first."

"I'm in no hurry." The creases cleared from Marc's forehead, and he exuded the impression of a man without a care in the world.

"Tell me what you think about these choices. Maybe I can give you a better idea of the final cost. We can still sign the contract today, but you'll know how much to borrow."

My stomach cartwheeled. How could Thomas be so pushy?

Marc's frown returned. "I like to take my time before making big decisions. Why don't you leave the drawing and samples with me? Let me study them at different times of the day. See how the light hits them. I'll get back to you before the end of the week."

The man's eyes narrowed. "How do I know you won't take my sketches to another contractor? I've spent hours working on this plan."

"I appreciate what you've done. Feel free to take the drawings with you. Leave me the samples."

Thomas rolled up the drawings and snapped a rubber band around the papers. "Don't take too long. I've got other customers waiting."

"Like I said, I'm not in a hurry. If somebody else makes a faster decision, I'll wait. No big deal."

I found it interesting Thomas claimed others were waiting for him. He'd acted so fast on Marc's request, I'd thought he was desperate for money.

Thomas stood.

Marc ambled to the door. "Thanks for stopping by tonight. Hey, I was out at the Richard Rice Plantation. Lots of expansion out there, and I thought I saw your truck. Did you make a bid with them on one of the projects?"

Thomas walked to the front door. "I bet every contractor within a hundred miles of the plantation hopes to get a contract there."

I leapt to my feet. "Why? What's so special about them?"

"They have more than one project in the works. If you do good on the first one, maybe they'll hire you for other projects. One of the great things about old places is something always needs to be fixed or updated."

Marc's shoulders straightened. "If you get the job there, would you still have time for me?"

"Absolutely. You can depend on me."

"Why?"

Thomas stood on the porch. "You and Peter were friends. Peter was good to me. I'll be good to you."

"I appreciate it." Marc remained standing by the doorway speaking through the screen door.

"Night folks."

We said good night in unison.

I slid my arm through Marc's. I was sure we made the picture of a loving couple. We watched Thomas drive away.

When his vehicle disappeared, I said, "There's something hinky going on."

"Why?"

"The very special kitchen remodel he showed you?"

"Yeah. The one he designed just for me."

"I've seen it before. It's not a Thomas King original." My head throbbed.

Marc's eyes widened. "Do you think he drew the same basic plan for somebody else? It's his, and he tweaked it for me?"

"No."

"How can you be so sure?"

"It's the same kitchen Juliet has. The plan came straight out of one of those architecture books you can buy at any hardware store or bookstore. Juliet's brother is a contractor in Savannah. Last year, he came up on weekends for a couple of months to work on her kitchen. Nate and I pitched in to help with the renovation. It saved her lots of money, and the landlord was so impressed he gave her two free months."

Marc sighed. "How'd you figure it out?"

I crossed my arms. "You might say I'm intimately familiar with Juliet's kitchen. Her brother, Griffin, showed us the plan and hung it on the wall until the project was complete. Juliet and I looked at it often and dreamed about the finished project."

"So it's not a Thomas King original."

"Not by a long shot."

Chapter Fifteen

AFTER THOMAS LEFT, Marc and I walked along the Waccamaw River on a worn path. The dogs ran ahead of us free of restraints. I'd convinced Marc to go with me to check out Peter's place, but I couldn't get Thomas's deception off my mind. "I know just because we've discovered Thomas is a liar, it doesn't mean he killed Peter."

Marc nodded. "True, but I keep wondering if he tried to cheat Peter somehow."

"If Thomas was going to scam somebody, you'd think he'd pick a less savvy target. Peter was an accountant involved in big business. It'd be hard to trick him financially. Somebody like me would be easier to deceive."

"Unless Thomas thought Peter was distracted by work and travel. I believe Thomas is arrogant enough to think he could fool Peter." Marc looked toward Peter's place. "Hard to believe he's gone."

"I know." My bottom lip trembled, and I bit it. Maybe with the lowering sun Marc wouldn't notice.

"Let's say Thomas and Regina are innocent. What about Danny?"

I halted and looked at the river. The lapping waves soothed my nerves. "You think Peter left his estate to Danny and his family? It'd be a motive to kill him if they knew."

Marc stuffed his hands into the pockets of his well-worn jeans. "Maybe. I'd like to know who the executor of the will is."

"I don't guess Peter picked Ms. Nichols if they were on the outs."

"His sister?"

"And Danny's mother."

"Uh uh." Marc shook his head. "I can't see it. If the family fought and split over the grandfather's will, why would Peter choose his sister as executor? It makes even less sense for him to leave his estate to her. Danny would've been a child, though. I think he'd be the most likely candidate to inherit everything if Peter wanted to keep it in the family."

The sound of jazz music drifted through the air. "Do you hear that?"

He cocked his head. "Yeah. There aren't any houses on the other side of the river and only mine and Peter's on this side for some distance." Marc turned toward Peter's house. "It's coming from the plantation house. Thomas must be working."

We were close enough to hear the music but trees obscured our view. "He keeps strange hours for a contractor, but there's also the black van I spotted earlier to consider. Maybe there's another contractor at the house. Electrician or something."

"It's possible. I usually try to run during the coolest times of the day, and I've noticed Thomas works late or early but rarely during normal business hours. How does he let sub-contractors into homes if he's not there? His weird schedule can't work for everybody." He pulled out his phone and tapped on the screen. "I'll add that to my list of questions for Thomas."

"Let's get closer to the house. Maybe we can see what's going on."

"Is this you backing off?"

Marc's words stopped me in my tracks. *Back off. Or else.* I'd been warned. "You're right, but how can I back down? Then again, how can I put Lacey Jane in danger?"

"Is that a rhetorical question or do you want my thoughts?" His dimple appeared.

"I'd like to hear your opinion." I twisted the leashes in my hands.

"Some might argue by catching the killer, you're protecting your sister."

"Right. Your logic works for me. Let's head toward the house but stay out of sight." I looked in the direction of Peter's home and unwound the leashes. "Sunny. Chubb. Come here."

Both dogs obeyed, and I leashed them.

I stood and looked at Marc. "Why are you being so nice? Helping me? Protecting me?"

Marc met my gaze. "Let's say I enjoy problem solving, and I like spending time with you."

My face grew warm. I focused on his comment. "Did you become a lawyer to help others solve their problems?"

"You might say that."

I reached for his hand and gave him a gentle squeeze. A feeling of rightness settled over me. Most people might have thought Marc had shut down his heart after losing his parents and being shuffled around the foster care system. I couldn't speak for others, but he seemed to be letting me into his life. I liked the feeling it gave me. And I'd make sure he didn't regret opening himself up to me.

We made our way closer to the house. Peter's house was positioned so the front door faced the river. Plenty of white rockers lined the space where a person could enjoy a glass of iced tea while enjoying a river breeze.

I held both leashes and knelt beside the dogs. Marc stood behind a sprawling oak tree on the edge of Peter's manicured yard. "I see at least eight different vehicles, and sure enough, there's a black van. The others don't look like they belong to contractors. No writing on the doors advertising any businesses. No ladders or special equipment on the back of trucks."

"Let me see." I reached for his phone. "I didn't know there was such a thing as a binoculars app."

"It comes in handy." He handed his phone to me.

I adjusted the focus and looked at the vehicles first. "You're right. They're all regular cars and trucks. Not subcontractors. In fact, one of them looks like the preacher's car. I wish I could see the back window."

"Why?"

"Pastor Larry has all kinds of love-one-another stickers on his window."

"What would bring your preacher to Peter's place?"

"Post-funeral get-together? Reading of the will?"

"Do you see Danny's car?"

"I don't remember what he drives." I handed the phone to him, wondering why I remembered emotions and people better than physical things than vehicles.

"Danny drove a black Lexus at the coffee shop." Marc returned to looking through the binocular app. "I don't see it or Thomas's truck."

"Could he have parked in back?"

"Anything's possible."

Chubb whined.

Marc knelt beside the golden retriever and rubbed his back. "It's okay, fella. I bet you thought this was your forever home. Sorry. You're stuck with me, but I'll take good care of you."

I rose. "Why don't you stay here and I'll work my away around to the back of the house?"

"No way. We stick together." Marc gave Chubb another pat and stood. "I'll follow you."

Sunny remained quiet and continued walking glued to my side.

I stuck to the shadows while making my way toward the back of the house. "The front porch lights are on as well as in the living room and dining room areas. It looks inviting."

"I see. Could a group of homeless people have moved into Peter's house?" Marc paused and raised the phone to his eyes. "I don't get it."

We continued on. Nothing was parked by the detached garage or in the grassy area. "It's clear, but I'd like to get a closer look at the cars in front."

"It's getting late and will be completely dark soon. Do you want to wait?"

"Yes. I want to see who exits the house." I ignored my hunger and retraced my steps to the front.

"Okay. May as well get comfortable." He sat and leaned against a tree. Chubb curled up in his lap.

I smiled and sat beside them. "Enjoy it while you can. At the rate he's growing, he won't be a lapdog for long."

Marc ran his hand over the retriever's head. "I'm glad you trusted me with Chubb."

"I had a hunch you'd be good for each other." I stroked Sunny who lay beside my stretched-out legs.

A horn honked multiple times, and the sound of a fast-driving vehicle grew louder.

The front door of the house opened. People poured outside and raced for the empty cars.

Sunny barked, and I grabbed hold of her collar in case she decided to run toward the commotion. "Hush, girl."

Marc bear-hugged Chubb. "Wonder what the excitement's all about?"

I scooted closer to the edge of the yard. "Let me have your phone."

He tapped his finger on the button to turn it on. "Here."

Chubb's fluffy, golden ears perked up.

I used Marc's phone to see who all ran from the house. I gasped. "It's not Pastor Larry. It's his wife."

"Do you see any of Peter's family?"

"No. In fact, I don't recognize anybody but Phyllis Mays. It's mostly men of different ages. Wait, there are two other women. Young. Like us."

Marc leaned forward. The cars started and tore out of the front yard.

Headlights swept over the two of us.

Marc tugged me to the ground. "We don't want to be spotted."

I flattened myself on a patch of grass and urged Sunny to lay beside me. "Should we leave too?"

"No." He pointed at the pickup truck driving toward the house still honking. "Let's see who's driving."

I grasped his arm. "It's Thomas."

Two men exited the front door of the house, carrying a table.

Marc struggled to keep his puppy still. "Do you know those guys?"

"One is Dylan King. I don't know the other one."

"Are they stealing furniture?"

The vehicle screeched to a halt at the bottom of the front steps.

"No. It looks like the shape of a poker table. Can I take a picture?"

"Sure."

Thomas jumped out of the truck without shutting off the engine. "What do you think you're doing?" Anger laced his words, and I was glad he wasn't yelling at me.

We lay in the wooded area. Close enough to hear and see but hopefully not be seen.

The guys on the porch kept moving toward the van with their table.

Thomas yanked his son's arm. "Tell me what's going on!"

"We lost our gambling place, and I knew nobody lived here anymore. We moved our poker game here. No big deal."

Chubb barked.

Chills covered my body.

All three men stopped and looked in our direction.

My ears rang. Could they see us?

Marc grabbed my hand. "Keep your head down and run."

The dogs and I followed. "Do you think they're going to shoot us?"

"I hope not. Just keep moving." After a few steps he glanced back. "And while you're at it, pray."

Thomas's loud voice cut through the thick air. "Who's there?"

Chapter Sixteen

IF MARC WANTED me to pray, he must be worried. I prayed and ran as if my life depended on it. "We can't lead them back to your place." My voice stuttered between my panted breaths.

"Follow me. I know a shortcut." Marc took the lead and gave Chubb enough space on his leash to keep up but not so much as to run in another direction.

Sunny remained behind me, but the increasing darkness challenged our speed.

Ow! My foot landed in a divot, and my ankle twisted. I bit back a moan and limped the next few steps. No way I'd let an injury get us killed. Moving back to a run, *ouch*, I downshifted into a jog and did my best to keep up with Marc and Chubb. *Lord, please protect us.*

Marc darted to the left.

I tailed him. Not as close as I'd have preferred, but nevertheless I mirrored his movements.

"Almost there." Marc continued the trek without looking back.

Part of me yearned to baby my ankle and slow the pace. The terrified part of me was glad Marc hadn't noticed my slip. He never slowed, and I did my best to keep up with him. Neither dog appeared challenged.

Soon we reached Marc's backyard. He sprinted across the grass and into the house.

By the time I entered, he was pulling food from the refrigerator. "In case Thomas shows up, we'll be here eating dinner. Leftover fried chicken."

My heart raced, and I tried to get my breathing under control. "What about chips and drinks?" I panted and perspired. No way I'd fool Thomas.

"I've got carrot sticks and apples. Let's put the dogs in the laundry room." He gave each animal a dog treat and shut the door. "They should be fine in there. I've got rugs on the floor and a full water bowl."

I grabbed two plates from the cabinet and placed them on the table, limping as I moved.

A vehicle rumbled nearby.

Marc dumped carrots on our plates along with two chicken breasts. "Sit down."

I took a seat and bit into my chicken so it didn't look like we'd just started to eat. I even pulled a couple of bites off and rolled them into a paper napkin to hide.

Marc half-filled two glasses with water and took a bite out of a green apple when he sat. "You might want to smooth your hair. It's kinda got a wild look."

That was embarrassing, but I removed the band supposed to be holding back a ponytail. Finger-combing my hair was the best I could do before attempting a messy bun. "Better?"

His cheeks bulged with food, and he nodded.

I giggled. "This is crazy."

Light swept through the room. Tires crunched on the gravel.

Marc swallowed and wiped his mouth. "Not so crazy after all. It looks like we've got company."

"I hope they buy our story. Are you still my boyfriend?"

"You better believe it."

Somebody pounded on the door.

Marc winked. "Showtime."

My stomach somersaulted, but I took another bite of chicken while Marc went to answer the door.

"Thomas? What a surprise. I didn't expect to see you so soon." Marc kept his hand on the door.

The man shoved his way inside and strode across the open space family room and into the kitchen. "Did you come to see me?"

Marc dashed in front of him and planted his hand against the man's chest to stop him at the kitchen entryway. "I don't know where you live. And I don't believe I invited you in."

I wiped my greasy fingers on a paper napkin and wiped my mouth. "Hello, Thomas."

Thomas looked at me, the table, then Marc.

I waved my hand over the food. "Would you like to join us? It's only leftovers, but I love cold fried chicken."

He narrowed his eyes to slits. "It's kinda late for supper."

Marc approached. "I get carried away working on boats and lose track of time. If Andi Grace hadn't insisted we eat, I'd probably still be in the boat shed. Not that it's any of your business."

"Alone and hungry." I shrugged.

Anger rolled off Thomas. He pointed at me. "You been here the whole time since I left?"

"I enjoy spending time with my boyfriend, but why is it any of your concern?" My breathing had returned to normal, but a trickle of sweat trailed down my spine.

"You always were a sassy thing. Acting like you were a better parent than me, and you were only a sister."

"Enough." Marc put a hand on Thomas's shoulder. "It's time for you to leave."

The man's expression changed so fast, no one would've known the anger flowing through him seconds ago. Except it'd been real.

Thomas held up his hands. "Sorry for the misunderstanding. Andi Grace and I go way back. We're all friends here. Right? I still plan to do your remodel. No harm. No foul."

Marc led him to the door. "If you plan to work for me, you'll need to improve your manners around Andi Grace. Pull yourself together. We'll talk tomorrow."

"Sure, man. It's all good. Sorry for disturbing your dinner. Y'all have a good night." He jogged to his truck and took off.

Marc came back inside after Thomas had disappeared. He opened the laundry room door and Chubb and Sunny joined us. "I can't tell if he bought our story."

"I need a Coke." I opened the refrigerator. Juice. Water pitcher. Bottles of something called Kombucha.

"I don't have any soft drinks."

I had a watered-down Coke sitting in the cup holder of my Suburban, but the ice had melted hours ago. It'd be flat and warm. "I don't know if I can date a guy who doesn't drink Coke."

Marc's lip twitched flashing me his dimple, then he laughed. Long and hard.

I leaned against the kitchen counter and laughed, too. I'd never seen Marc completely let go this way.

At last Marc sat at the table. "Sounds like I need to pick up a twelve-pack next time I'm in town if this relationship is going to survive."

"A really good boyfriend would keep some at the house and some in the boat shed for me." I used a napkin and ran it along the back of my neck and forehead.

"Duly noted." He waved to the other seat. "Why don't we finish eating?"

"It's not going to be the same without—"

"Don't say it." He chuckled.

I returned to my place and took a bite of chicken. "You know, Thomas broke up whatever was going on at Peter's place. If it was an innocent gathering, everybody wouldn't have rushed away. Even Dylan and his friend hurried off."

"Actually, we assume Dylan left."

That stopped me. "You're right. We ran before finding out what happened to him."

"I'd say his dad wasn't happy to discover Dylan had a group of friends partying at Peter's place."

I slumped in my chair. "Friends? I'm not sure what the connection was between those people. Also, did you notice how awkward the table was? I'm sure it's like the poker table for sale at Regina's place. She told me she's sold three of them in the last month."

Marc's brow puckered in thought. "Do you think Dylan and his friends were playing poker?"

I hopped up and paced. Pain flared in my ankle, forcing me to return to my seat. "Phyllis Mays ran out of the house. The other day she told me she'd come into some money and could afford to pay Juliet to color her hair. What if she gambles?"

"South Carolina has strict laws concerning poker and various forms of illegal gambling. We need to call Sheriff Stone. Maybe he can find some evidence at the house."

"What kind of evidence? If Dylan took the table and cards—wait a minute. Do you remember the ace of hearts the day I found Peter's body? I gave it to you, and later we turned it over to Wade."

"Yep. You hired me so you could show me the card. My guess is this isn't the first time Dylan's run games." Marc moved to the counter and pulled his wallet out of a wooden bowl. "I'll call the sheriff."

I had to admit, that impressed me. Not only did Marc know where to find his wallet, he knew where to find Wade's business card. The only organized part of my house was the office where I kept a work schedule and pet files.

Marc dialed the number.

I loaded the dishwasher then took Chubb and Sunny outside for a walk while Marc discussed the situation with Wade.

Overhead clouds blocked the stars. A sliver of the moon peeked between the white puffs.

A pop sounded. Like a creature stepping on a dry branch. Or a person. I froze where I stood. Was somebody watching us?

Chubb and Sunny barked. Rapid, loud, and ferocious snarls. They'd gone into alert mode. Oh, yeah. Somebody was close to our territory.

"Let's get inside. Come." Sunny understood and followed me. I hobbled to the backdoor and opened it.

Chubb continued his nonstop yapping. "Chubb, come." The dog gave one last bark and joined me at the entrance.

I nudged him inside, slammed the door, and locked it.

Chubb refused to calm down. He growled at the door.

"What in the world? Chubb, quiet." Marc raised his voice.

The dog geared down to a low rumble in his chest.

"We heard something out there. He's protecting me."

Marc knelt and rubbed the puppy. "Good boy. Way to go defending Andi Grace."

Chubb gave Marc an adoring look.

With one last scratch behind the retriever's ears, Marc pushed from the floor and pulled his phone from his pocket. "Sheriff Stone was heading straight to Peter's house, but I'm going to call back and ask him to stop here first."

I nodded and sank into the kitchen chair I'd occupied earlier. Never before had I been so scared for my personal safety. Immediate and intense. Many times over the years, I'd worried about the future and having enough money to provide for the kids. This was a different kind of threat, and I didn't like it. "Wait a minute. Can you ask him to send a deputy to check on Lacey Jane?"

"Sure." After he made the call, he sat beside me. "How bad is your injury?"

I didn't have the strength to pretend my ankle didn't hurt. "Bad. Especially for a person who makes a living walking dogs."

Chapter Seventeen

MARC FOLLOWED ME all the way home and walked me to my front door. The key ring slipped from my fingers and fell to the ground. I picked them up and dropped them again.

"Are you nervous to go inside alone?"

"No. I'll have Sunny, and there are two other dogs inside I'm sitting for. I'm sure it's fine." My words might've sounded braver if my voice hadn't wobbled.

He took the keys from my trembling hands and unlocked the door. "Why don't you let me help take the dogs out? Then you can hunker down for the night."

"I already feel guilty letting you follow me home." I stepped inside and turned on the lights. "I've taken care of myself for years. This is ridiculous." If I said it out loud, maybe I'd believe it.

"You've never tangled with a killer before. There's no shame in backing off." Two pairs of my cross trainers had been kicked off and left in the front entry as well as a pair of flip-flops. Marc scooted them to the side with his foot.

"I don't know what to do next. I want to prove my innocence and catch the killer. If it weren't for his threat against Lacey Jane, I'd be more determined to help catch him. As it is, I've put my sister in harm's way and disrupted your life."

"Hey, you're not interfering with my schedule. I needed to come to town and buy Cokes for my girlfriend."

"Yeah. Right." His words warmed my heart and I laughed. "The other dogs are in the kitchen."

"Do you want me to look through the rest of your house while you let them out? I can check under beds and in the closets to make sure nobody is hiding."

My shoulders relaxed at his offer. "You're so nice. Thanks. I warn you, though, my house isn't as neat as yours."

"No sweat. I learned to be neat in one of my foster homes. I also learned not to get too attached to things because I never knew when

I'd get moved and lose items I thought belonged to me." His face reddened. "I don't know why I said that."

"You didn't get to keep your stuff?"

"Some families kept what they bought for me. Their money. Their stuff. In high school, I found different jobs so I'd have a little money of my own."

"What'd you buy?"

"I opened a bank account and saved up for the proverbial rainy day. I became a minimalist neat freak."

I gave him a small smile. "Neatness has never been my strong suit. My mother often told me I'd never be able to keep a roommate in college if I didn't learn to be organized."

"It didn't stop you from raising your siblings. I'm sure it's not as bad as you think. I'll meet you in the kitchen." He turned right and started searching the bedrooms.

I let Sunny and the other dogs out the back door and rinsed some dirty dishes before loading them into the dishwasher. What was Marc thinking about my house? And my messiness? Who cared? It wasn't like he'd break up with me for being a slob. He was my pretend boyfriend. Did I wish it was real?

With a soft footfall, he reentered the kitchen. "Not a soul in sight. You locked the front door?"

"Yes." I pulled dog treats out of a plastic bin. "My sloppiness didn't scare you away?"

"The sight of an organized office surprised me. Even the desktop was neat. The charts and calendar proved you can be neat if you want."

"Trust me, it's an effort to be organized." Another trait Peter had instilled in me in order to run a successful business.

"I didn't find the killer hiding in any of the rooms. Are the dogs safe?"

I shrugged. "The yard is fenced in, but you never know when a visiting dog will try to dig out. I find it safer to watch than to trust. Except for Sunny, of course."

Marc stepped onto the deck.

I turned on the outside lights to illuminate the backyard and joined him on my spacious twelve by sixteen deck.

He smiled. "The white picket fence seems to fit your personality."

Sunny barked from the right corner of the yard. The other dogs raced over and barked too.

My first instinct was to quiet the dogs, but what if somebody was there trying to get to us?

Footsteps pounded on the grass.

A dark form moved across the back of the yard. My pulse skyrocketed. "Somebody's out here."

The dogs dashed after the runner.

Marc pulled out his phone and turned on the flashlight.

"Go inside and call Sheriff Stone. And turn off the lights."

Sunny leapt at the person and bit his leg. The other dogs continued their frenzied barking.

My legs refused to move.

A dog's yelp sounded.

"Stop!" Marc yelled and raced toward the intruder.

A rip sounded. Then a thud.

Sunny joined the cacophony.

A shot rang out.

A dog squealed.

Marc hit the ground.

I ducked behind my grill.

The dogs howled and barked. It was hard to tell what animal made which sound.

Marc hurried to the dogs. Sunny lay on the ground panting, and the other two stood guard.

No. Not Sunny. I raced to Marc and the dogs. "Did he shoot her?"

"Yes."

I screamed and dropped to the ground.

"Andi Grace, Sunny's alive. You don't have time to fall apart." Marc slipped his arms under my sweet German shepherd's body and crossed the yard. "Andi Grace. Open the door."

I caught up with him on the deck, ripped open the door, and held it for Marc and the Westies.

"We need to get her to the vet."

I ran my hands over sweet Sunny. "What about you? Are you okay?"

"I'm fine. Focus on Sunny."

Sirens sounded in the distance.

I cleared the kitchen table and raced to the linen closet for a sheet. Back in the kitchen, I spread it on the table. "Lay her there. I'll call Doc Hewitt."

Marc stayed by Sunny's side while I made the call.

He spoke to my dog. "You're going to be okay, Sunny. Andi Grace's got this. She'll take good care of you."

As soon as the vet picked up the phone, I started talking. "Doc Hewitt, this is Andi Grace. Sunny's been shot. I hear sirens, and I don't know if the cops will let me leave. Can you come to my house?"

"On my way." He disconnected the call.

I studied Sunny's wound while Marc cared for the other dogs and settled them into their crates.

Marc joined me. "It sounds like the sheriff's almost here."

"Would you pull a towel out of the top drawer?"

Marc brought me a soft kitchen towel.

I held it on her wounded shoulder to stem the flow of blood.

The doorbell rang, and somebody pounded on the door.

"I'll get it." Marc left me standing over my precious friend.

Chapter Eighteen

I REFUSED TO LEAVE Sunny's side until Dr. Hewitt arrived. Sunny was so much more than a dog to me. She'd been my friend, comforter, and defender since the day she'd appeared in my life. Sometimes I believed she'd been sent from God.

The first person to arrive was Wade Stone. He stormed into the kitchen and skidded to a stop at the sight of me holding bloody rags against Sunny's wound. "What happened?"

I opened my mouth. Instead of words coming out, my lips trembled and tears filled my eyes.

Marc walked around Wade and rubbed my back. "Sheriff, can you and I talk in the living room? We've called the vet. It'd be mighty decent of you to let her focus on the dog right now. She'll be happy to answer your questions when she knows Sunny is okay."

Wade pointed at me. "I'm not leaving until we talk."

I nodded. On a normal day, I would've been ticked at Marc speaking for me. At the moment, all I felt was relief. The two men left me alone with Sunny.

Dear God, please let her be okay. Help Doc get here fast. I remained standing over my dog.

Marc handled Wade and two deputies, leading them through the kitchen to the backyard.

From their crates, Heinz and Chloe barked like ferocious terriers. No doubt they'd bite into a leg or ankle if given the opportunity to defend me. Sunny whimpered.

"You're going to be okay, girl." I uttered soothing words in hopes of comforting her.

The doorbell rang. All of the men were outside.

Not wanting to stop applying pressure to the wound, I called out, "Come in."

Hurried and heavy footsteps thudded over the living room floor. Doc Hewitt appeared across the table from me. "I got here as fast as I could."

"Doc." My voice wobbled, and I almost sank to the floor in relief. "Thank you so much for coming. I think it's only a flesh wound." Even though I wasn't a vet, I'd helped Doc Hewitt enough to have an educated guess.

"Let me see what we're dealing with." The veterinarian took over.

I washed my hands but kept my gaze on Sunny.

After a few minutes, Doc Hewitt nodded. "I agree. You've done a good job cleaning the wound."

"Do you think she needs X-rays?"

He adjusted his bifocals. "No. Somebody taught you well. I have no complaints on how you handled the injury."

Somehow, I managed to smile. "Yes. You did teach me well."

The front door banged shut, and deep voices drifted into the kitchen. I peeked into the living room to assure myself it was the good guys.

Marc and Wade were in a deep conversation, and the deputies must still be searching for leads in the backyard. I owed Marc. Big time. He'd taken charge of the sheriff and deputies, allowing me to care for Sunny.

I glanced at Doc Hewitt and Sunny. "I probably need to speak to Sheriff Stone."

"Go ahead. We'll be fine." He was preparing to stitch up the gash and never looked at me.

My stomach clenched. Too many close calls tonight had left my stomach in knots. Poor Sunny was paying the price.

The men stopped talking when I joined them in the living room.

"Did y'all find any clues?"

Marc rubbed my shoulder.

Wade held up a clear plastic bag with a piece of material. "Part of the assailant's shirt snagged on your fence."

Black cotton. Jagged edges and a partial hem.

"It looks like maybe a polo shirt." I should know. I'd laundered enough for my brother over the years. People might say I was sloppy, but I'd always been clean.

Wade nodded. "Could be. I'd like to hear your version of what happened tonight."

I wanted to return to Sunny, but Wade expected me to do the adult thing. "Thomas was wearing a white T-shirt when we saw him at Marc's place."

Marc gave me an encouraging squeeze on the shoulder. "Doesn't mean he didn't change. In fact, it'd make sense to wear black. Less chance we'd spot him in the dark."

Wade said, "Let's sit."

I moved to my flowery red couch and dropped onto one end. My mother had read many stories to me on this very couch. Despite the night's events, there was a degree of comfort when I thought about my mom. I faced Wade, who sat in the ivory wingback chair. The same chair my dad used to sit in to lecture me when I'd misbehaved. Maybe it was why I felt like I was in trouble. Or it could've been because Wade was the sheriff and wore a gun at his waist and could've easily arrested me for Peter's murder. I took a deep breath. Time to cooperate. "What do you need to know?"

Wade placed a recorder on the table and pushed a button. "Just tell me what happened tonight. From your point of view."

Marc left the room, and I missed him. I shook off that thought. I didn't need a man to make me strong. The last twelve years should've proved how capable I was. I took a deep breath. "I'll start with hearing the music at Peter's house. Okay?"

"Yes."

I took another deep breath and began. Halfway through the story, Marc slipped into the room, sat beside me, and handed me a glass of Coke in a sweat-proof glass full of ice cubes.

"Thanks. How's Sunny?"

"Dr. Hewitt is stitching her up."

I nodded and turned back to Wade. "Marc was kind enough to follow me home. After our encounter with Thomas King, I was kinda nervous."

Wade nodded. "I understand. What happened here?"

I took a gulp of my drink and reviewed the events with Wade. "Then you arrived. Do you think it's Thomas King?"

Wade punched the button on his recorder. "I don't know. Be careful around him, but don't assume it's not somebody else. Let me handle the investigation, and you stick to dog-walking." His blue eyes pierced me. "Do you understand?"

"Yes, sir." Okay. Maybe addressing a man my own age as sir was over the top.

Marc stood. "Sheriff, is it safe for Andi Grace to stay here by herself?"

"I'll make sure a car patrols this area tonight." He gathered his belongings and strode to the front door.

I followed the men. "Are you going to question Thomas King?"

"I've got a deputy heading to his house as we speak, and I'm going to join them. The sooner we get there, the better our chance he'll slip up." He gave me another pointed stare. "If he's guilty, of course."

"Of course. Did you find the bullet?"

"Not yet. For the record, we don't need your help looking."

I nodded. "Will you check for a gun at Thomas's house?"

Marc touched my arm. "Andi Grace, trust Wade to do his job." His voice had a hint—just a hint—of a "back off" warning.

My skin prickled. I wouldn't analyze whether from embarrassment or from Marc's touch. "Sorry, Wade. I'm just so worried."

His expression softened. "I understand, Andi Grace. We'll ask about weapons. But maybe you should give Thomas a break."

My head jerked back. "What do you mean?"

"When we were young, his wife disappeared with Dylan. Thomas couldn't afford a private investigator, and the police couldn't locate them for over a year."

Thomas hadn't been on my radar until I was responsible for raising Lacey Jane. "How do you know this?"

"I just do."

"What happened?"

"The FBI found Mrs. King and Dylan in Texas. His picture was on a milk carton, and a kid going to school with Dylan saw it and told his parents. By the time Mrs. King was arrested, she'd done a good job of brainwashing Dylan."

"Brainwashing how?"

"The usual. His dad was a terrible person. Didn't love them. That kind of garbage. Add that to the fact Dylan blamed Thomas for his mom's arrest. You know how hard it is to be a single parent. Imagine how much harder if you've got those hurdles to cross."

How did I not know about Dylan's kidnapping? Had I been so focused on my family and Danny I hadn't cared about anybody else's problems? Shame on me. "Thanks for sharing his story, Wade."

"I'm not saying the man is innocent, but you know the old saying. Walk a mile in a man's shoes. You might cut him some slack."

"I'll try to be nicer." Unless he turned out to be the killer.

Marc stuffed his hands in his pockets. "The most important thing is to be safe."

Wade nodded. "I agree."

I summoned up my courage. "Does this mean you've ruled me out as a suspect in Peter's murder?"

In Wade Stone's inimitable way, he sidestepped my question. "The case is wide open. Good night." He left us standing by the front door.

As Marc closed the door, I twisted my mouth. "Maybe when we hear who inherited Peter's estate, we'll have a better suspect." I tipped my head. "I'd never heard the story about Thomas."

"I guess we should give Thomas the benefit of the doubt, but don't let down your guard."

"Right. I'm going to check on Sunny." I headed to the kitchen. Sunny was still laying on the counter with her eyes closed and breathing heavy. "How's she doing, Doc?"

"She'll be sore, but no permanent damage. I need you to add more soft towels or blankets to her kennel. Let's make it as comfortable as possible."

I hurried to the laundry room and pulled a soft quilt from a shelf. Back in the kitchen, I fluffed the towels in the crate and placed the quilt on top. A big space for a big dog needed lots of padding. "Ready."

The Westies had grown quiet and watched us deal with Sunny.

Dr. Hewitt pointed to Marc. "Do you mind carrying her? My back isn't as strong as it used to be."

Marc spoke soft words to Sunny before lifting her to his chest. At the door of the crate, he knelt with Sunny in his arms. The man's arms bulged as he leaned in and placed my dog on the mound of softness.

My heart swelled. What a nice man. He'd be a great father one day to some lucky children.

My pulse spiked. Where had that come from? I was a practical woman and didn't have time to imagine what Marc would be like as a father.

Marc as a father. I'd raised Nate and Lacey Jane. The threat. I found my phone and called my sister.

"Hello. Andi Grace?"

"Where are you?"

"At my apartment. Why? Where are you?"

"I'm home. Pack a bag. I'm going to call Nate to take you to his place for the night. I'll explain what's going on later. Don't answer the door for anybody except Nate. Do you understand?"

"What's going on?" My sister's stubborn streak often caused trouble.

"Please, don't argue. I'm calling Nate now. Will you go with him?" A bubble of hysteria wove its way into my voice.

Marc stared at me wide-eyed.

"Yes, but sister, you've got some explaining to do."

"I promise to tell you everything as soon as I know you're safe." I disconnected and called Nate, going into big-sister mode on him like I had Lacey Jane. I couldn't help if Marc thought I was a whack job. Lacey Jane's safety came first.

ONE O'CLOCK IN THE morning, sleep eluded me. It'd gotten to the point every tiny noise propelled me to pray. When it'd become a lengthy one-sided conversation with God, I got out of bed and channel surfed until I'd found a movie worth watching.

I kept my phone at my side in case I needed to call for help. On the table sat a cup of sleepy tea I'd brewed earlier. Juliet had given me the tea months ago, but this was the first night I'd tried it. The taste wasn't bad, but it left a slimy feel in my mouth. Still, if it helped me sleep, it'd be worth drinking.

My phone vibrated with a text message from Marc.

`Are you okay? Do you want some company?`

The middle of the night didn't seem like the time to act brave.

`I'm watching movies and pretending I'm not scared.`

`Heading your way.`

The night didn't seem quite as frightening knowing Marc cared enough to check on me. I'd been too afraid to put on pajamas in case the bad guy showed up and I needed to run. So I didn't have to change clothes, but my hair needed brushing.

After making myself presentable, I fixed air popped popcorn and found a Dick Van Dyke marathon on TV. Laughter would be good. Something simple and fun. I pushed the pause button so we wouldn't miss anything.

The doorbell rang, and I hurried to answer it. "Come on in. I made popcorn and melted real butter."

"Sounds good." Marc entered with Chubb at his side.

The puppy sniffed and angled toward the kitchen.

Marc followed me to the couch and plopped down next to me. "It's been a while since I've had popcorn."

"This is so much better than microwave popcorn, but nothing beats what you buy at the theater."

Chubb returned, curled up on the braided rug in front of the TV, and dropped his head on his paws.

The Westies whined.

"I'll be right back." I led the fluffy white dogs into the family room where they checked out Chubb.

Marc said, "How's Sunny?"

"Doc gave her pain medicine, and she's asleep." I crisscrossed my legs and hit the play button. My body was wired tight. I was a mixture of nervousness at having Marc here so late at night, and relief he was here. "Here's a glass of water for you and Coke for me."

"Water's good." He reached into the big bowl and seized a handful of fluffy white kernels. "I've seen this episode before."

"Me, too. My goal was something funny because I've had enough scary."

At the end of the episode, Marc turned down the volume. "Why don't you go to sleep? The dogs and I'll protect you."

I dropped my head back on the couch. "Do you think Thomas shot Sunny?"

"Your guess is as good as mine."

"If not him, what about Dylan? We know he's involved with the gambling or whatever was going on at the house tonight." My eyes grew heavy.

"Yeah, but does he own a gun? It's hard for me to picture Dylan shooting a dog or killing Peter."

"We can ask Wade." I reached for my notebook and wrote down the question. "What about your friend who wants to build a casino?" I yawned.

Marc cracked his neck. "He's got a little age on him. It's hard to picture him running from the dogs and jumping over the fence. However, I can imagine him killing Peter and shooting Sunny."

"Me too, from what you've said about him. Even though I don't know him as well as you do." I clenched my back teeth trying to hold in a yawn. "I think tomorrow morning I'll question the preacher's wife."

"About what?"

"Gambling."

"Don't you think it's dangerous? Especially for a woman who's supposed to back off?"

I shrugged. "Obeying the note didn't remove me from danger."

His brows crept up. "I wouldn't exactly say you obeyed the note."

His censure made me cringe. "You've got a point, but who is Phyllis going to tell?"

"For starters, Dylan. If Mrs. Mays is one of Dylan's regular players, he's not going to be happy you warned her away."

Poo. He was right. "I'll think about what to do. Can you question Mr. Reeves?"

Marc stared across the room in thought. "In my mind, he's the most likely candidate. I imagine Peter would've opened the door to the man." He turned his focus back to me. "I know I would have."

I gripped his warm arm with my cold fingers. "If Mr. Reeves is guilty, then it's possibly pre-mediated murder. Not a crime of passion."

"Agreed. Now go to bed, Andi Grace."

"Okay. Be careful, Marc." I stood and headed out of the room but turned at the last moment. "Thanks for coming over."

"Anytime. I want you to know you can count on me."

His words sounded sincere, and his smile warmed my heart. When I laid my head on my pillow, no visions of murderers or dead people coasted through my mind. Tomorrow would be soon enough to decide my next plan of action. I closed my eyes and slept.

Chapter Nineteen

AT A DIGNIFIED TIME of the morning, I waited for Marc at the Daily Java for breakfast. When he trotted across the parking lot, he still wore his clothes from the middle of the night but had added a ball cap. I smiled—was this self-confident man concerned about how his hair looked? "Hey. There's a line inside, but I didn't know what to order for you."

Marc looked past me and squinted, peering through the glass. "I need protein. If they have a bacon and egg bagel, get one for me. I'll save us a table on the patio since I have Chubb."

While waiting my turn to order, I listened to the morning gossip. In my opinion, the coffee shop was second only to Juliet's beauty salon in the gossip department. I overheard words like divorce, money, affair, and gambling. My ears perked up. Gambling? I stood still in line and tried to hone in on who mentioned gaming.

I'd given up by the time I reached the counter. "Hi, Sis. You doing okay?"

"Just peachy. What can I get you?" My sister frowned.

"Are you mad at me?"

She nodded.

"Why?"

"Suppose you give me your order."

"Fine, but we need to talk. Sisters stick together."

"Do you mean we don't keep secrets from each other?" Lacey Jane had her long brown hair pulled into a neat bun.

"Exactly." If anybody had a right to be miffed, it was me. In my opinion, Lacey Jane had been too friendly to Danny.

"What about your new boyfriend?"

"Boyfriend? I'm not dating anybody." At her raised eyebrows, it hit me. "You mean Marc?"

"Yeah. I had to hear it from a customer you two were dating."

I lowered my voice. "We're friends. That's all. You should know not to believe rumors."

Lacey Jane's frown lifted. "Your order?"

"One large, iced, sugar-free vanilla latte with almond milk. A healthy smoothie with green stuff and two breakfast sandwiches. Extra bacon on one."

My sister quirked an eyebrow, leaned left, and looked toward the patio. "You want to tell me again not to listen to rumors?"

"You'll laugh when you hear the story. Join us on your break." I handed her a twenty. "Keep the change."

She passed a beeper to me and turned to the next customer.

Erin Lane was standing at the table when I joined Marc and Chubb. "Hi, Erin. Looks like business is booming."

She hugged me and whispered in my ear. "Are you okay?"

"Sure. Why?" I pulled back.

"I heard you had some excitement at your house last night." Her gaze left me and landed on Marc.

Ridiculous how fast word traveled in a small town. I shivered. "I wouldn't call what happened exciting. Somebody shot Sunny. I liked to have died, but she's okay. Doc Hewitt came over and took care of her."

She studied me with a hint of a smile. "I noticed a red truck at your place this morning. Can I assume it belongs to Marc?" One neatly trimmed eyebrow quirked up.

I sat. "This is exactly how rumors begin."

Erin plopped herself beside me at the little bistro table Marc had saved for us. "What gives?"

Chubb growled.

Marc leaned forward, resting his forearms on his thighs. "I went home after the sheriff left, but I was concerned the intruder might return. I texted Andi Grace, and when I discovered she was jittery, I went over. We had four dogs to chaperone us. We watched a little TV, and I stayed on the couch when Andi Grace went to her room."

Erin pressed her lips together then turned back to me. "I'm glad you're okay."

My sister appeared with our food. "When the beeper goes off, you're supposed to pick up your order." She giggled.

I'd completely ignored the device during our discussion with Erin. "Sorry."

"No problem. It actually happens more often than you'd imagine. I'm just giving you a hard time." She set the tray on the table and took the beeper. "I have a break in fifteen minutes. Can you stay that long?"

"I'll be here." I'd wait longer in order to clear the air with Lacey

Jane, but I was grateful it wouldn't be an hour.

Erin stood. "Marc, I might like to talk to you about a wood kayak for Corey."

He pulled a business card out of his wallet. "Give me a call."

I arranged our plates and drinks on the table and handed the green tray to Erin. "Are you and Corey free for dinner tonight?"

"Corey has a board meeting at six."

"Why don't you call me when he's leaving, and we can meet for ice cream instead of dinner?"

"Sounds good. Marc, will you be there?" Her voice lilted.

He linked his fingers with mine. "I never turn down a chance to eat ice cream."

She didn't miss his action and squinted her eyes. "See y'all then."

I whispered. "I hope that's okay."

"It sounds like something a couple would do." He bit into his breakfast sandwich and before I'd eaten half of mine, he'd wolfed his down. "I've gotta go. See ya later."

I savored my breakfast. It didn't take long for my sister to arrive with two iced coffees. She loosened her bun. "I thought it might be getting hot enough for cold drinks."

I nodded. "Absolutely. The day's heating up."

Lacey Jean propped her arms on the table and lowered her voice. "What's the deal with you and Marc Williams?"

We were alone on the patio, but I still kept my voice low. "We're pretending to date in order to get information from Thomas King."

"I thought you were going to quit looking for Peter's killer. You know, because of the threat on my life and Sunny getting shot. At least that was the impression you gave me on the phone last night."

"That was my intention." I reached for my glass.

"So what changed your mind?"

"They're coming after me. What if you're next and I didn't do anything to stop them?"

Lacey Jane slumped back in her chair. "I guess I understand your logic, but . . . . What if they come after me *because* you're snooping?"

"Either way could be dangerous." I sipped my iced coffee but never took my eyes off Lacey Jane. "What's going on with you and Danny?"

She looked at the table. Not at me. "There's nothing to tell."

"I saw him hug you yesterday. Don't fall for him."

My sister's eyes widened, and she leaned forward again. "Do you still love Danny?"

"No." Angry, yes.

"Then why would you care if I dated him?"

"Honey, when life got bad, Danny broke up with me. You and I need to date men who are dependable and honorable. I don't think Danny has either of those traits."

She tipped her nose in the air. "He's grown a lot in the last twelve years. Matured."

The last thing I wanted was to push Lacey Jane into Danny's arms. "I can't stop you from dating the man, but do you really want to go out with somebody whose past includes breaking your sister's heart during the darkest period of our lives?"

"You always seem to take life in stride." She ran her finger along the edge of the table. "I had no idea how bad Danny hurt you. You never acted very upset."

"What?" I counted to ten in French. "My entire world had crumbled at my feet. How could you think I wasn't upset?"

"You sold the house and bought another one. I never saw you cry over Danny." She crossed her arms over her chest.

"Oh, baby girl. The ink was still wet on my high school diploma. I was supposed to go to college. Instead, I needed a job and enough money to take care of the three of us. I couldn't afford the house payment on our old home. Do you remember how big it was?"

She nodded.

"I didn't know what I was doing half the time. There were wills and contracts to figure out. I cried myself to sleep every single night for months. Danny wasn't there to listen to my grief over losing Mom and Dad. And I couldn't share with Mom about Danny dumping me. I was a mess on the inside, but I couldn't let you and Nate see me like that."

Long seconds ticked by. A truck in desperate need of a new muffler drove by. I continued to wait for a response from my sister.

At last Lacey Jane leaned forward. "I'm sorry. I had no idea you were suffering too."

"I was the big sister. It was my job to take care of us." I shook my head. "I prayed a lot in those days. God gives power to the weak, and I prayed for power and wisdom. God sent some amazing people into our lives, and we survived."

"You're right." My sister stood. "I need to get back to work."

"Sure. Be careful." I really wanted to warn her to guard her heart from Danny, but enough had been said for one day.

Chapter Twenty

A FEW HOURS LATER, I struggled over what to wear. I'd decided my usual shorts and T-shirt weren't dressy enough for a date, even if it was to the ice cream shop and even if Marc was only my pretend boyfriend. Erin was one of those beautiful women who raised the bar on appearance. I didn't want Marc to be embarrassed by my choice of outfits. At last, I decided to wear a denim skirt and sleeveless red, white, and blue top. Silver hoop earrings and flip-flops completed my ensemble. Not too shabby for a make-believe girlfriend.

Erin and I arrived at the ice cream shop before the men. As predicted, the woman had out-dressed me by wearing a pair of white capris, heels, and a silk blouse. Bling earrings rivaled her engagement ring and wedding band.

We claimed an outside table and waited for the guys.

Erin stretched her legs. "What a nice night."

A gentle breeze cooled my skin. "It is nice. Since Peter's death, I've felt off kilter."

"It must've been horrible for you to find his body." She placed her hands on the table. Erin's sensible-cut fingernails were the only clue she worked in a coffee shop with baked goods.

"Yeah, it was terrible. I still can't figure out who'd want to hurt Peter. Was there anything going on with the plantation board?"

"You need to ask Corey."

My pulse leapt. "Are you saying there is a problem?"

"Corey met with Peter and Asher Cummings after the last board meeting. Something about the financial report. Asher thought the figures were off and asked Peter to look over the numbers."

"I understand why Asher Cummings would take his concerns to Peter, but why your husband?"

Erin sat straighter. "My husband is the CEO of Richard Rice Plantation."

A chill raced up my back, having nothing to do with the breeze. Corey Lane was CEO. Peter was an accountant. "How does Mr.

Cummings fit in? Was he the only person who noticed a discrepancy?"

"His company made a huge donation for the cafe, and he was paranoid the board wouldn't be responsible with the money. Asher demanded every penny being accounted for."

"Isn't that a normal request for a nonprofit?"

"There's always a little fudge factor."

Before I could argue with her logic, Corey appeared. He wrapped his arms around Erin and kissed her neck. These two never shied away from showing their affection. One day I'd love to be in the same kind of relationship. The challenge would be to find a man who loved me and wasn't afraid to show it. A man devoted to our relationship and not afraid to face hard times together. A man who loved God above all else and loved me second. Was it too much to ask?

Probably.

"Sorry I'm late. Did I miss ice cream?" Marc appeared. Angels didn't sing, and fireworks didn't explode. I'd be a liar, though, if I said there wasn't some chemistry between us. His gaze connected with mine and sparks flared.

If this red, hot, and tingly sensation was the definition of flushed, then I was flushed, thanks to the look Marc had given me. "Let's order." To my further embarrassment, my voice croaked.

Marc's dimple caused my stomach to flip-flop.

Erin and Corey walked to the counter, and I followed with Marc by my side. "Did you have a good day?"

"I spent most of the day repairing a Boston Whaler. How about you?"

"Phyllis Mays will meet me tomorrow. Because today is Wednesday, she had to help get food ready for a church supper. We're going to get our nails done after my morning dog rounds."

Marc rubbed his wrist. "Manicures?"

"Yep." We scooted up in line.

"Did you hurt yourself?" I pointed to his wrist.

"I tripped over Chubb in the shed earlier. Forgot he was there."

I felt Marc's wrist. "Did you get it looked at and is Chubb okay?"

"The dog is fine, and I took some ibuprofen before coming over here."

"You need something on your stomach if you took ibuprofen. What are you going to order?"

"The strawberry-kiwi smoothie sounds good. Have you tried it?"

I nodded. "It's good but probably not healthy enough for you."

His mouth dropped open, but a twinkle graced his eyes. "You're going to give me a hard time for making smart choices?"

"I have no room to judge, but I've noticed you make good choices when you eat and order drinks. Even your kitchen is stocked with healthy options."

Marc waved me forward.

I spoke to the young man behind the counter. "I'd like two dips of Rocky Road in a waffle cone."

Marc quizzed the kid on smoothie options.

In the mirror on the back wall of the ice cream shop, I watched Erin and Corey. Sitting at a table for four, they leaned close to each other. I expected to see them kiss. Instead, they talked. Both frowned. Corey darted his eyes from his wife to us. Erin seemed to have taken charge of the conversation, and Corey nodded a lot.

Before I knew it, Marc elbowed me. "Here you go."

"Thanks." I took the waffle cone stuffed to overflowing with ice cream. I reached for a long spoon and napkins before returning my attention to the mirror.

He slipped his arm around my waist and leaned closer. "Should we act like a devoted couple?"

"Uh, I don't want to get chocolate on your shirt. I'm sometimes messy." I slipped away.

Marc finished the transaction. "What's up with you?" He held his bright pink smoothie in one hand and touched my shoulder with the other.

"Sorry. I was watching Erin and Corey in the mirror. They're not happy about something."

We walked across the shop.

At the table, the Lanes both smiled at us like their previous conversation had never happened.

Marc held my chair out then sat to my right.

"Thanks." I licked the chocolate ice cream and got a chunk of marshmallow. How had I let Marc pay? Too busy watching the Lanes. "Hey, thanks for this. Next time will be my treat." Is that something a real girlfriend would say? Was the man *always* expected to pay? It didn't seem fair, especially if I had a job.

"You're welcome." Marc didn't seem fazed.

Erin said, "How long have you two been dating?"

Like a coward, I took another bite, leaving Marc to answer.

He stirred his smoothie with the large straw. "Not long. I pretty much fell for Andi Grace the first day we met. What about you two? Have you been married long?"

Erin's eyes sparkled. "Five years. Corey swept me off my feet, and when I left college to take over the coffee shop, he followed me to Heyward Beach. We ran off to Charleston and got married."

I wiped my sticky fingers on a white paper napkin. "I never understood why you eloped. Did your parents not approve?"

"You know how my mother is. It would have taken at least a year to have the kind of wedding she wanted for me. Meanwhile, my dad wanted me to go back to Clemson and finish my degree. Corey and I decided we didn't want to wait, so we eloped."

Corey slid his arm around Erin's shoulders. "When it's right, you just know."

I didn't want to waste time considering his words. We were here for answers. "Corey, I guess you've heard I found Peter's body."

"Yeah. It must've been terrible."

"It was. It really got me to wondering who killed Peter, and I can't figure it out. Did you know him well?"

Corey shrugged. "We were both on the board of directors of Richard Rice Plantation, but I wouldn't say we were friends."

"Who do you think killed Peter? Could it have been one of the board members?"

His eyes widened and he stared at me like I was crazy. "I have no idea."

I pressed on. "I heard there was some conflict among the board members. Financial issues. What about Asher Cummings?"

Corey pushed his banana split to the center of the table and propped his long arms on the table. Erin's husband was tall and thin, with scruffy hair, but smart as all get out. "It's really none of your business, Andi Grace. Asher, Peter, and I discussed some money issues, but they aren't public record."

He wasn't going to deter me. "I know Asher was at Peter's house the week he died. Do you think he's capable of murder?"

"Not a chance. Asher is as honest as they come."

Erin placed a slim hand on her husband's arm. "Corey's right. Nobody ever says a bad word about Asher. The man is full of integrity, but he can make it hard to move forward with the expansion projects at the plantation."

Marc wiped his mouth with a napkin in the brightly lit ice cream shop. "What do you mean?"

Erin answered, "He never moves forward on a project until every penny has been raised. He always says something like you're not being honest with people's donations if you can't complete whatever you're raising money for."

Corey frowned for a fleeting second then reached for his banana split. "I'm pretty sure the sheriff won't waste his time questioning Asher."

Maybe the sheriff wouldn't question him, but I had a few things I'd like to discuss. Like was Corey trustworthy? How had he become CEO of the plantation at such a young age? What was his story before meeting my friend Erin? I took a deep breath. "When it comes to murder, I think everybody possible should be questioned until they catch the killer."

Marc reached for my hand and squeezed it. "Did Andi Grace tell you we were the first two people the sheriff questioned?"

Erin laughed. "Marc, I don't really know you, but there's no way Andi Grace is guilty. Trust me. I'm a good judge of character."

I smiled at my friend. Her words touched my heart until I considered her husband was on my suspect list. How well did she judge anybody?

Thirty minutes later, Marc and I sat in the front seat of my Suburban. We both had elbows propped on the console and positioned our faces close to each other. If the Lanes looked our way, they'd think we were talking mushy words of love. Instead, I asked, "What do you think about Corey?"

Marc shrugged. "He was quick to defend Asher Cummings. If Corey was guilty, wouldn't he have tried to make Asher look guilty?"

"I don't know Asher except by reputation. He seems to be an honest man everybody respects. I've never even heard his name uttered in the beauty shop."

"Why would he be a topic of conversation in a woman's salon?"

"Gossip, baby. Gossip." I chuckled. "Not that I add to the gossip, but I always listen."

He gave me that same teasing expression I was coming to understand. "Isn't listening just as bad?"

This time I shrugged. Was it? Maybe. "Juliet is one of the most devout people I know. She challenges me to be a better person. I'll think about your question, though."

"I'm just messing with you. As long as you don't repeat what you hear, I'm sure it's fine."

My thoughts churned. Did I allow gossip to affect how I saw people? Living in a small beach town, the locals knew each other. Tourists flooded the area throughout the summer, but the rest of the year we were a small community. "I'm going to work harder to not listen to gossip. At least after we solve Peter's murder. I figure the beauty shop will be the first place to hear about Peter's will."

Marc ran a hand over his face. "I hope I'm never a topic of gossip at the beauty shop."

"You're too good-looking not to be discussed, and you're not married. Once people get to know you better, you'll be a hot subject." What else could you say about a handsome man who made your heart accelerate every time you saw him? Hunk was too old-fashioned and made me think of cheese. Gorgeous worked for both men and women. Cute didn't seem like a mature enough description for the man, and attractive wasn't adequate. I'd keep thinking, but for now hot worked.

"Another good reason to stay in my boat shed working alone. Just me and my mutt."

I reined my attention back to Marc. "If you're not careful, you might become a hermit."

"There are worse things."

"I'd die if I couldn't interact with people and dogs. Being a hermit would also make it hard to solve this murder, which brings me back to Asher and Corey. Thoughts?"

"Just between you and me? Not beauty shop gossip?"

"Absolutely. Our conversation is private."

He met my gaze in the dim interior of my Suburban. "Something doesn't feel right about Corey Lane. He's cocky, arrogant, and brash. But he appears to be devoted to his wife, which is a good thing."

That didn't answer my question, exactly. "Don't you think he's awful young to be CEO?"

"It's not impossible to believe. Maybe he has a background in non-profits."

"I don't see how. He graduated and moved here. At first, he seemed to hang out at the coffee shop helping Erin. Before long, he was CEO. Can you use some of your lawyerly investigative techniques and dig into his background?"

Marc looked at his watch. "I've got a lot of work tomorrow."

"How about starting tonight? My house has wi-fi." I didn't want to be a clingy girlfriend. Probably a clingy pretend girlfriend was even worse. "We need answers in order to move forward.

"Andi Grace, nobody can ever accuse you of backing down from a challenge. I guess my being at your place will play into our dating image."

"Right." My spirits lifted. I could tell he was about to agree.

"Okay. You've talked me into it." He opened the passenger door. "I'll follow you."

In less than fifteen minutes, I pulled into my driveway, and Marc parked his red truck behind me. Let the neighbors talk. It wouldn't be the first time I was the focus of local gossip, and it probably wouldn't be the last time. Not much could be done to stop people from spreading rumors.

A guy in dark sweats and a hoody ran on the sidewalk. I did a double take. The June night was way too hot to wear so much clothing. The runner must be cooking in those clothes. If it was a new fad, I wouldn't participate.

I headed to the front porch and reached to unlock the door.

Marc's hand shot out across me. "Wait. Did you leave the door open?"

Fear spiraled up my spine at the sight. My door stood ajar. I'd been warned and ignored the message. Was the killer inside waiting for his next victim?

Chapter Twenty-One

INSTEAD OF DIALING 911, I called Wade on his personal number I'd saved to my contact list.

"Stone here."

I tapped the circle to convert to speaker phone so Marc could hear. "Wade, it's Andi Grace. We're on speaker phone, and Marc's with me. I just got home, and my front door's open. Like not just unlocked, but open. What should I do?" I tightened my grip on the phone so I wouldn't drop it with my trembling hand.

"I'll be there in five minutes. Get away from the house."

"No problem." I might be getting a reputation for impulsiveness, but I wasn't completely off my rocker.

Marc reached for my hand and led me to his truck. He handed me the keys. "Sit here with the engine running. If the situation goes sideways, leave."

I gasped. "Where are you going?"

"I'm going to check around back. How many dogs are in the house?"

"Three." At some point, I needed to rethink allowing pets to stay at my house. As much as I loved the dogs, they were an extra complication this week. I was responsible for their safety and would hate for one of them to get scared or hurt.

"Don't you think it's odd they aren't barking?"

"Yeah. I have a gate on the right side of the house. Just reach over and lift the latch." I squeezed the plain keyring in my hand. "Do you think the dogs are okay?"

"We'll know as soon as Sheriff Stone arrives. Sit tight." Marc squeezed my hand.

I wasn't used to playing damsel in distress, but the thought of the dogs being hurt left me weak.

Marc disappeared into the darkness around the side of the house like I'd directed. At the rate things were happening, it seemed like a good time to invest in outside lighting. Serious lights, not the froufrou ambience things.

I propped my arms on the steering wheel and strained to see into the night. No sign of movement.

Wait a cotton-picking minute. The runner dressed in sweats. Seriously. Who wore sweats in this heat? Unless you had a death wish, you wore jogging shorts and a sleeveless shirt. A lot of guys didn't wear any kind of shirt. Which brought me back to the mysterious runner. I'd bet money at one of the poker tables that he was the one who broke into my house.

I had nothing of real value. No cash and only sentimental trinkets. Sunny and the other dogs were the most valuable things inside my home. The runner had been alone.

Flashing blue lights and a siren signaled Wade's approach.

I jumped out of Marc's truck and waited until the official vehicle stopped. "Hey, did you see a runner?"

Wade lowered the window. "Yeah, a few blocks away."

"I think he's the one who broke into my house." I waited while he relayed the information to a deputy. "Marc's looking around the backyard."

"I told you to stay back."

"I sat in the truck like a good little girl, but we didn't hear the dogs and grew concerned, so Marc went back there."

Wade stepped from his vehicle and switched on his flashlight. "Stay with me."

"Really?"

"Yep. I don't trust you to stay out of trouble."

I stayed quiet and followed him to the side of the house.

Marc ran to us. "The back door is unlocked, and all three dog crates are empty."

"Not the dogs! I've got to find them." I turned and ran toward front door.

Marc raced past and rounded on me, blocking my path to the house. "You've can't go inside until Wade says it's safe."

I glared at Marc and counted to ten in French. My logical side said to back away gracefully while my heart longed to search for the dogs. I sighed. "I need to do something."

"Let's call friends to look for the dogs."

Wade joined us. "Sounds like a good idea. Let me and my deputies clear the house. You stick with Marc."

Marc and I headed to his truck while Wade and two deputies searched my house. "Will you call Nate? I'll contact Lacey Jane. Tell

Nate to get Juliet and drive to Heinz's home. I'll text them the location."

"I don't have his phone number."

I shared the contact information then we made our calls. I also posted pictures of Sunny and the Westies on social media. Lacey Jane had been on a date. She and the guy headed to Chloe's home. My hope was Chloe and Heinz had been set free and would return to their homes, but that theory didn't explain why Sunny hadn't come back here. Although she could be a mother hen, especially if she sensed the other two dogs were in danger. She'd been injured though by the guy with the gun. Who knew what her condition was?

After contacting my siblings, I called Dr. Hewitt and asked if the Westies had tracking devices. He promised to go office and call me right back with the answer. I disconnected.

Marc tapped his cell phone on his thigh. "I called Eli Reece. He's getting some guys together to search."

"How do y'all know each other?" Eli ran a water sports business on the beach.

"Despite what you think, I'm not a complete hermit."

Slammed. Again. "Sorry. I appreciate the guys pitching in to help."

The front door opened, and light poured onto the porch and sidewalk. Deputy Hanks, Deputy Sawyer, and Wade exited my house.

I reached for the handle. "Let's go."

Marc scrambled out and stopped me at the front of his truck. "Slow down. Wade'll update us when he's ready."

It killed me to watch the three men converse while my sweet Sunny was missing. She'd already been hurt once since Peter's death and subsequent investigation. "When we find Sunny, I may not let her out of my sight again."

The deputies strode to their vehicles, and Wade approached us. "We got fingerprints off the crate latches. Going to run them through the system."

I gasped. "My fingerprints will be on them."

"Of course we'll take that into account. Nobody caught the runner. You've got two gates on your fence. Both were open. I assume the side gate was due to Marc, but the back one is a different story. I think the intruder must have let the dogs out through there. We also found Styrofoam packages with plastic wrappers wadded up. The labels indicated sirloins. Plus there was a screwdriver. Any chance you cooked steaks recently?"

"No. How'd this creep get into my house?"

"Lock bumping."

My mouth dropped open. "Say what?"

"Thieves use a special key, insert it into a tumbler lock, bump the key with a hammer or screwdriver, and they open the door. You've got an older house. It might be past time you increased your security."

"I've always felt save here." I shivered and wrapped my arms around myself. "Wade, do you think he lured the dogs outside with food?"

Wade nodded. "It wouldn't be the first time. Might seem cartoonish, but the method is effective."

My phone buzzed. "It's Dr. Hewitt. Hold on a second." I slid my finger over the screen and spoke into the phone.

"Andi Grace, both dogs have GPS dog trackers on their collars. It looks like the dogs are on the beach near the pier."

"Thanks so much, Doc."

"Have you found Sunny?"

"No, sir." My throat grew tight, and I hoped she was with the other dogs.

He sighed. "I should've given you a tracker, even though you couldn't afford it. We'll remedy that soon. Why don't I meet you at the beach?"

"Thanks. See you there." I shared the news with Marc and Wade.

Marc pulled his keys from his pocket. "I'll drive you."

Wade ran his hand along his jaw. "I'm going to hang out here for a bit. Either until you get home or until I get another call. Let me know what you find."

I nodded and hopped in Marc's truck.

He backed out of my drive and drove down the street. "Don't guess there's a shortcut?"

"There's always a shortcut. Turn right here." I gave him directions and soon he pulled into the parking lot by the pier.

Four teenaged boys were popping wheelies on their bikes. Marc swerved in their direction. "Hey, any of you guys see three dogs?"

The tall one puffed out his chest. "Yeah. The big one snapped at us."

My blood boiled. "She wouldn't snap at you for no reason. Did you pick on the little dogs?"

Marc held up his hand to stifle my words. "Which way did they go?"

The smallest kid pointed behind us without uttering a word.

"Thanks." I felt sorry for the little guy. Why were the kids out after dark?

We parked, and I shifted my concern for the kids to the back burner of my brain. We ran from the sandy parking lot, and hit the beach. I heard a dog bark and cupped my hands over my mouth. "Sunny. Chloe. Heinz." It wasn't a full moon, but there was a bit of light in the sky.

Marc turned on his phone's flashlight. "I think the sound came from over there."

I admired Marc's clear thinking and turned on my own flashlight app. Together, we trudged through the thick sand until we hit the packed-down area and picked up speed. "Sunny!"

Another bark sounded from the pier. An old black pickup truck drove onto the beach. I did a double take and spied Doc Hewitt behind the wheel. He headed toward the ice cream and bike shop.

A pain in my side testified I wasn't in as good of shape as I thought. I pushed through the ache in my side and my tender ankle. I almost matched Marc's pace.

Doc Hewitt braked and leapt out of his truck with more agility than most men his age. "I see them."

All three dogs barked, and I poured on more speed. I was too close to lose the animals again.

Chapter Twenty-Two

I REACHED SUNNY, who stood at the base of a sand dune watching the Westies. The men ran after the little dogs and caught them. Doc Hewitt pulled treats out of his pocket and passed one to each dog.

"Oh, Sunny. My poor baby." I collapsed on the sand and held my German shepherd. "First some horrible man shot you, and tonight he kidnapped you. Dognapped. I'm so sorry." I burst into tears and buried my face in Sunny's neck. I had no power to hold back the emotion ripping through my soul. She'd been a faithful companion for years, and now I'd failed her. Not once. Twice. "Whoever did this to y'all is gonna pay."

Doc Hewitt cleared his throat. "I'll take these two little ones back to the clinic and check them out. Meet me there when you're able. I'll look over Sunny when you get there." The slight warble in his voice proved he wasn't completely unaffected by the plight of the dogs.

I hugged Sunny tighter and tried to catch my breath.

"Here." Marc held out a paper napkin. "Best I can do on short notice."

I took the offering and wiped my eyes before blowing my nose. Not my prettiest moment, but it couldn't be helped. The mere thought of losing Sunny wrenched my soul.

Marc squatted and rested on the balls of his feet. He ran his hand over Sunny's back. "Even though Sunny made it this far and seems fine, Doc Hewitt should examine her."

"I agree." I shifted to my knees and pushed up. "Sunny, let's go."

She turned in the sand and followed me with slow, deliberate steps.

I thanked God for no more apparent injuries.

Marc took my hand in his, and the three of us walked to his Silverado.

"You make a good pretend boyfriend."

"Hmm." He opened the passenger door. One side of his mouth crept up. Not quite a smile but almost.

Sunny tried to jump in and whined.

Marc knelt and lifted her. "Do you want her in your lap or the back seat?"

"How about I ride in the back with her? She'll be more comfortable with the extra space." I slid into his Silverado, and he placed Sunny beside me. I ran my hand along the previous injury around her shoulder. The bandage was damp, but it didn't look like bloodstains in the dim light. I buckled up.

Marc drove steady to the vet clinic, and I appreciated his caution.

I ran my hand along Sunny's side. Her breathing had returned to normal. I'd never know the full extent of what she'd been through but she appeared to be okay. "Should we call Wade?"

"I already did. He had to deal with an emergency situation. We're to inform him when we head back to your place. He doesn't want any more excitement there tonight. Have you alerted your brother and sister?"

My energy waned, and I dreaded calling them. "I'll text them we found all three dogs."

The clinic was off Highway 17, and Marc turned into the parking lot.

I needed to see about the Westies. Sunny raised her head and looked at me with sad eyes. "We're going to get you checked out too, girl."

Marc helped her out and raised a hand for me.

I grasped his hand and held on until my feet stood firm on the ground. Without saying a word, we walked into the clinic at the Sunny's pace. Doc had left the door unlocked for us, and I secured the lock and deadbolted it once we were inside.

A few cars whizzed past on the highway. I glanced out the window. "I don't think anybody followed us."

"I know we weren't followed."

His words reassured me. Marc was a great help in a crisis. Calm and dependable. Hard to believe for the last twelve years I'd been the steady person. Never cried in front of other people, even after the funeral for our parents. Not to say I never cried, but I always held back tears until I reached the privacy of my bedroom. Sunny was the only witness to my occasional bouts of weeping. I'd even steeled myself not to cry at coffee commercials. So what happened tonight? Was Sunny my kryptonite?

"Wade knows we're here. I bet he sends a deputy by before long."

Marc touched my shoulder, and I turned from the window. "Forget about the killer and focus on the dogs."

"You're right." I strode down the hall toward the exam room with a door open and lights on. "Doc Hewitt, we're here."

"I heard you come in. Do you have paperwork to approve giving the dogs medication?"

"Yes, but I can call the owners if you'd feel better."

"No need. I think a dose of the same medication they take during storms will take the edge off and help calm them." He wrote notes on paper instead of the computer most of his techs used. It'd be up to his employees to decipher and document. "Why don't you dose these two while I take Sunny across the hall to examine her?"

"We ran into some boys near the beach. I'm pretty sure they antagonized the dogs, but I don't know if they physically hurt them. Sunny would do all she could to protect the little ones."

Doc Hewitt nodded. "Yep. It's in her DNA. I'll give her a thorough exam in just a minute."

"Sorry. I know you will. I guess I'm a little on edge."

Doc winked at me. "There's no drug I can give you to calm your nerves, but interacting with the animals usually helps."

I smiled but my face felt numb.

Marc had been standing in the doorway and moved aside. He slipped his arm behind me. The closeness gave me strength.

Sunny followed Doc Hewitt to the room across the hall. She'd been here many times as a puppy when I worked here. They'd formed a special bond, and Sunny never feared a trip here.

Marc said, "I'll go lift Sunny onto the exam table and be right back."

"Good idea." I should've considered offering, but my thoughts were muddled.

Heinz barked, and I turned my attention to the Westies. "You're safe now." I knelt and loved on both dogs.

Marc returned and drew close. "Can I do anything to help?"

"This is a good time for you to learn how to give dogs medicine." I opened a cabinet, retrieved a bag of miniature marshmallows and two tablets, each in an individual blister pack. "Some people hold a dog's mouth open and shove medication down their pet's throat, but I discovered stuffing the tablet in a marshmallow is just as effective and more pleasant. I've also tried sticking a pill in peanut butter on a cracker, but most dogs lick their tongue on the floor afterward."

"Sounds messy." He picked up Chloe and approached me.

"I may not be the most organized person, but I don't like peanut butter smeared on my wood floor." I held out one marshmallow with an anxiety pill in it for the Westie.

"She's shaking in my arms."

"I'm sure tonight was a terrible ordeal for the dogs." I rubbed her head.

"It was terrible for all of us." He lowered Chloe to the floor and picked up Heinz.

My heart softened like butter in a straight-from-the-oven biscuit. I decided to tease Marc instead of focusing on his kindness. "You make a great pretend boyfriend."

A flush crept up his neck. "Uh, thanks. I guess."

I wrapped the tablet into the sticky marshmallow and popped it into Heinz's mouth. "It's not easy to give you a compliment."

"Probably because I'm not used to getting compliments."

Poor Marc. What a sad life he must have lived after his parents died. I wouldn't cry in front of this man twice in one night, though. Not going to happen. I longed to hug him. Instead, I picked up Chloe. "Let's check on Doc and Sunny."

I headed for the exam room and decided Marc Williams would learn to take a compliment. I'd shower him with words of affirmation because, as far as I could tell, he was a good and decent man.

An hour later, we made it home. The sheriff's truck sat in front of my house. "Looks like Wade is here."

"Sure does." Marc pulled into my drive slow and cautious. "He's sitting on your front steps."

Wade sat on the porch and his feet rested on the bottom of three steps. The railing needed a fresh coat of white paint, but maybe it was too dark for Wade to notice.

Sunny repositioned herself when Marc pulled to a stop.

I waited for Marc to walk around and help get Sunny down. Once on the ground, she circled the front yard and stopped near a magnolia tree.

Marc opened the back door for the Westies, who'd snoozed on the short drive home.

Wade joined us. "Everybody all right?"

Marc passed Chloe to me and Heinz jumped out before we could help him.

I nodded. "The dogs seem fine, considering whatever happened to them. Doc Hewitt gave all three hydroxyzine to take the edge off. Did anybody show up here?"

Wade shook his head. "Not while I was on watch. Had a car accident reported at Murrells Inlet on Highway 17, and I went up until Highway Patrol could arrive. One driver was drunk, and we hauled him to jail. Because I was gone for a while, I'd like to go through the house again with you. Make sure it's safe."

Relief rushed through me. "Absolutely."

Marc said, "I'll take the Westies to the backyard so they can do their business before bedding down."

"Sounds good. Thanks, Marc." Sunny and I followed Wade into my house, while Marc and the Westies headed to the backyard.

Wade turned on the foyer light. "You need to get a lock for the gate. Do you have floodlights in back?"

"They burned out."

"Time to replace them." He entered the living space and turned lights on as he moved from one room to the next.

"Have you eaten?" The man had been running all over the place tonight.

Sunny trudged past me and entered her large crate. Most of the time she'd arrange her blankets. Tonight, she hunkered down and closed her eyes.

"Not yet."

It was after midnight. He must be starved. "When does your shift end?"

"We're shorthanded, and I'm pulling a double." He opened the pantry door.

I reached around him, grabbed a bag of potato chips, Oreos, and a loaf of wheat bread. "How about a ham sandwich?"

"I wish I had time. Do the locks work on your windows?"

"As far as I know." I laid food items on the kitchen counter. I might not be much of a cook, but I sure knew how to make school lunches. I'd make something for Wade to take with him.

He sighed. "I'll check as I go through the rest of the rooms."

Marc tapped on the back door.

I opened it for him, and the Westies looked as worn out as Sunny. They entered the same crate. "Most nights I wouldn't let you two stay together, but we'll make an exception tonight."

Marc washed his hands and dried them on a paper towel. "Looks like Sunny's already out. Where's Wade?"

"He's checking the other rooms. I'm fixing him a ham sandwich. Do you want one?"

"Sure. It seems like my smoothie was days ago. How can I help?"

I opened the refrigerator and pulled out ham, lettuce, mustard, and mayo. "You've done more than a lot of friends would've tonight. Why don't you sit and relax?"

"Not more than a boyfriend would." He winked at me and my legs turned to gelatin. But instead of relaxing, Marc pulled glasses from the cabinet and filled them with ice.

Wade reentered the room. "The lock on your office window is loose. You can find what you need at the hardware store to replace it and get something for your gate. Shouldn't be too expensive. Ask for Walter. He'll be glad to help. It's how he's stayed in business so long."

Walter had owned the store as long as I could remember. "Okay. Do you want mayo or mustard? You can take it with you."

"Mayo. Thanks."

I slathered Hellman's onto the bread then wrapped the sandwich in tin foil. "There you go. How about a Coke?"

"Sounds good." He reached for the Oreos and helped himself to a few.

I pulled a soft drink out of the fridge for him. "You stay safe out there."

He gave me a cocky grin. "Yes, ma'am."

Marc said, "I'll see you out."

I returned the food, except for the condiments. One shiny red apple sat on the top shelf. Marc would be shocked to see me choose a healthy option. I snagged the piece of fruit and poured water into the glasses.

Marc clumped into the kitchen. Dark circles lined his eyes.

I stood at the counter. "Do you want mustard?"

"Sure." He kept his voice low. "Do you have tools?"

"My daddy's toolbox is in the garage. Why?"

"I hope you take Wade seriously. Fix the windows and put a lock on the gate. Can you do it?"

"Sure. I'll look online for a video teaching how to change the window locks."

Marc yawned.

"Hey, why don't you take your sandwich and eat it on the way home. I don't need a babysitter, and it's late."

"I'd be glad to sleep on your couch again."

"No. I appreciate all you've done for me, but Chubb's probably missing you. Besides, you'll sleep better at your house."

As soon as I'd made the sandwich, Marc departed, and I headed for bed with my apple. This night hadn't gone anything like I'd expected. The three dogs sleeping in my kitchen would get an extra dose of love tomorrow. I'd take care of my dog walking duties, and before the day ended, I'd find out more about Corey. Starting with was he a runner and what would he have to gain by killing Peter?

Chapter Twenty-Three

I ENTERED THE coffee shop after walking my last dog of the morning. Did I have other things I could do related to my business? Absolutely. AG's Dog Walking and More demanded more of my time than just caring for pets. Advertising, social media, buying supplies, bills to be paid, and bills to submit for payment. Tons of details big and small needed my attention.

However, the previous night's scare had left me shaky, and I wanted to see my sister. We'd spoken on the phone before falling asleep the night before, but I needed to see her with my own eyes.

As I reached for the shop's door handle, a florist's deliveryman walked out. "Morning, Andi Grace."

"Hi, Mr. Leasor. It's a beautiful day."

"Sure is. Have a good one." The man limped toward the bright purple van with everything from roses to daisies painted on the side. The words Heyward Flower Shop were emblazoned on the driver's door and again underneath the picture. Maybe I should advertise on my Suburban. It couldn't hurt. Except the killer would always know where I was.

I entered the coffee shop and meandered over to the counter where Lacey Jane and Erin admired an enormous vase of red roses. "Whoa, is it your anniversary?"

Erin blushed. "No. Corey sent them with a note saying he loves me."

"They're beautiful." Was it normal for a man to send his wife over a dozen red roses on a Thursday for no reason?

Thursday. It'd been a week since I'd found Peter's body. Hard to believe he was gone and hard to believe how fast the week had flown by.

Erin picked up the vase. "I'll be in my office. Lacey Jane, it's time for you to take a break."

My sister's eyes brightened. "Yay."

Soon Lacey Jane and I occupied a corner table with two cups of coffee and blueberry muffins. I scooted closer to my sister. "What's the story on the flowers?"

"Not any old flowers. Roses."

"Hard to miss." I laughed. "You know I'm a daisy kind of girl."

"Me too, sister." She poured Stevia into her coffee and stirred. "After Erin and Corey met y'all for ice cream, they went home. Corey decided he needed milk and left. He was gone for well over an hour, and Erin convinced herself he was either dead or having an affair. She was fit to be tied by the time he got home."

My heart raced. Corey didn't have an alibi for a while the night before. "What did he say?"

"He decided to go for a run and forgot all about the milk."

My heart accelerated. "Who goes out for milk and ends up running instead?"

"It's weird, isn't it?"

"Definitely." I poured creamer into my coffee and added raw sugar.

My sister waited while I stirred my coffee then sprang her question. "What's going on, Andi Grace?"

I explained about the runner, the missing dogs, and my house being broken into. "The man I saw running wore dark sweats and a hoodie. I thought he was crazy because it was so hot."

"Do you think it was Corey?"

"I don't know." I hesitated to confide my strategy. Marc and I planned to meet at my house to research Corey. "Do you know much about him?"

"He acts like he's crazy about Erin. I'm more inclined to believe he'd steal your dogs than cheat on his wife."

"What about kill Peter?"

Lacey Jane gasped. "What? You can't seriously think he's a murderer."

"Somebody is, and it's probably somebody we know." I sipped my coffee. Despite the heat of the day, I appreciated the warmth seeping through my chilled body.

Movement in my peripheral vision drew my attention.

Danny stalked toward us, and he didn't look happy. "I guess you're pleased with yourself."

I drew back in my seat. "I don't know what you're talking about."

My ex-boyfriend snarled at me. "You mean you haven't heard from the attorney? My uncle left you in his will."

"How nice of him." I didn't care how small of a token Peter had left for me. For some crazy reason, it felt good to know he cared enough to remember me. One of his favorite paperweights would be wonderful.

"Nice? Nice?" Danny's face reddened. "I don't know what kind of funny business you pulled, but my family will fight you."

My face grew hot. Could Peter have left me his fancy new laptop? He knew I needed to upgrade my computer system. "I can't believe you'd be so petty to take away whatever token Peter left me. I was his friend. Day in and day out. You may be a blood relative, but you were in Georgia for school and work. Peter and I formed a bond, and I'll be honored with whatever he left me."

"Yeah? I'd be honored too if he left me the bulk of his estate. You better prepare for the battle of your life." With those words, Danny threw an envelope my way then turned and stormed out of the coffee shop.

Lacey Jane squeezed my hand. Her face paled. "I've never seen Danny so mad."

"Me, either. Please, don't get tangled up with him." His verbal attack left me shaking.

"Do you think it's true? He left you his home and stuff?"

"How can it be? Peter and I were friends. Not family."

"May I?" Lacey Jane pointed to the envelope.

My hands shook so bad I probably couldn't open it. "Go ahead. It'll be good practice for you to read a law document."

I held my mug with trembling hands and sipped the delicious brew while my little sister read the papers.

At last she met my eyes. "When Danny said the bulk of Peter's estate, he wasn't kidding. Plantation, vehicles, and furniture. You're also listed in his insurance policy. Baseball memorabilia goes to Danny. It's appraised at a few thousand dollars. His sister gets the family Bible, other books, and pictures."

This had to be a cruel joke. I set the mug down with a plunk. "I never expected to be in Peter's will. You know what I thought when Danny said I was getting something? I thought he might give me his laptop because it's newer than mine, and there's a paperweight I always admired. Never in a million years did I expect anything like this."

"What are you going to do?"

My brain had gone into overload. "I don't know. I—I can't fathom this. And Danny's going to fight me so there may not be anything to worry over."

The coffee shop door swung open, and in walked Wade. Make that Sheriff Stone because he looked like he was in official law enforcement mode. His brow was furrowed, and he beelined it to our table.

I should've expected it. All along I'd figured whoever inherited Peter's estate was a suspect. It appeared Sheriff Stone had the same idea. "Lacey Jane, if I'm arrested, take the will to Marc. He's my lawyer. He'll know what to do."

"Andi Grace, I'll find Marc. We're not going to let you get arrested." Her hand clutched my arm.

"His number's in my phone." I slid it across the table.

Wade glared at me.

I didn't like the height disadvantage. I wanted to stand but didn't want to appear nervous. "Hi, Wade. I guess you heard."

"We need to talk. At the station."

"Are you arresting me?" It became hard to breathe.

"I don't think you want to have this discussion here."

I glanced around the place. Everybody had quieted, and all eyes studied us. I stood.

Lacey Jane hopped up and hugged me. "Don't answer any questions without representation. I'll find Marc." She took the envelope and my phone and disappeared.

Wade stepped back and made a motion for me to leave. He followed so close if I'd stopped, he would've plowed into me. Emotionally, I already felt like he'd mowed me down.

Time slowed to a crawl before Marc joined us in the interrogation room. A glance at my watch showed it'd been less than an hour. No way I'd survive prison if arrested and convicted. I'd about lost my mind in the short time since Wade had picked me up.

I hadn't cried, though. So I'd give myself props for holding myself together.

Marc entered the room wearing khaki shorts and a T-shirt proclaiming *Rule Number One: Do not fall off this boat.* He for sure looked more like a boat builder than a lawyer.

Panic set in. I should've hired the wiliest attorney in South Carolina to get me off murder charges. Not a man who'd walked away from practicing law.

Then Marc's gaze met mine. He gave me an encouraging nod before turning his attention to Wade. That one action filled me with hope. His faith in me was more valuable than some high-powered attorney from Charleston.

Lord, thank you for bringing Marc into my life. Please help the truth come to light and get me home.

Then my mind flashed to details. Three dogs waited for me at my house. The urge to text Lacey Jane hit, but I sat in this room with no cell phone and no purse. Only God and Marc were here with me. God knew the truth, and Marc believed in my innocence. I'd be okay.

I had to be.

Chapter Twenty-Four

HOURS LATER I popped two ibuprofen tablets into my mouth and swallowed them down with Coke. The immense relief I'd felt when Wade told Marc I could go might've set a world record. My hopes had soared until Wade revealed I wasn't off his suspect list. There wasn't enough physical evidence to hold me. Yet.

Marc drove to a convenience store and bought icy cold soft drinks and junk food. I drank the Coke and ripped open a bag of M&Ms while Marc drove us to the nearest beach. We sat in rusty beach chairs and watched children build sandcastles. Teens practiced surfing and rode boogie boards. Parents chased their little ones, and bright colored umbrellas lined up in rows parallel to the ocean. The sights and sounds almost made me feel like it was a normal day. Almost.

Clouds floated over us from the west. I closed my eyes and drifted off in the warmth of the day. When I opened them Marc smiled.

I felt my face for drool. None. "I can't believe I fell asleep."

"It's probably a result of the stress. I hate to ruin the moment, but we need to discuss what's going on. Do you understand the probate process?"

"When my parents died, nobody fought me over the will."

He nodded. "If Danny's family doesn't fight you, it may still take months before you can move into Peter's place. Possibly a year."

The timeline didn't bother me because I wasn't even sure I wanted his plantation. If he hadn't left the bulk of his estate to me, Wade wouldn't have taken me in for questioning. The interrogation this morning had focused on my relationship with Peter and financial issues.

As the afternoon drifted by, Marc continued to remind me there was no concrete evidence linking me to the murder. The beach crowd thinned, and we walked to the pier for ice cream. I ordered my usual rocky road in a waffle cone. Marc ordered pralines and cream. His choice of ice cream and the Coke he drank earlier wasn't his norm. He was concerned, too.

The sky was dark when I got home. Lacey Jane had taken care of the dogs—as in all the dogs on my schedule for the afternoon. The lamps beside the couch made the living room cozy and inviting.

A soft snore came from the recliner in the corner.

"Lacey Jane, what are you doing here?"

She woke up and yawned. "I wanted to hear everything. Marc texted me you were headed home, but I must've fallen asleep."

I dropped onto the couch. "Thanks for helping me today with the animals. Did Erin give you any grief over leaving work?"

"No. She's knows I'm a good employee. Most mornings I beat her to work. By the time she arrives, the coffee is percolating, and the ovens are warm."

I studied my little sister for a second. "I'm proud of you."

"Thanks." A light blush colored her cheeks. "I can't believe Sheriff Stone arrested you."

"Whoa. He didn't arrest me. He only took me in for questioning." I kicked off my shoes and curled my feet under me. "I probably would've done the same. It looks like I had the most to gain from Peter's death."

She shifted in the chair. "Tell me everything."

I recounted how Wade had tried to question me, but I'd taken Lacey Jane's advice and kept quiet until Marc arrived. He'd guided me on what questions to answer and which ones to avoid. Wade had worded some of the same questions in different ways and tried to trip me up with my replies. "I remained consistent with my answers, then he left us alone for a while. Marc told me not to say anything, so we sat there quietly. At last Wade returned. I'm convinced he ate lunch and left us to stew. I'm kinda sorry I fixed him a sandwich the other night."

Lacey Jane shook her head. "No, you're not."

I sighed. "You're right. He's doing his job. I only hope he'll be tough on the killer when he catches the person. Put the screws to him or whatever it takes to get a confession."

"What does Marc think?"

I plumped a pillow and leaned against it. "He says we need to clear my name."

"How?"

"The only way I can think of is to catch the real killer."

"I was afraid you'd say something like that."

"One thing I don't get is how Danny knew about the will before I did. Why wasn't I contacted?"

Lacey Jane sat straighter. "I looked it up. The executor has up to three months to notify you."

I sank deeper into the pillow. "I guess Danny's not the executor since he tracked me down. Still, why wasn't I contacted?"

"Maybe the executor is a friend of the family and wanted to alert them." She held up my phone. "You had a couple of calls from unknown numbers today."

Were the calls from the executor or potential clients? I decided to figure it out later. "I won't inherit anything if I'm arrested and convicted of Peter's death."

"I know you want to catch the killer." Lacey Jane stood and moved to the front door. "Be careful, Andi Grace. This person has already killed once, and he seems intent on preventing you from finding the truth."

I followed and gave her a good, long hug. "Thanks again for helping today."

"It was a real eye-opener, and I think I'm on the right track on becoming a paralegal. When I finish the program, I'll be even more helpful."

I laughed. "Let's hope I don't need this kind of help ever again."

I fell asleep with Sunny at the foot of my bed, and I even let the Westies sleep in the same crate again. It seemed as if we all needed extra comfort.

My dreams drifted from the murder to the interrogation to getting locked up. Then I dreamed about the freedom to inherit Peter's land.

I woke up with a pounding heart and pure exhaustion. In no time, I downed my first cup of coffee. The second cup I savored by adding mocha creamer and organic sugar.

Marc texted me.

We need to meet. My place?

I replied.

Heading your way right after I walk the dogs.

Despite my words to Danny the day before, excitement rose in my soul as I drove past the plantation on my way to Marc's home.

Peter's place had enough land for me to expand my growing business. If in good shape, the carriage house would make a great area to board more dogs instead of just checking on them. I could enclose an area for the dogs to play in and maybe I could start dog training classes.

I drove to Marc's place with the intention of exploring Peter's land. Hold up. Not Peter's land. My land. Maybe. At least if a judge ruled in my favor.

My favor. Did I really want all of Peter's property? And what about college? I questioned pursuing my old dream of journalism versus expanding my business.

Could it be my dreams had changed? I loved animals, and they responded well to me. I gave my head a mental shake. I needed to slow down. Just because Peter left me his estate didn't mean I had to take it. Plus, if I kept the place, I'd have to deal with George Reeves knocking on my door. My head spun.

I reached the turn for Marc's place. Not seeing his truck, I headed for the boat shed. When I pulled up, Chubb ran out to greet me. My fears and stress diminished at the sight of Marc's golden retriever. Peter's land had enough space for an animal shelter. Every animal deserved a good home. Were animals my destiny instead of journalism? I needed to make time to think and pray about it, but a peace filled my heart at the thought.

Marc exited the building and waved, with Chubb at his heels.

I hopped out of my vehicle and loved on Chubb.

"Good morning." Marc leaned down and scratched behind Chubb's ears. "Did you get any sleep?"

"Not really. My brain wouldn't stop. I reviewed Wade's questions in my mind over and over. Did I give him good enough answers for him to turn his attention elsewhere?"

"Your answers were solid, and they were the truth."

I sat on a wooden bench in the shade of an oak tree. "I also kept wondering why Peter left the bulk of his estate to me."

Marc's eyes widened. "You're sure he just thought of you like a little sister?"

"I was eighteen when we met. Still a kid." My face warmed. "There was never anything romantic between us. I never even had a crush on the man. Don't get me wrong, he was good to me and my family, but he was too old. Yuck."

"How old are you?"

"I'll be thirty on the Fourth of July. What about you?"

"Thirty-two." He sat next to me, and Chubb lay on a grassy spot at our feet. "Ten years isn't a big age difference."

I considered his words. "You're right. Maybe I was in survival mode the summer I met Peter."

He settled next to me on the bench. "I get it. Why do you think Peter would leave you so much?"

I hiked my shoulders. "Pity?"

"I doubt it's the reason. It could be he knew you'd use integrity in dealing with his property. What are you going to do with it?"

"Danny plans to fight me for everything. In my wildest imagination, I never dreamed Peter left me anything in his will. Of course, I still struggle to believe he's gone."

Marc elbowed me. "I got the best gift of all."

I tipped my head and frowned at him. "Danny didn't mention you were listed in the will."

Marc pointed to the golden retriever. "Chubb. Unless you think the family will fight me for him. Then I'd get fired up, put my law credentials to good use, and meet them in court."

The dog's ears perked up, and he gave Marc an adoring look.

I smiled. "I told you I have the gift of matching pets and people."

"You made me a believer, despite the fact I didn't think we'd be a good fit." His arm drifted along the back of the seat, bringing us closer together.

Butterflies fluttered in my belly. As much as I wanted to rest my head on his shoulder, I resisted temptation in case his move was an innocent gesture. "Have you got time to walk around Peter's property?"

"I've got a better idea. Wait here." Chubb followed Marc into the shed.

I gazed toward the river. A blue jay called to his mate. A reply came from the distant trees.

I relaxed at the sight and sounds of nature. *Lord, what do you want me to do? Was journalism a childish dream of mine? Have you called me to care for animals? You know I love all animals but especially dogs. Is the gift of Peter's land a sign you want me to build an animal shelter? I'm so confused. All these years I thought I was taking care of Nate and Lacey Jane until I could start my own life. Is it possible I was already living the best life for me?*

A *vroom* pulled me out of my prayer. I opened my eyes, and Marc rode out of the boat shed on a four-wheeler.

I leapt to my feet. "What in the world?"

"We'll cover more ground this way. Come on."

I hesitated. Riding on the four-wheeler would put us close together. Would the action reveal how I felt about Marc? I understood his logic though. I rose to my feet and strode to Marc. "Okay."

I'd ridden four-wheelers with friends before. I'd pretend like this time was no different. I seated myself behind Marc, and he took off. "Where's Chubb?"

"I gave him a big bone to chew on. I fenced in a secure area for him in the shed. He's fine."

We picked up speed, and I stayed quiet, enjoying the view and the time with Marc. He wouldn't be my pretend boyfriend forever, but I hoped we'd always be good friends.

I leaned forward. "Can we go by the carriage house?"

"Sure. Why?" He adjusted our direction.

"If I really do get this property, I thought it could be a good place to board dogs."

"Might take some remodeling."

"If Thomas isn't the killer, I could ask him for an estimate."

"No. Even if he didn't kill Peter, I'm still not sure about his business ethics. Maybe I can help. Let's see what we've got to work with." He drove at a reasonable speed. Not like a grandma, but not a speed demon either.

Soon we reached our destination, and I hopped off the four-wheeler as soon as he shut off the engine.

Stones crumbled at the corners of the carriage house. "Ugh. I'd hoped for more. You know, a lot of carriage houses in big cities have been converted into homes."

"Let's check inside. It could be decent."

I followed him to the stone building and ran my hand over the smooth surface.

Marc slid open the door and swiped at a cobweb in the doorframe. "Nothing like the coolness inside a building like this."

"Yep." I breathed in the damp air. "This isn't what I imagined."

"Peter once told me a previous owner kept race horses to the right and carriage horses in stalls on our left." Marc moved in the direction where race horses once hung out. "This will take a ton of work to modernize for dog kennels. One of the barns might be a better option."

"Okay." I refused to allow myself to feel upset. Whatever we discovered this morning, it had to be better than the previous afternoon. This was a time to dream, so I tamped down my disappointment.

"There's a mule barn and a regular barn closer to the main house."

"Regular barn?"

Marc shrugged. "I've never lived on a farm."

"Plantation."

"I stand corrected."

"You kinda live on a plantation now. Right? You and Peter each own parts of Hewitt Kennady's original plantation."

"True, but mine is a small plot of land compared to the original. I pretty much have my home, a little land, the boat shed, and the dock." He took my hand. "Let's get out of here."

"One day I'd love to fix this up." I pulled back before going with him into the warm sunshine. "Maybe artists could use it. Rent it out for an inspiring retreat."

Marc seated himself on the four-wheeler. "It takes a lot of money to run a place this big. There's more to see, but I need to get back to work. Besides money, you'll be investing time into running the plantation the way it should be."

I fisted my hands on my hips. "Are you saying I should refuse to take it? Am I not educated enough to handle this place? What about Mr. Reeves? Do you worry I'll give up and sell the place to him?"

Marc made a T-formation with his hands. "Timeout. I didn't accuse you of anything. You're definitely smart enough to handle this property. The question is do you want it to suck the life out of you in the process? You're young, with your whole life ahead of you. Do you really want to be stuck here taking care of old buildings and all of this land?"

The irritation drained right out of me. I'd sacrificed my twenties for my siblings, and I'd do it all over again. No regrets. "You make a good point. Maybe it's the thought of all this freedom. Being outside and breathing fresh air. After yesterday's fear Wade would lock me up, I may have gotten carried away today."

"Don't get me wrong. This is an amazing gift from Peter, but there's a lot of responsibility. Make an informed decision. If you decide to sell to George Reeves, that's your prerogative. Peter and I agreed not to sell to the man, but it's your land now. Make your own decision."

"To make an informed decision, I need to see what all there is. Are you willing to continue the tour?"

Marc's smile weakened my knees. "We'll see as much as possible today and finish another time. Hop on."

So I did.

Chapter Twenty-Five

AFTER OUR TOUR of the barns, we drove in the warmth of the morning sun to the main house. "You know the last barn is in decent shape. I think it'd work for a doggie day care."

Marc tilted his head. "What about the heat? You'll need air-conditioning in the summer and heat in the winter. At least January and February."

I wouldn't let the truth bring me down. "You're right. Juliet's brother is a contractor I trust. Maybe he can give me an estimate when he's visiting one weekend."

"Speaking of contractors." Marc pointed to the back of the house. Thomas's truck was parked and loud rock and roll blasted from the porch. Marc pulled the four-wheeler into the shade and stood. He offered a hand to me.

I gripped his hand and got off. "I guess it's time to face the music."

Marc chuckled. "You might want to stick to your day job and not try to be a comedian in Myrtle Beach."

"Ow. That hurt." I grabbed my heart and laughed. "Just kidding. Let's see what Thomas is working on."

Marc reached for my hand. "Don't forget. He thinks we're a couple. Peter paid him for everything. Even if the new room isn't your style, don't agree to any changes because he'll want cash up front."

"I'm surprised Peter hired Thomas." I knocked on the back door. When nobody answered, I turned to Marc. "I guess we'll walk in."

"It's going to be your house."

"Except it doesn't feel real." In fact it felt wrong to be rewarded for Peter's early death.

"Even so, act like you believe it." Marc opened the door and waved me in.

I entered and followed the sound of rock and roll. Thomas was in the new addition. "Hey, Thomas." I waved to get his attention.

He climbed down from the ladder, crossed the room, and turned off the paint-splattered boom box. "Howdy. What can I do you for?"

I swiped my damp hands on my shorts. "You may have heard I inherited this house."

Marc walked around the room, surveying the progress.

Thomas ran a hand through his lanky dark hair. "Do you want to make changes? We can work it out."

Wow. Marc had a handle on this guy. Was he being considerate or trying to get more money out of me? "No, but I'd like to see Peter's plan for this space."

"No problem. I've got my copy over here." He moved to a piece of plywood supported by two sawhorses. "Why don't I show you instead? It'll be easier."

"Okay."

"This is the fireplace, of course. It'll have a white mantle, and Peter planned to hang a big TV over it. Windows on either side of the fireplace, and this wall has two more windows. Over here, he wanted—well, it's a wall."

I followed the direction he pointed. Something was off kilter with the wall.

Thomas said, "Canned lights in the ceiling. Light gray walls and heart of pine flooring."

"Crown molding?"

"No."

I played along, even though I didn't believe Thomas. "It should be very nice. I'd still like to see the original plan and contract."

Marc shot me a warning look and stood between us.

I said, "It looks great, Thomas."

Marc stopped when he reached the architectural rendering. "Your plan shows a wall of windows along here, but I only see two openings."

Thomas frowned. "This allows for more furniture along the walls."

Suspicions crept in. Would windows have cost more? "Do you have a change order I can see?"

"No." His mouth tightened.

My heart raced like it usually did when I faced a confrontation. "I'd like this room to be exactly like the original plan unless you can show me a signed document."

Marc closed his eyes and rubbed his forehead.

"Fine. A wall of windows it is." The anger in Thomas's voice was unmistakable.

I nodded. "I'm going to look around a bit upstairs. We'll let you know when we leave."

Marc and I exited the room, and Marc headed straight to the refrigerator. "I bet you'd like a Coke."

"Yes." Plus lots of chocolate. But no need to reveal all of my secrets.

Marc opened the fridge. Instead of water bottles and soft drinks, there were cans of beer.

I gasped. "Are you kidding me?"

Marc made a beeline to Thomas. "Does anybody else besides you have a key to the house?"

His eyes narrowed. "Why?"

Marc's chin lifted a fraction and his legs spread out as if ready for battle. "Because the refrigerator that held nonalcoholic beverages the day Peter died is now full of beer. Care to explain?"

"I, uh, I maybe didn't lock up one night."

I crossed my arms. "There's enough for a party. What's going on, Thomas?"

The man's face reddened. "If you don't trust me, you can hire somebody else to finish the job."

I set my hands on my hips. "I'd want a partial refund and analysis of what money has already been spent and for what. Peter taught me good accounting practices."

Thomas fisted his red-handled hammer and raised his arm.

My knees quaked, but I tried my best to keep a straight face. If he thought I was frightened, he'd have the upper hand. Forever.

Marc stepped between us. "You best put your hammer away and cool off. Don't come back until tomorrow. If you decide to quit and refund what Peter paid you, just let me know. We'll work it out with the executor of the estate."

Thomas stormed out of the room, uttering obscenities until the kitchen door slammed shut.

I blew out a breath. "Do you think he'll quit?"

"No way. He doesn't have the money to pay the estate back. Most contractors would have a team of men here working on this room. Thomas may not have known you'd inherit the house, but he knew somebody would. I bet he thought he'd pull a quick one by changing the windows. It's cheaper to put in two than a whole wall of them. We need to change the locks on this house. Pronto. Any chance you got a lock for your back gate?"

"No. Once Danny dropped his bombshell, and Wade took me in for questioning, I forgot all other plans." I glanced at my watch. "Actually, I need to walk a couple of dogs and check on the Westies and Sunny."

"Can it wait a few minutes?"

"What do you have in mind?"

"As long as this place belongs to you, let's go through Peter's files."

"I've got a better idea." I hurried to the pantry and grabbed some reusable shopping bags. "Let's gather them up so we can take our time."

"Andi Grace, you are one of the smartest people I know. Never sell yourself short."

I couldn't give him a verbal reply. His kindness washed over me like a soothing shower. Whether he meant them or not, I'd cherish his words.

Chapter Twenty-Six

AFTER I'D TAKEN care of my dog-sitting duties, I hightailed it home. In the kitchen, I spread Peter's files in alphabetical order on the counter. Sunny, Heinz, and Chloe played in the backyard. On my way home, the executor of Peter's estate had called me. Alan Farmer was a local attorney Peter had hired to draw up his will and be executor. He promised to email me a copy of the will and admitted I'd inherited almost everything. I didn't see the need to tell Mr. Farmer that Danny had already given me a copy of his copy. I wanted my own.

My emotions seesawed between excitement and fear, and fear was winning. I was most afraid of being arrested. I should've stopped to buy a lock for the gate and my windows. Impatience overrode everything else. I needed to go through the files and didn't look forward to any more delays.

Maybe I'd stumble upon a clue or two. Thomas might not be the killer, but he was up to no good.

The front doorbell rang, and I froze. The dogs barked from the back deck, and the bell rang again. With a racing heart and slow feet, I made my way to the door. A glance out the window revealed Marc. I whipped open the door. "What are you doing? I thought you'd be working until dark."

"One of the nice things about June is the long days." He held up a brown paper sack with the hardware store's logo. "I reached a stopping point and came to town."

"Come on inside."

"I think it's best to work on the gate first. Chubb's in back with the other dogs. I hope that's okay."

"Sure. Have you eaten?"

He shook his head. "Too busy."

"I'll order something. Do you like Chinese food?"

"Yes. Chicken with broccoli and hot and sour soup." He jogged down my front porch steps, and I speed-dialed my favorite Chinese restaurant.

After placing our order, I returned to arranging Peter's files. Some I moved to the kitchen table. Richard Rice Plantation, remodel, and family were the three I planned to study before going to sleep.

Sunny barked once.

I hurried to let her inside, and the other three dogs followed. I gave each one a treat and filled four water bowls.

Marc appeared at my side.

How had I missed his entrance? If I was in danger, I'd need to sharpen my skills of observation. "That was fast."

He shrugged. "I'm used to working with my hands. I'll start with your kitchen window and work my way around the house."

"Okay. I'm going through Peter's files and alphabetizing."

The dogs had moved from lapping up water to munching on dog food.

Marc removed the lock from the window near the door. "Sounds like a good plan. We need to find out who Peter's executor is and see if they'll agree to hire a locksmith to change the locks at his place."

"The executor called me on the way home. His name is Alan Farmer." I told Marc about my conversation with the attorney.

Marc's eyebrows rose. "Peter hired an attorney to be his executor. Very interesting."

"That's what I thought." I turned back to the files, but my eyes drifted to the one on the table labeled Richard Rice Plantation. Picking it up, I sat at the table and opened it.

The first page contained a list of board members in bold font and large size. Corey Lane was CEO. John Paul Young was listed as the CFO. Asher Cummings, Lonnie Wolfe, Dick Rice, Paula Houp, Catherine Anne Baransky, Ronnie Stevens, and, of course, Peter Roth made up the board. According to Corey, Asher had been confused over the board report.

I turned the page. Numbers. Lots and lots of numbers. I hopped up and pulled a Coke out of the refrigerator. "Would you like a drink?"

Marc chunked the old lock into my waste basket and installed the new one. "I'll wait until our food gets here. Did you find anything in the files?"

"Not sure. I need to make sense of the numbers and Peter's chicken scratchings." I pulled a pen and pad out of a drawer and started deciphering the notes and arrows.

When I started a crossword puzzle or sudoku, I got lost. The same proved true for solving Peter's files. I never heard the doorbell ring and didn't realize dinner had arrived until Marc waved a brown paper bag under my nose.

"You hungry?"

My stomach growled. "Actually, I'm starved."

We washed up and soon sat at the kitchen table, eating. I dug into sesame chicken, and Marc started on his soup. The spicy tang hit my taste buds. The food was so delicious, I speared a second bite of chicken while I kept chewing the first bite.

"When you concentrate on a task, you're all-in. Have you found anything in the files?"

I shot him a smile. "As a matter of fact, it appears there's a problem at the plantation. Not mine, but the Richard Rice Plantation. If I'm interpreting Peter's notes correctly, Asher Cummings came to him with doubts about the financial report. It looks like the company Asher works for gave a five-hundred-thousand-dollar donation earmarked for building a café on site for tourists."

Marc whistled. "That's huge."

I took another bite and nodded.

"What's the problem?"

I wiped my mouth with a paper napkin. "At a recent board meeting, they discussed bids for construction of the café. John Paul Young and Corey were only focused on the low bid."

"Low bid wins, right?" He opened his plastic container of chicken and broccoli.

"Maybe." I studied my notes. "It looks like Asher was concerned if the café was built for anything less than five hundred thousand, they couldn't spend the excess on anything except the café. At least not without his company's permission."

"I get it. They gave it for the café, and you have to use it for café."

"Exactly." I took another bite. "He's concerned about the integrity of the plantation."

"Yeah. If they spend the extra on another project, it's dishonest."

"I think we should talk to Asher Cummings tomorrow. See if he can shed light on the issue."

Marc pulled out his phone and swiped it. "I'm meeting a boat owner in the morning about building a wooden kayak for his daughter's eighteenth birthday. Can you wait until early afternoon so I can go with you? There's also the issue of Thomas and asking Mr. Farmer about changing the locks and alarm codes."

My pulse vibrated in my temple. Peter's death had complicated my life in many ways. It was hard to imagine living in the big, old plantation house when I was so very comfortable in this home I'd lived in the past twelve years. I didn't need the space for myself, but it'd be great to have the land to expand my dog walking business. I needed to pray, but life was hitting me fast and furious these days.

"Andi Grace, are you listening?"

"Yeah. I'll call Mr. Cummings in the morning and see what I can set up." If the only time the man could meet was in the morning, so be it. I appreciated how much Marc helped me, but I could handle this on my own if necessary.

Chapter Twenty-Seven

NATE RODE SHOTGUN with me to Peter's plantation, Friday morning. "I really appreciate you coming with me. I hated to bother Marc again. I was shocked when Thomas called this morning and apologized before asking me to meet him."

"I'm glad you called me." He tapped his fingers on his worn jeans. "It's a lot to take in. You owning a plantation on the river."

"Don't get excited yet. Danny plans to fight me."

"Jerk." His fingers tightened into a fist. "He never was good enough for you."

I counted to ten in French. "I'm afraid our little sister may be interested in dating him."

"What?" Nate's tone was a growl.

"I think she was crushing on him until he showed his obnoxious side when he confronted me about the will. I hope his ugly outburst opened her eyes."

"I'll talk to her. Danny Nichols is not going to get away with breaking both of my sisters' hearts."

I turned down the plantation lane surrounded by trees. We rumbled along in the shade until we entered the clearing in front of the house. "Last night Thomas scared me. If Marc hadn't been with me, he might have struck me. I want to make sure you're aware of the danger."

"I'll stay alert. He's not going to hurt you on my watch."

I circled round so the Suburban pointed down the driveway, in case we had to make a hasty retreat. "Do you think I should've called Wade?"

My brother rubbed a thumb along his chin. "It might be a good idea for somebody to know our location." Nate slipped out of the truck and inspected the landscape.

I called the sheriff. It rolled to voice mail. "Hi Wade. I wanted to let you know I'm at Peter's plantation to speak to Thomas King. Last night Thomas threatened me, and I suggested he could refund me the balance of what Peter paid him if he wants to quit. This morning he asked me to come here to discuss the situation. My brother is with me, but in case we disappear or turn up dead, you'll know to start your investigation by questioning Thomas. Thanks."

I joined Nate by an enormous crape myrtle. "What do you think?"

"As a professional landscaper, I'm impressed. Peter didn't go cheap with anything out here."

"Wait until you see the inside. Ready?"

"Let's get it over with."

I led him to the back of the house and took a deep breath before entering. Thomas was at work on the mantle. A Bruce Springsteen song played on the boom box. I kept a safe distance in case the man decided to take a swing at me. "We're here."

Thomas whipped his head around. "Do you always travel with a bodyguard?" He shut off the music.

"Come on, Thomas. You know my brother. He wanted to check out the yard."

"Right. Landscaper extraordinaire." Thomas guffawed.

Nobody messed with my siblings. I threw my shoulders back. "You're right. Nate does extraordinary work, but that's not why you asked me to come today. Have you decided to finish the room exactly like the original plan, or do you want to refund the balance of Peter's money?"

His nostrils flared. "I don't leave projects unfinished."

"Can you handle working for me?" I'd rather work with almost any other contractor, but probate could take months, and anyway, I wanted to hear his reply.

"I've seen your bossy side. I don't imagine you'll have any trouble telling me what to do." He tipped his chin up in a holier-than-thou stance and crossed his arms. His stringy dark hair fell back.

Nate frowned. "You best treat my sister with respect, or you'll have me to answer to."

Thomas frowned. "Understood." His voice rumbled deep in his chest.

I needed to take charge in case Thomas took longer than the probate. "We're going to change the locks. You'll get a new key, which can't be duplicated. The alarm codes will also be changed. We can activate and deactivate them with a phone app. You'll need to call and let us know when you come and go so we can arm the system." I was confident we'd talk Mr. Farmer into my plan.

His eyes widened. "Say what? Don't you trust me?"

"Somebody's been in this house and stocked the fridge with booze after Peter died. That's on you, Thomas. If it happens again, it's on me. As long as you call me the minute you leave, there won't be a repeat occurrence."

"You blaming me for whatever happened here?" His voice boomed through the stillness of the morning.

Nate stood at my side.

I lifted my chin. "Only you, the sheriff, and I had keys to this place. I didn't throw a party. It's down to you or the sheriff."

"Is that all, your highness?"

Nate's fists hit his hips. "No need for sarcasm. From what I've seen of this meeting, I doubt you can work for Andi Grace. Why don't you give her a refund and move on to your next project? It'll make all of our lives easier."

Thomas raised his hands in a defensive gesture. "We're good. I didn't mean no disrespect. Y'all know how excited I am to work on this project. This room is gonna be spectacular." He rambled on about completing the renovation. "I just wanna do Peter proud with this job."

I couldn't keep listening to his lies, but my gut told me he'd never return the money to Peter's estate. I had to make sure he completed the project.

Nate touched my arm. "What do you think? Let Thomas finish?"

"Sure, as long as he agrees to my conditions." I took a deep breath. "I do have a copy of the original plan with Peter's notes and contract."

Thomas's face paled. "Okay. I won't have to make you a copy. If you don't mind, I best get back to work on this mantle."

I stopped Nate from walking away. "Thomas, the contract said the project will be complete by July fourth." My birthday.

"The death and sheriff have thrown me back."

"When do you think it'll be done?"

The man studied the room. "Give me until August first."

"No. I'll give you an extra week, even though you've not lost seven days of work."

His shoulders hunched up, and he looked ready to argue.

Nate held up his hand, his eyes cold and hard. "I'm a businessman, and when I agree to a deadline, I make sure I meet it."

Through pinched lips, he growled. "Then it'll be ready by the eleventh of July."

"You need to leave when we do. I'll show Nate around the house while you finish up for the morning. When the locksmith changes the locks, you can return to finish."

"You need to give me an extra day then."

"July eleventh. That's what we agreed on." I turned, scurried out of the room, and dragged my brother upstairs. "I want to show you around the place. See how prim and proper all of this is? It's not me, and I can't imagine living here."

Nate held a finger over his mouth. "Let's whisper until Thomas clears out."

We walked through each room upstairs before I led him around the main floor, never saying a word. To my surprise, there was no sign of Thomas when he got back downstairs.

I locked the house, and we headed back to Heyward Beach. "Thoughts?"

"It's an amazing house, but it doesn't suit your personality. You're more relaxed—*er*, casual—than the person who'd live there."

"Do you think I should let Danny's family have it?"

"No. Peter willed it to you for some reason. How do you picture yourself here?"

"I could never live in the main house. I'd like to—" I stopped. He'd think it was too silly.

"What?"

"I'm just toying with the idea."

He rolled his hand like a Ferris wheel. "Keep going."

"I could make one of the barns a place to board dogs. There's an area where I can train them for owners who need help. There are other buildings on the plantation, but I'm not sure what all I have. I mean, if it becomes mine. Marc's going to look over the will and see what my chances are. You know he's my attorney now. He's probably sorry he ever met me. I'm on the sheriff's suspect list for Peter's murder, and Danny's family has threatened to take me to court. I trust him to keep me out of prison. I'm not as concerned about the plantation." I was rambling, but the whole situation still made me nervous.

"Sweet for you. So if you get the place, you're going to grow your dog walking business into more?"

"Right. It seems appropriate. Peter helped me get my business started, and because of him, it'll grow."

"Are you sure this is what you want to do? What about your dream of being a journalist?"

I pulled into the parking lot of Nate's Landscaping. "I've changed over the years. This is my new dream."

He looked at his watch. "I've got to run. I'm glad you called me this morning. If I finish early enough tomorrow, why don't we take some four-wheelers out to the plantation and check it out. You, me, and LJ. It'll be an adventure like old times."

"How about if I include Juliet?"

Nate's eyes brightened. "Jules is always included."

I smiled. It was rare for my brother to call anybody by their given name. "I'll give her a call."

"You always impress me, reaching out to others, Ange."

"I hate that nickname."

He shoved open his door. "It's adorable, like you."

I laughed. "I never could get mad at you."

He hopped out. "Are you kidding? Seems like you got mad at me plenty over the years."

"Not really. I just wanted to make sure you grew up to be a decent person, and I expected you to behave. If I'd just been a sister, you would've liked me better."

He sobered. "I don't know if I would've survived foster care. LJ and I owe you a lot."

I shrugged. "You would've done the same in my position. Family sticks together."

"Amen. See you later." He tugged on his ball cap with his business logo.

I drove to the coffee shop and called Asher Cummings from the parking lot. His deep voice came through the line. "Hi, Mr. Cummings. This is Andi Grace Scott. I was a friend of Peter Roth and wondered if I could speak to you."

The deep tenor added a musical lilt as he responded. "What's this about?"

"Peter's death and the Richard Rice Plantation. It'd be easier to speak face-to-face. I'm at Daily Java and could bring you a cup of coffee."

"Throw in a chocolate chip cookie, and I'll meet you there."

"Absolutely. You've got a deal."

I texted Marc to be polite—he'd wanted to be part of the meeting. But I could do this without him. I had my list of questions and was prepared.

It didn't take long for me to order, and Mr. Cummings popped up before I had our coffee and had started to search for a table.

We chose a table in the back corner of the coffee shop. It was mid-morning. A group of ladies doing a Bible study sat around a large rectangular table made from reclaimed barnwood. Outside, two young mothers sat while their toddlers used sidewalk chalk to entertain themselves. A man who looked to be in his forties worked on his laptop and nursed a large cup of coffee.

"Lacey Jane warmed your cookie."

Asher Cummings's pictures on social media didn't do the man justice. Well over six feet, blond hair brushed the top of his ears, a moustache, and bright blue eyes. "Nothing like a chocolate chip cookie fresh out of the oven."

I already liked the man. Not pretentious. "I'm sure you're a busy man, so I'll get straight to the point. I'm the one who found Peter's body, and I wonder if his murder is related to the Richard Rice Plantation. I want to be honest with you. Yesterday Danny Nichols told me Peter left his place to me. The family will fight me, but I've started going through Peter's files."

Asher stirred the cream and sugar he'd dumped into his coffee. "I feel like I should warn you to be careful. Have you found anything useful in the files?"

I liked him better and better. "Cummings Security Company donated a half-million dollars for a café at the plantation, but it's your company, and I'm sure you're aware." I fumbled through sharing my discovery with him.

His blue eyes narrowed. "You realize the donation isn't public information."

Quickly, I nodded. "Yes, sir. Marc Williams is the only other person who knows. He's my lawyer and was Peter's neighbor, and he helped me go through the files. We won't go public with the information." I took a sip of my coffee. "Mr. Cummings, who do you think killed Peter?"

He shrugged. "Why are you so curious? You should let the authorities handle the murder."

"I learned the hard way cops don't always catch the bad guys. I'm a suspect, but I'm innocent."

"How'd you learn the hard way?" He added more sugar to his coffee and stirred it.

"Twelve years ago, my parents were killed by a hit-and-run driver. The police never caught the driver, and I've always felt guilty for not doing something. They deserve justice."

"I guess you were a kid then."

"I was eighteen and planning to go to college."

His keen gaze studied me. "What'd you do?"

"I stayed home and raised my brother and sister, and Peter helped me establish my dog walking business. I feel like it's my responsibility to help catch his killer. Plus, it'll get me off the suspect list. So what do you think happened to the money your company donated? Stolen? Used for something other than you intended?"

He leaned forward and folded his long fingers together. He wasn't skinny, nor was he fat, but he was a big man. I was glad we appeared to be on the same side of justice.

"Somebody is monkeying with the figures. There should be plenty of funds for the café but the project stopped due to lack of money. It's impossible and the reason I approached Peter. I don't know if it's Corey Lane or John Paul Young, or if they're in cahoots."

"CEO and CFO working together. What's going on with the money?"

"Corey has a paid position, and he gave himself a raise. You know his wife owns this coffee shop." He tapped a finger on our table.

"Yes, sir. She's my friend, but I barely know her husband."

He took a long, slow breath.

I said, "I'm sorry. Maybe I should've told you right away. This is confidential. I don't intend to share anything you tell me with Erin Lane or anybody else."

"Why don't you go online and look up Corey Lane on *Find the Truth*." He reached into his pocket and slapped a fifty on the table. "This will cover the full report."

My palms grew damp. "Mr. Cummings, can't you just tell me?"

"Call me Asher, and the answer is no. I don't want to sway your conclusion."

"Do you think Corey is the killer?"

His gaze drifted toward the trees lining the street. "I know he shuffles money around to suit his needs. It doesn't bother him to pay monthly bills with money raised for a specific purpose. It's wrong."

"Like the café money? Is that why he was intent on taking the lowest bid, no matter what?"

"Probably. The companies making the low bids usually do shoddy work. The money my company donated was specified to go to building the new café. It'd be wrong to use any of the donation for daily expenses or to buy more horses. It's wrong to use it for anything other than the café. I said so to the board. Corey tried to smooth things over and assure us the full amount would be used appropriately. Bunch of hogwash. At least we agreed to wait on deciding which bid to accept."

My thoughts drifted to Juliet's brother. "Are you still taking bids?"

"I don't see why not, but a person would have to hurry. We meet the first Monday of the month."

"Yes, sir. Is there anything else you can tell me?"

He finished his cookie without uttering a word. After wiping his mouth, he looked at me with a twinkle in his eye. "Andi Grace, I hope you get Peter's plantation. If I think of anything else, I'll give you a call."

"Would you mind if I share this with Marc Williams? He's already seen the files, and he's an honorable man. Like you."

Those blue eyes sparkled again. "Thanks for asking. Feel free to tell him."

I handed him my business card. "Call me anytime. Day or night. About the only time I won't answer is when I'm in church."

"I knew you were a good girl. Stay safe." He took my card and left the shop. I sighed. It was great to meet a man with such integrity. If I was lucky—no, if I was smart, I'd only marry a man like Asher Cummings.

My phone vibrated. Marc Williams. I shivered. Marc was also a man of integrity, and he might not be too happy I'd met Asher without him.

Chapter Twenty-Eight

I UPDATED MARC on my progress and discovered he was annoyed to be left out of the conversation with Asher. I'd figured he'd be pleased to know I didn't run to him over every little thing. We ended the conversation by making plans for him to go over Peter's will in the evening. We hung up, and I tackled my afternoon of dog walking appointments. I also returned Heinz and Chloe to their homes. They'd been fed, exercised, and bathed and were ready to nap. Their families were scheduled to return in the evening. The Westies were a true joy, but I hadn't given them enough attention. I needed to get my life back on track.

On the way home, I swung by the grocery store and purchased hamburger, potatoes, and salad in a bag. The least I could do for Marc was feed him a home cooked meal.

I took a quick shower and applied makeup, which was a rarity for me. Curling my hair instead of tying it back in a ponytail was more proof of how much I'd begun to care about Marc. I wore nice shorts and a button-up sleeveless purple blouse. Now to tackle the food prep. Not my strong suit.

I nuked the potatoes for five minutes then buttered and salted them before wrapping them in foil and sticking them in the oven. The doorbell rang, causing my heart to flutter. I took a deep breath and went to greet Marc.

The sight of Thomas froze the smile on my face. "Thomas. What can I do for you?" Why was he here?

He stuffed his hands into the pockets of his faded cut-off denim shorts. "What would you think about painting the walls charcoal gray? It's less than a thousand dollars to change colors. We could also add a ceiling fan and surround sound."

"You know, I really don't have a lot of extra money, and the house might not be mine if the family fights me. Let's stick to the original plan." My voice wobbled. "I appreciate you thinking about it, though."

Marc arrived and parked in front of the house.

Thomas frowned. "You're making a mistake."

And then the thing tugging at the edge of my mind hit me. "Hey, you didn't call me when you left the house."

"So I forgot. You know now."

Anger flushed through me. "That wasn't our deal. You're supposed to call me or Alan Farmer the minute you leave so I can set the alarm." Earlier in the day the executor had agreed to my idea of changing locks and alarm codes. Mr. Farmer had even sent a man over to install locks that were difficult to pick and made special keys that were harder to duplicate than average. And as I'd asked, Thomas wasn't to enter or leave without contacting one of us first.

"What's a few minutes going to matter?"

Marc strolled across the yard. "What's going on?"

Thomas spun. "I was just asking your *girlfriend* about making some nice changes to the remodel."

I met Marc's gaze. "I decided to pass since we're not sure who the house will go to."

He turned to Thomas. "Is there anything else we can do for you?"

"We still need to go over the plan for your place."

Marc shrugged. "I'm in no hurry. Go ahead and finish Andi Grace's room."

With a low growl, Thomas stomped past Marc, bumping him in the shoulder. The man never said sorry or goodbye. He'd driven away before Marc stepped inside, and I locked the front door and bolted it.

"I need to arm the security system at the plantation house." I picked up my phone and punched the numbers into my app. "How was your day?"

"Productive. I'm glad it's the weekend, though."

I nodded. The weekends often involved more work for me with families taking short trips. If I was able to start a kennel, boarding animals would be much easier. I could schedule dog training classes during the week, but there was no way I could picture myself living in Peter's house. "Hey, tomorrow afternoon Nate and I are going to tour the property on four-wheelers. My sister and Juliet may join us. I know you and I've already done it once, but it might be fun. What do you think?"

"You and I only hit the areas close to the house. There's a lot more to explore." We made our way to the kitchen, and he plopped down on a barstool and tapped a folder. "Let's discuss the will first."

I washed my hands and opened the package of hamburger. "I'm listening, but I don't know if I want to inherit Peter's place or if I want you to tell me it's not possible."

"Then I don't know if this is good news or bad news." His smile calmed my nerves.

"Go ahead. I can take it." I divided the meat into four patties and hoped keeping my hands busy would lessen the impact of Marc's revelation.

"I spoke to Peter's lawyer. Danny's the only one in his family trying to fight you. The others don't care."

"What are his chances?"

"Alan Farmer assures me the will is solid. Peter had kept in touch with Danny, and the lawyer said Peter believed his family were money grubbers. He loved them, but he didn't trust them. He feared they'd sell the land to George Reeves. You're the new owner and can move in when probate is over."

I washed my trembly hands and dried them.

"Are you all right?" He stood and moved closer to me. He gazed at me with his gray eyes.

I swallowed hard. "I guess. It's a bit overwhelming."

Marc reached for my hand. "Why don't we sit outside for a bit?"

The warmth from his touch calmed my nerves. "Okay. The burgers can cook while we talk. Would you like some iced tea?"

"Sounds good. Give me the burgers, and I'll start grilling them."

After he stepped onto the deck, I poured our drinks into Tervis tumblers decorated with sunflowers. I added a slice of lemon and sprig of mint to the tea. Just because I wasn't a great cook didn't mean I was ignorant of gracious entertaining.

Sunny stood beside Marc at the grill. I filled her water bowl before sitting on my vintage red metal glider. "You could've brought Chubb over tonight."

He flipped a burger. "He tested a kayak with me this afternoon then swam in the river. He was exhausted, so I left him snoozing in his crate."

I crossed my legs. "It's a good thing he can swim since you live on the river and build boats."

"You'll be living on the river too if you move into Peter's place." Marc sat next to me and draped his arm across the back of the seat. "What are you going to do with this place?"

"I still can't picture myself living in Peter's house. It's too prim and proper. Not to mention it's too big. Your home is much more comfortable. I wouldn't have any trouble moving into your place." Why couldn't I have given Marc a simple answer? "You, uh, you know, I meant if Peter's house was like yours. I'm not asking to move in with you." I needed to just shut my mouth. I was only making things worse.

Marc threw his head back and laughed. "We may have met a few days ago, but I already know you wouldn't proposition me."

"Right." I reached for our glasses sitting on the picnic table, handed him one, and chugged mine. "George Reeves is still on my list of suspects."

"It's possible, but he's a businessman and not emotionally invested in the project."

"Thomas is a businessman."

"True, but I don't think you realize how wealthy George Reeves is. I looked deeper into his background after you and I discussed suspects. George wants it, and he has a vision. I just don't think it's worth killing someone to him. On the other hand, Thomas barely makes it from one job to the next. He's not scrupulous, and his has a mean side. If we were down to two suspects, I'd pick Thomas."

I shared my thoughts on Asher Cummings. Marc drank his tea and when I finished, he checked the burgers.

My doorbell rang, followed by a knock.

"Somebody must be anxious to see me. I'll be right back." I snatched our glasses and deposited them on the kitchen counter on my way to the door. I wasn't expecting anybody, but I figured one of my siblings or Juliet would be on the front porch. Instead, I was greeted by Danny's parents, Fred and Leslie Nichols. Two bad surprises in one day. I blinked.

With her arm up like a football player, Mrs. Leslie pushed into my home. "Of all the nerve. First, you take advantage of Danny, and then you worm your way into my brother's life to the point where he left you everything. I don't need his money, but I'm going to make sure you don't get it either."

I struggled to breathe. Take advantage of Danny? Was she nuts? I bit my lip and refused to cry. "Your brother introduced himself to me after my parents died. He was kind and caring. Unlike my *boyfriend's* parents."

Mr. Fred closed the door with a gentle click and touched his wife's shoulder. "Hon, be reasonable."

Mrs. Leslie turned on her husband. "You always had a soft spot for the girl. You and Danny. Not me. I saw her money-loving tendencies long ago." Her focus turned back to me. "What did you do to get Peter's attention? Were you having an affair?"

"No!" The accusation ripped my heart. "I never thought of Peter in a romantic way. He became a friend when I was forced to grow up too fast after my parents died."

"Why?"

"Why what?" I looked toward her husband for help. For a lawyer, he was awful meek around his wife.

"You must've done something." Mrs. Leslie screeched. "Why did he care about you?"

She had me there. Why had Peter gone out of his way to help me? "I don't know."

Her eyes narrowed and if she could've fired lasers at me, I'd be dead.

The back door banged. I heard Marc's gentle steps in the kitchen and Sunny's nails clicking on the floor. The scent of grilled burgers and baking potatoes drifted into the family room.

I clenched my fists. "Why do you hate me so much? You never spent time with Peter. Danny was the one who broke up with me after my parents were killed. I never asked you for a thing during that time or since then."

"If you hadn't dated our son, he could've made better grades. He could've dated girls more suited to our social class."

Mr. Fred said, "Stop, Leslie."

Marc entered the living room with forceful footsteps. "Andi Grace, what's going on?"

I looked at him. "Marc, I'd like you to meet Danny's parents. Fred and Leslie Nichols."

"Marc Williams." He extended his hand, and the two men shook.

I swallowed hard. "They want to fight me over the will."

Marc squared his wide shoulders. "I've been through the will and spoken to Alan Farmer. Contesting the will is a waste of time. Mr. Nichols, I believe you're also an attorney. I'm sure you know Mr. Farmer has a good reputation for preventing loopholes and being a fighter."

Mr. Fred stuffed his hands into his khakis. "I'm aware, but how do you know?"

"I'm an attorney and a friend of Peter's. We were neighbors. Do you have a copy of the will?"

Danny's father nodded. "Yes."

Marc was more helpful than any anxiety pill on the market. *Lord, thank you for Marc being part of my life. You always send people my way when I need them most.*

Mrs. Leslie stepped forward. "Fred, we can't back down."

"We'll talk in the car. We should let these people eat their dinner before it gets cold."

I opened my eyes as the couple moved to the front door. "Please don't come back to my home." The spunky part of me wanted to add "here or at the plantation," but it wouldn't help matters to fan the flames of Mrs. Leslie's anger.

Danny's parents left without saying goodbye. I didn't care.

Marc pulled me into a hug. His arms tightened around my shoulders.

"Why does everything always have to be so hard? Does it feel like we're fighting somebody from every direction? North, east, south, and west. They keep coming at us."

"You're strong, and your faith is strong. You can handle it, Andi Grace. I believe in you."

I held on tight. "I'm so tired of fighting."

"You'd be bored if it was easy. You're a champion for the underdog. It would be simple to say you don't want Peter's estate. It'd also be easy, and maybe smart, not to help find his killer. I've already discovered that's not you. You're a hero."

I laughed. "Not hardly."

"Yes. You are. You rescue dogs, and you make people feel good. That's your gift. Accept your gift."

Doubt filled my thoughts.

Marc tightened his hold. "Instead of taking Peter's land and selling it for big bucks, you're thinking about how you can help stray animals and how you can work with families and their pets. I can keep trying to convince you, or we can eat. I slid the burgers into the oven, so they're warm, but they could dry out."

"You're right. Let's eat." I pulled back a tiny bit but remained in Marc's arms. "Peter sought me out, in a way. He reached out and helped us pull our lives together. We were strangers before the day at the real estate office."

"I remember you saying you'd never met him before you began looking for a house."

"Right. He'd been renting a place and had decided to put roots down in the area."

"You said the cops never caught the hit-and-run driver."

"Right. Why?"

"I'm not sure. Danny's mother seems to be an angry woman. Was she always like that?"

"Maybe. I don't want to think about those people right now, unless you think they could have killed Peter." Here I stood in a handsome man's arms, and we were discussing murder.

"It wouldn't be the first time somebody was murdered by a family member." He stepped away. "I'm starved. Let's eat."

I missed the warmth of Marc's arms. "Do you think once Peter's killer is caught I can look into my parents' death? Is twelve years too long?"

"It's never too late to solve a cold case."

His words pleased me. Gave me hope even. I pulled the burgers and potatoes out of the oven. "I'm sorry about the Nicholses showing up. My normal life is not this full of drama. I guess if we were really dating, you'd be ready to break up with me."

"No way."

Despite the heat smacking me in the face from the oven, a shiver danced up my spine, making my body tingle. One day some woman was going to be very blessed to call Marc Williams her boyfriend. Unfortunately, it wouldn't be me. I was a realist. The man was in a different league. Smart, handsome, funny, and kind were only a few of the great qualities that made Marc Williams.

But right now, I'd enjoy a cozy dinner for two with Marc. Afterward, we'd discuss Peter's murder.

During dinner we talked about boating. The conversation and food were delightful. Afterward, we sat on the deck drinking lemonade. Sunny snoozed at my feet, and I settled into my seat and crossed my legs.

Marc reclined in the Adirondack chair to my side. "Asher Cummings is one of the good guys."

I drew a line through his name and added him to the innocent side under Regina Houp. "We're left with Corey Lane and John Paul Young from the Richard Rice Plantation. I'm going to leave George Reeves on the list, as well as Peter's family."

Marc steepled his fingers. "Let's not forget Thomas and Dylan King."

"Hard to forget them." I underlined their names. "I don't feel like we're getting anywhere."

"Don't get discouraged. We're making progress. I discovered

Corey Lane grew up in a bad neighborhood in Greenville, South Carolina. His dad left the family, and his mother worked two jobs. Corey also started working at a young age. His high school cross country coach confirmed Corey was determined to get out of poverty. He studied hard, ran, and worked at a retirement community on weekends and summers. His coach said Corey shared financial tips he learned from the older adults. He was determined to make money, no matter what. All admirable traits until you think about 'no matter what.'"

"How did he afford Clemson?"

"Scholarships." Marc cleared his throat. "I earned scholarships myself. No shame in that."

"I agree." I tapped my notepad. "I'd like to think Erin has good judgment and wouldn't marry a killer. The thing is, she grew up wealthy and never really struggled financially. If she wanted a new dress, shoes, or haircut she paid for those things. Never had to save . . ."

"What?"

"Erin never had to save a penny. Phyllis Mays is a different story. Phyllis recently came into money but never explained how. It's not any of my business, but most people aren't ashamed to say they've inherited or earned some extra money."

"You think she's embarrassed to name the source?"

I doodled a dollar sign on my notes. "What if she got the money buying lottery tickets? Her husband is against the lottery, so she has to keep it a secret."

"You buy lottery tickets at the grocery store or gas station. Public places where she could be seen by neighbors and parishioners. I don't see how she'd keep that a secret."

"Do you remember the ace of hearts I found?" I quit doodling. "The news has mentioned traveling poker games around Myrtle Beach. We saw Dylan rushing out of Peter's house. It looked like he was carrying a poker table. Phyllis was there too. What if they're involved in some kind of illegal gambling operation?"

"Your theory would explain why Phyllis didn't reveal how she came into the money." Marc rubbed his hands together.

I jumped up. "Let's go get ice cream."

"Really? Why?"

"Most Friday nights Pastor Mays and Phyllis go to a movie and out for ice cream at Scoop It Up. They joke about popcorn being their main course and ice cream is their dessert. We should hurry in case they went to an early show."

"Fine. I'll drive."

Sunny seemed tired, so I left her with a doggy bone and full water bowl. In no time, I sat in the passenger seat of Marc's truck and directed him around the back roads so we'd miss the major vacation traffic.

I tapped my toes. Heyward Beach in June. Even my shortcut was crowded. If we could only get to the ice cream shop in time. "Thanks for coming with me."

"You've got me hooked on finding the killer. This is more than the research I used to do for my old law firm, and I'm enjoying it. But we need to stick together and be careful." He braked at a stop sign and our gazes collided.

My mouth grew as dry as a desert in August. Marc supported my quest to find the killer.

The car behind us honked, breaking our moment of closeness. Solving a murder for the first time, and also meeting a man I cared about at the same time rocked my equilibrium. No more boring Andi Grace. I was on my way to the ice cream shop with a fabulous man.

As long as we arrived in time for me to speak to Phyllis, I'd have another puzzle piece. Big or small, it'd give us a clearer picture of Peter's murder.

Chapter Twenty-Nine

I SCOOPED THE LAST bite of rocky road into my mouth as Phyllis walked through the ice cream shop's glass door. She dashed to the ladies' restroom, and I followed while Marc worked on his banana split.

There were only two stalls and two sinks in the pink-tiled room with a hot air hand dryer. I made plenty of noise washing my hands, and soon Phyllis took her place at the other sink.

I smiled but felt my jaw tighten. "We need to talk."

Her eyebrows rose. "About?"

I blocked the door and turned the dead bolt. Nobody could walk in and interrupt our conversation.

"Have you lost your mind? Larry will be waiting on me to order. What's going on, Andi Grace?"

"I was about to ask you the same question." I stood between her and the door to freedom. "How did you get extra money?"

She frowned and shook her finger at me. "Honey child, that's none of your business."

I straightened and threw my shoulders back. "You can talk to me or Sheriff Stone. Might be less embarrassing to confess right here."

"I haven't done anything wrong." Her reddening face said otherwise.

"Then you won't mind telling me about the money."

Phyllis clamped her lips together.

"You know Peter was murdered. It could be tied in to the gambling at his home."

Her shoulders slumped. "Larry can never find out. Please, you can't tell him."

At this point, the facts were still muddled. I truly had nothing to blab. "I won't tell your husband, but I won't promise to keep it from the sheriff. What's going on?"

Phyllis took a few deep breaths.

I pushed. "Do you gamble?"

The blood drained from her face, and her eyes bugged. "How'd you know?"

"I saw you race out of Peter's house one night after his death. Don't you think it's morbid to meet at a dead man's home to gamble?"

She shuddered. "Yes. Once I heard the location, I almost backed out."

"But?"

"I'm hooked. I need help, and I don't know which way to turn."

"Is Dylan King in charge?"

She waved both hands as if fanning her face. "Yes, but he has a partner."

"Who is it?"

"A young guy from Georgetown. A football player, I think. He pretty much stays in the background."

"Did you kill Peter?"

"No." The word came out swift and fierce. "I have an alibi. I was at an auction the night Peter died. I saw Paula Houp and her niece. We spoke. Lots of people saw me."

Okay. Easy enough to check. "How often did you play at Peter's?"

She twisted her wedding band around her finger. "Once Thomas King began working on Peter's house, Dylan held gambling nights at the plantation when Peter was out of town."

"Who else is involved?"

"Nobody you'd know. Some locals from Myrtle Beach and some tourists. A few men join us from Conway."

Her words jolted me. "How do tourists know about the gambling ring?"

"It's possible they heard about it from hotel employees." Phyllis shrugged. "Can we keep this between ourselves?"

I placed my hands on her shoulders. "You need to tell Larry before somebody else does. I won't, but one day he'll find out."

"The news will crush him and ruin our marriage."

"Have a little faith. Your husband loves you." I gave her a quick hug and turned to unlock the door. "Tell him."

She avoided eye contact.

Two teenage girls in swimsuits stood, waiting for the restroom. The skinny youth wearing a neon green bikini said, "You're not supposed to lock others out."

"Sorry." I hurried to Marc. "Ready to go?"

"Let's roll."

I smiled at Pastor Mays, who stood to the side of the counter, no doubt waiting on his wife before ordering. I hoped she confessed the truth to him before he found out another way.

SATURDAY MORNING, I met Marc at Peter's place. *My* place unless Danny and his family fought me for it. His mom had threatened me, and the woman was tenacious. But I'd give it all up to have Peter back. Alive and well.

I inhaled deep of the fresh morning air. Marc and I sat on the tailgate of his truck drinking Daily Java coffee and whole grain bagels slathered with cream cheese. The river lapped the shore with a soothing sound. A brilliant bluebird flew past us, stopping in a pine tree. In the distance a frog croaked.

Marc lifted his coffee cup. "Nice way to start the morning. Thanks."

"Seemed like the least I could do since you're taking me around the property." This was the day to explore more of the massive property.

"I find it strange Peter never gave you the full tour."

I shrugged. "We mostly talked about dogs, my family, and my business." The bagel in my belly morphed into a lump of concrete. Had I deluded myself all these years thinking Peter and I were such good friends? "It seems like we weren't as close as I imagined." The question that kept tugging at the edge of my mind returned. "Why do you think he helped me when we barely knew each other?"

Marc stared straight ahead. "I don't rightly know. Maybe he was one of those people who saw a problem and took action. Like you."

"What do you mean?"

"You're trying to find the killer, despite no training." He sipped his coffee. "Your parents died, and you sacrificed for your brother and sister to have a better life. You see a problem and act. Admirable trait—if it doesn't get you killed."

Cold seeped into my bones. "Do you think Peter found a problem and died for it?"

"If you ruled out Regina and a lovers' spat, I'd focus on money trails."

"Money. Like gambling, Thomas adding on the room, and the Richard Rice Plantation's financial issues."

"Very good trails to follow." Marc leaned my way. His hand came out, and he ran his thumb over my lower lip. "Cream cheese."

Heat flooded my face. I hoped like everything I didn't have it in my teeth as well. At that very moment I decided the next time I'd buy fruit cups.

Marc chuckled. "Ready to roll?"

I swallowed the last sip of my coffee and held out the brown paper bag. Marc added his trash to mine, and I crammed it in the corner of his truck. "Let's do this."

I climbed behind him on the four-wheeler, and Marc took off so fast I was forced to wrap my arms around his midsection. Okay, so maybe I wanted to snuggle close to the man.

Marc slowed at one point. "Cotton fields are to the north. Rice fields are close to the river. A farmer rents the field over there and grows pumpkins, potatoes, and peas."

"All start with the letter P."

"Clever." We sped up a path big enough for a tractor.

"How did Peter manage everything, in addition to his regular job?"

"He didn't sleep much, and he hired help for some areas. A lot of the buildings need work." Marc pointed out the breeding stables, which were in a different structure than the coach house, where the coach horses had been kept originally. We passed the greenhouse, gardener's house, kitchen garden, flower garden, storehouse, spinning-house, guest quarters, smokehouse, old kitchen, and icehouse, and, of course, Peter's plantation house, where Marc drew to a stop. "What do you think?"

"It's too much. There's no way I can care for all of this property."

"What about your plans to expand your dog business?"

My stomach swirled. "I just never imagined how big the property is. Did you show me everything?"

"This is all Peter showed me. Why?"

"What about slave quarters?" I slipped off the vehicle, and he followed me to the back steps. I sat in the shade, still waiting for a reply.

"This land is only a portion of the original plantation. The slaves had homes, but they're on somebody else's property now." He sat next to me.

"Are they on your land?"

"No. Compared to the other landowners, I have very little. I was focused on property on the river for boats."

"Makes sense."

Marc removed his hat and ran his hand through his hair. "Now that you've seen it, do you think you'll keep the place or sell it off?"

Sadness overwhelmed me. "I feel unworthy of inheriting so much.

I've been comfortable in my little home and decided you're right. Taking care of this place could suck the life right out of me."

"Does that mean you're selling?"

"I don't know. Peter didn't want to sell, and he trusted me with it. I've got a lot of praying and thinking to do before I make a decision. I'm really a simple girl. No dreams of being rich."

The sound of an approaching vehicle brought me to my feet. "Do you hear that?"

"Yep. Somebody's coming."

I ran to the front of the house and a black van appeared. Dylan. Whether he was here to help his dad or set up for a poker game didn't matter. I intended to discover the truth.

Chapter Thirty

DYLAN WAVED AND drove to the back of the plantation house.

Anger surged through me, and I dashed behind him. When I rounded the corner, Dylan stood by the van with wide eyes.

Marc had planted himself in front of the boy. Arms crossed and ball cap on backward showed how serious Marc was. While Marc might only be a few inches taller, he appeared to tower over Dylan. Must've been all those amazing muscles.

I didn't need a man to fight my battles, and I jumped into the fray. "Dylan, I wasn't expecting you this morning."

"I came to help my dad."

"He's not here."

"Sometimes I start without him."

My temple throbbed. "Did he give you a key?"

Dylan reached into the van. My breathing hitched in my chest. Was he going to pull a gun?

Marc stepped in front of me.

Dylan tugged his keys from the ignition and held them in front of us. "Don't see how it's any of your concern, but I've had a key for some time."

Marc didn't budge. "It's Andi Grace's business because Peter left the plantation to her. We'll follow you inside."

Dylan strode to the door. "If it's Andi Grace's house, why don't you have your own key?"

My key sat in my SUV's cup holder, but I didn't tell him.

Sure enough, Dylan's key didn't work. He turned and faced us. "What's going on?"

I held my head high. "We changed the locks when we discovered you were holding poker games, gambling nights, or whatever it is you're doing here."

"Me?" His voice squeaked.

"I've got a witness. Did Peter discover what you were doing and confront you?"

"What? You're crazy."

"Somebody murdered Peter. Was it you?"

"No way." He backed away from me with hands up. "I'm not a killer."

"Somebody murdered Peter, and you had a key to the place. You're up to no good. Maybe you didn't want Peter to turn you over to the cops. The two of you argued, and you pushed him. He fell, hit his head, and died."

He shook his head so hard it should've have given him vertigo. "No. I admit we gambled here, but that's all."

He probably wouldn't hurt Peter on purpose, but it could've been an accident. "You're not welcome here, Dylan. Not to help your dad finish and not to have parties." I took a step closer to make my point. "Do you understand?"

"Yeah." He spit on the ground then marched to the van.

Marc followed him and spoke loud enough for me to hear. "There's also a new security system. Your father doesn't know the codes. Andi Grace is giving you a second chance. I suggest you take it."

Dylan's reply was to jump in the van and take off with tires squealing and a cloud of dust.

I joined Marc. "Thanks for having my back."

"Anytime. I think he got the message."

Sandy particles from Dylan's quick departure continued to float through the air. "Me, too. The question is, did he kill Peter?"

"I don't know, but stay alert."

"Trust me, I will. I'll also keep him on my suspect list."

Marc nodded. "Good girl. I'd say we've had enough excitement for one morning. Let's go to the river."

"Sounds like a nice plan."

Marc and I took his kayak on the river and followed the property lines on the water of the original plantation. Afterward, we ate sand-wiches and raw veggies on his dock. Sunny and Chubb chased each other on land and splashed in the water. It had turned into the perfect summer day. The only disappointment was Nate had gotten tied up helping a new widow who couldn't make up her mind on what she wanted. Lacey Jane and Juliet backed out when they heard Nate couldn't make it. I suspected a little match-making, but in this case, I didn't mind.

I allowed myself to breathe, and God's peace flowed through my veins.

Marc pulled water bottles out of his cooler and handed me one. "You look relaxed."

"I am." I nodded and drank deeply from the Tervis bottle Marc had given me.

"Spending time on the river is always good for me." Marc stretched his lean, long legs from where he now sat in an Adirondack chair on the dock.

I considered his words. "You know I've had a lot of fun times on the water, but today was different. Not fun exactly, but peaceful."

"When things got crazy growing up, and I had no control over my life, I hightailed it to the nearest river, lake, or beach. Life still makes more sense to me when I'm around water."

I ran my hands over the smooth chair arms. "Did you make these?"

Marc nodded. "Yes. Years ago. Woodworking also helps me get centered."

Over the years, I'd learned to lean on God for survival. He'd give me wisdom about the plantation. I refused to become a slave to a piece of property, but I'd be smart with my inheritance. "Marc, inheriting this land might open the door for a conversation with George Reeves."

He raised his black Ray-Ban sunglasses and speared me with his gaze. "Bad idea."

I shook my head. "No, it's a great idea. I can contact him and say I heard he'd made an offer to Peter. I'll set up a time to meet him, and when we get together, I'll bring up Peter's murder. It'll unfold naturally. Easy peasy." My face grew warm. Too bad I'd ended my argument with a childish phrase.

"What if Reeves killed Peter?" Marc leaned forward and rested his forearms on his thighs.

"You said he wouldn't kill over something so insignificant."

He held up his hands. "It's only a theory. Not worth risking your life."

"I'll only agree to meet him in a public place." I scooted to the edge of my seat.

"If you arouse his suspicions, he might try to hurt you later."

"I'll take Sunny with me."

"Your dog has been attacked once already."

"Good point." I pushed off the chair, moved away from Marc, and sat on the wooden dock, where the dogs snoozed. I swung my legs back and forth, allowing my toes to skim the nice cool water. No way I'd risk Sunny again. She might appear scary to strangers, but she wasn't.

She was tenderhearted and had been hurt protecting Chloe and Heinz. If George Reeves tried to harm me when Sunny was around, she'd defend me. I didn't want to endanger my beloved pet again.

The dock creaked and rocked from Marc's slow, steady steps. He stopped beside me. "I didn't mean to upset you, but we need to be smart."

Smart wasn't always my strong suit. Too often I reacted before thinking through my options. "You're right. What do you suggest?"

"You shouldn't meet George Reeves, but if you insist, then take your lawyer."

I smiled. "The man I hired when we found Peter's body?"

"Yes. Little did I realize what all having you as a client would entail. You've been questioned about Peter's murder, inherited Peter's estate, you may have to fight Danny over the will, and now—"

"Will you go with me to meet Mr. Reeves?"

He sighed. "Against my better judgment, I'll schedule a meeting."

"Thank you." In a short time, Marc had become a close friend. I'd lost Peter, but my friendship with Marc was different. We were more equally yoked.

As much as I'd cared for Peter, hanging out with Marc was more comfortable. To be completely honest, we also had a little chemistry. I took a deep breath. Since the day Danny broke my heart, I hadn't allowed myself the luxury of romance. There hadn't been time. Deep down, there'd also been the fear of another broken heart.

Marc claimed he was planting roots in the Low Country. He wasn't going anywhere, and neither was I. Maybe it was time for a real romance.

Chapter Thirty-One

AT TEN O'CLOCK Monday morning, I sat in front of a large modern glass desk in downtown Charleston. Marc sat in a sleek black leather chair beside me, and we faced George Reeves. His cowboy hat rested on the bookshelves behind him, and he ran a hand through his thick dark hair. A few gray streaks wove through the dark strands.

"Ms. Scott, your attorney here is one of the reasons I can't offer you top dollar for the plantation Peter Roth left to you." His southern drawl and good-old-boy smile had no doubt charmed many people over the years, but his eyes had a calculating coldness.

I scooted to the edge of my seat. "Are you saying if Mr. Williams would sell his land to you, my land would be more valuable?"

Mr. Reeves nodded and reached for an unlit cigar in his ashtray. He rolled it between his thumb and pointer finger. "My plan is for a hotel and casino. I need enough space for shows, and I want to be approachable for boat and land traffic. I'll need to have a marina for boats and yachts. To make it work, I need both properties." Again, he flashed the fake smile.

"Why?" I scratched notes on my pad.

"To build a bigger marina. It's part of my vision for the casino property." He leaned back in his chair. "At this point there are no land-based casinos in South Carolina. I plan to change that, but just in case it doesn't get approved, I'll need a couple of casino boats."

Was he bluffing? "If I sell to you for a lower price, then will you make a higher offer to Marc for his land?"

"It's possible, but I'm not going to make any promises today." George turned his gaze to Marc and pointed at him. "If you and Peter had agreed to my initial offers, construction would be underway by now. I'm losing money on this project every day."

Marc shrugged. "I'm here today representing Andi Grace. Nothing more."

I said, "George, since you mentioned Peter, who do you think killed Peter?"

He turned his attention back to me. "In my experience, it usually comes down to money. Who stood to gain the most by Peter's death? The answer seems clear to me."

I gulped. "Who?"

"You, my dear."

Fury swept through my body like a tornado. I stood on shaky legs. "Peter was my friend. Nothing else. I never dreamed he'd leave me a penny, much less his house."

The fake smile turned into a sneer. "You mean his plantation."

"Right."

He set down his stogie and linked his fingers on top of his glass desk. "I was in Mississippi the week of the murder. My wife was with me, and I have more than one witness. You're the one who gained the most from Peter's death."

Marc stood and circled my elbow with his fingers. "We're done here."

A few minutes later I sat in the front of Marc's truck with the air-conditioning on full force. "He thinks I killed Peter."

"You shouldn't be surprised. He's not a nice man." Marc drove with one hand and loosened his blue silk tie with the other. "He meant to rattle you with his words. He deflected the attention from himself."

"Although he said he has plenty of witnesses. If he's telling the truth, I can take him off my suspect list." I reached for Marc's tie and placed it on the back seat.

"You're doing a good job of eliminating suspects. Who's left?"

"Corey Lane and Thomas King. Maybe Dylan."

Traffic thinned as we cleared the city limits. "You hungry?"

"Starved. One of the dogs I walked this morning refused to take care of business, and I didn't have time to eat."

He turned off the main road. "I know a place with amazing fried chicken. It's a little off the beaten path."

"You eat fried chicken?" What had happened to the healthy-eating Marc Williams?

"My mouth is starting to drool just thinking about it. Miss Mabel also has the best macaroni and cheese in the county. Maybe the state. Prepare to be amazed."

"Sounds like comfort food to me."

"Delicious food." Marc pulled into the sandy parking lot of a concrete building in desperate need of a fresh coat of paint, leaving me to doubt his recommendation. However, lunch turned out every bit as delicious as he predicted. Miss Mabel had stepped out of the kitchen and hugged Marc. Nobody ever took our order because Marc always ordered the same thing. In addition to the chicken and macaroni and cheese, we had bowls of green beans and fried green tomatoes. Every bite had been delicious and left me in serious need of a nap.

On the drive back to Heyward Beach, we bounced around theories on the murder, some serious and some far-fetched. At last Marc dropped me at my house and took off to work on an old canoe.

Late that afternoon, Sunny and I entered Lovely Locks. I'd taken care of the pets on my afternoon schedule and wanted to spend time with my best friend. "Hey, Juliet."

She turned from removing permanent rods from an elderly woman's hair. "Hey there. What's up?"

"I thought you might like to join us for a walk on the beach."

"I would except I missed lunch today. Can we eat first?" She tossed some rods in the sink.

"I'll run over to Daily Java and pick up sandwiches."

"Sounds good. I'll text you when I'm done here."

I drove to the café so Sunny would be energetic for our walk. I pulled in and parked in the shade. In my rearview mirror, I spotted Danny's fancy Lexus. I counted to ten in French and practiced a few greetings before heat forced me out of the vehicle. Sunny stayed at my side as we entered the café. At the back-corner table, Danny sat with his laptop open and a mug at his side.

"Hey, what are you up to?" Lacey Jane circled around the counter and hugged me. "Sorry about backing out Saturday."

"No problem. I'm here to pick up sandwiches for Juliet and me. We're going for a walk on the beach. When do you get off?"

"Seven."

"Do you want to join us?"

"Thanks, but I've got plans." My sister avoided eye contact. "What would you like?"

I placed an order and paid. While Lacey Jane prepared our food, I strolled to the back of the building and stopped at Danny's table. "Your parents paid me a visit this weekend."

His head jerked back. "Really?"

"Yes. They accused me of scheming to get Peter's money. I can't believe you think I'd do something low down and rotten."

Danny stood, and Sunny growled.

"Easy, girl." I rubbed her back.

"I don't think you'd trick my uncle out of his money, but you've got to admit it's weird."

"Weird for him to leave money to a person who cared about him? We were friends. You can't choose your family, but you can choose your friends. Peter chose to be my friend, and he chose to leave me his estate. I won't apologize, because I didn't manipulate him in any way."

Danny huffed. "I'm not accusing you of anything."

I took a deep breath, unsure if I believed him or not. "Thanks. See you later."

"While you're here, I've got a question."

"What?" I tightened my grip on Sunny's leash.

"I'd like to ask your sister out on a date."

My stomach plunged. "Are you asking for my blessing? To date my sister?"

He jingled change in the pocket of his trousers like he had when we were in high school. "I guess you could put it that way."

"Danny, I don't care who you date, but if you break Lacey Jane's heart, you'll have Nate and me to answer to." Years before I hadn't let him watch me cry. I'd held my head high when he dumped me, but I would stick up for my little sister.

"I don't plan to break her heart."

I bit my tongue and left him standing there. Momma had taught us to keep our mouths shut if we didn't have anything nice to say, and nothing nice came to mind.

With a smile, Lacey Jane handed me a paper bag and two drinks. "I added chocolate chip cookies. My treat. What happened with you and Danny?"

"Be careful, sweetie. His family threatened to sue me over Peter's will. Don't say anything to them they can misconstrue and drag us to court over."

My sister bit her lower lip. "Danny said he's changed since y'all dated."

"Maybe he has. I've forgiven him, but I don't want him to hurt you." I tugged on my sister's hair. "You saw how angry he was the day he confronted me here."

"Yeah, but we all get angry at times."

I paused, considering her words. "True. Be careful, baby girl."

Lacey Jane nodded. "I will."

I exited the café with the food and a sinking feeling in my gut. My sister was older now than I was when I dated Danny. I only hoped she was wiser. Danny wasn't on my list of murder suspects, but he ranked number one on the heartbreaker list.

AT THE BEACH, Juliet and I devoured our food before starting a power walk along the beach. Sunny kept up with us. No problem.

Juliet said, "Sheriff Stone stopped by the beauty shop this afternoon."

The hairs on the back of my neck tingled, but maybe I was overreacting. "For a haircut?"

"No. He was looking for a shoplifter who stole some silver pieces from Paula's shop. I hadn't seen anybody, so he left. He's one fine-looking man."

"I thought you were interested—" I almost blurted out my brother's name. A relationship between my best friend and my brother could turn out beautiful, or it could go sideways, leaving life awkward for all of us.

"In who?"

"Never mind. Did he question you about me?"

"I'm afraid so. We talked in the break room, so none of the customers heard us."

So my fear wasn't unjustified. "What did he say?"

"He asked if I thought you killed Peter. I told him there's no possible way you'd ever hurt anybody. You get along with everybody."

Relief swept through me. I had good friends who always had my back. "Thanks. I saw Danny at Daily Java. He asked my permission to date Lacey Jane."

Juliet stopped and grabbed my arm. "What'd you say?"

"I told him not to break her heart."

"Do you trust him?"

"He said he's changed, but I don't believe him after the episode over the will. I've never seen him so angry."

"Maybe it was a one-time thing."

"Time will tell. So you're interested in Wade?"

Juliet released my arm and took off at our previous pace.

Sunny and I caught up with her. "You didn't answer me."

"I don't have my heart set on him, but if he asked me out I'd go. What's the latest on you? Maybe Wade will ask you out. Or what about Marc? You two seem to spend quite a bit of time together."

Her abrupt subject change made me curious but I bypassed it for now. "I'm definitely interested in Marc." If you can't be honest with your best friend, who can you share with? "It's the first time I've felt something for a man since Danny."

"Right man at the right time?"

"Who knows? He may not be interested in anything besides friendship. He's helping me solve the murder. Today we ruled out George Reeves." I updated her on my suspect list, and we turned to retrace our steps.

"What are you going to do with Peter's place?"

The mere question sent my heart into overdrive. "There's a lot of responsibility tied to this inheritance. It's part of South Carolina history, but I don't want to live in the house like Peter did." I described the property to Juliet.

"I love the idea of you incorporating your business and even expanding to dog training and rescuing pets. Wouldn't you have to live on the property, though?"

I slowed my pace. Sunny and Juliet followed my lead. "Yeah. You know I'm a beach girl, and I love my little house. Bungalow. Cottage. Whatever you want to call it, I love my home on the island. What am I going to do?"

"We'll pray about it. Something good will come of this gift."

"I hope you're right, my friend."

Chapter Thirty-Two

A MONOTONOUS series of bird chirps woke me up Tuesday morning. I texted Erin and asked if I could meet her and Corey for breakfast at the coffee shop. They agreed, and I hurried to take care of the animals in my care.

When I entered Daily Java, Erin waved at me from a table by the windows. "Your sister told me what you'd like. Hot vanilla caramel latte with a chocolate chip muffin."

"It looks yummy."

Corey finished his cup of black coffee. "I need a refill then we can talk."

I nibbled on my muffin and sipped my latte. "This is delicious. I'm going to get spoiled coming here so much."

"I appreciate your business."

Corey rejoined us and straddled the chair with his long legs. "What's on your mind, Andi Grace?"

I looked around the coffee shop, and nobody appeared interested in our conversation. "Can you keep this confidential?"

Both nodded, and I could tell I had their full attention.

"I was wondering if you could guide me on turning part of Peter's plantation into a museum."

Corey said, "You mean your plantation. Take ownership in the place. What'd you have in mind?"

"It's still in probate, but I want to be prepared if it works out. Can I donate the house to be toured? Like a museum or whatever. I'd like to keep some of the barns and turn them into dog kennels, a training facility, and a dog shelter. The kennels would be for me to keep dogs when their families go out of town. The shelter would be a different structure for stray or abandoned dogs." I held my breath waiting for his answer. Would he see through my request? I needed more information on his business habits.

Corey nodded. "Sure, it's possible. Would you like me to come out and see what you're working with?"

"Yes. It may not be big enough, but I want to be prepared."

"I understand. How about we meet there at one?"

"I can make it work. Thanks so much, Corey."

"I'll see you then." He stood and kissed Erin.

"I'll be in front of the main house. Thanks again."

Erin placed her empty mug on the wood table. "I'd love to join you."

"Absolutely. It's one of the reasons I wanted to meet with both of you."

"Not for a free breakfast?" Her smile didn't reassure me she was joking.

"No. One thing I've learned is if I can't afford to pay for something, I don't get it. I just thought it'd be more convenient for you to meet here." I opened my little crossover hipster bag and pulled a ten from my wallet.

Erin patted my hand. "Today is my treat."

"Hey, I understand what it's like to run a business. I'm not going to take advantage of you." I left the money on the table and stood. "I'll see you at one."

In my Suburban, I cranked the air on high and headed home. My thoughts swirled around Erin. Did she think I was making a play for her husband, or did she think I was trying to bum a free meal? Was a muffin and coffee truly a meal? I hadn't asked her for anything. She'd been waiting for me with the food. I didn't want to cause my sister to get fired, and I never caused a scene. Never ever, which was one reason considering me as a suspect in Peter's murder was ridiculous.

My thoughts drifted to the Lanes. Had Erin's mood changed when Corey left us alone? We'd gotten along fine the other night. The two of them had argued when alone but seemed good when the four of us ate ice cream together. Rumors around town indicated Corey was a womanizer. If they were true, it made sense that Erin didn't totally trust him around other women. Lacey Jane had told me Erin had been mad at Corey when he'd supposedly gone out for milk. Hence, the red roses. There was more to that story. Like he'd worn black and led my dogs away from the house so he could find the files I'd taken from Peter's place. Or had Corey killed Peter and meant to plant evidence at my house?

I pulled into the drive and parked. The best way to show Erin I had no interest in her husband was to reiterate I was in a relationship. I called Marc.

The sound of Marc's voice through the line gave me a warmth. "Hi."

"Hi. I hope it's not too early to call."

"No, ma'am. I've been awake and working for hours. What's up?"

"I've called to bribe you. If I bring you lunch, could you spare a few minutes to go with me to Peter's house and meet the Lanes?" I explained the situation.

"Not a problem. Come a little early, and I'll show you my latest project. I'm restoring an antique thirty-two-foot Prowler. It's a beauty. Bring Sunny along and the dogs can play here while we go to *your* house. Not Peter's."

"It's going to take a while for me to get used to saying that. I've never had anything handed to me on a silver platter before. Although Danny can fight me or something else might happen in probate."

"Peter's lawyer would know if he'd changed his will. Relax."

I laughed. "That's the other problem. It's hard to relax when I know I'm still a suspect in Peter's murder and I've got to make some kind of decision about the plantation."

"Take a deep breath."

I made a loud production of inhaling and exhaling. "Yeah, much better. I'll see you at lunchtime. Boat shed?"

"Chubb and I'll be there."

I smiled. Marc truly was a nice man. I pushed open the door and headed inside. It might be a good idea to try to fix my hair and look nice for my pretend boyfriend. Then I'd spray it with the expensive hairspray for humidity control. While I was at it, I might even apply a little makeup. With enough practice, I might get the hang of being a girlfriend.

I'D BEEN IMPRESSED with the Prowler Marc was working on, and he'd been impressed with the Cobb salad I brought him. It wasn't homemade, but I'd given him a healthy lunch option.

We now stood in the living room of the plantation house. Corey and Erin had explored the place, and they spoke in hushed tones in the kitchen.

I ran my hand over the grand piano. "Do you play?"

Marc shook his head. "Not really. I play guitar and tinker on the piano."

"Seriously? Did you take lessons?"

"I learned at one of my foster homes. One of the older boys taught me some basic chords, and I learned the rest on my own. What about you?"

"I took piano lessons as a child, but it's been years since I've played. Our piano was one of the things I sold when we moved. It brought a pretty price. Lacey Jane lost out on more lessons, but at the time I thought we needed the money."

"It takes strength to make the tough decisions."

His words thrilled me. No judgment from him, and he'd even paid me a compliment.

The Lanes entered the room, and we ended our conversation.

I leaned against the piano. "What do you think?"

Corey said, "I need to do a little research and figure out what makes it special here. We need an angle to attract tourists and locals so they'll want to visit here in addition to Richard Rice Plantation. The views of the river can't be beat. It'd also be a nice venue for weddings and afternoon teas."

"Except I don't want to be in charge of events. I want to focus on growing my business."

Marc slipped his arm around my shoulders. "Maybe you could hire somebody to be in charge of events. What about running a bed and breakfast?"

"Erin could handle it better than me. I don't think I have the gift of hospitality, and I don't enjoy baking."

Marc chuckled. "In the short time I've known you, I've figured out you're a caretaker but not much of a cook."

Erin said, "I could sell you baked goods if you decide to run this as a B&B, but you'll still have to serve beverages."

"And clean and wash sheets and so on and so forth." Running a B&B wasn't something I wanted to do. I'd taken care of my siblings, and I'd do it all over again, but it was time to make some decisions based on my desires. Caring for dogs was a better fit. "Erin, I don't suppose I could hire you to run this place. You could be in charge of turning the house into a B&B and find ways for the plantation to make money."

Her mood had mellowed since our private conversation this morning. "The coffee shop is a full-time job, but if I think of anybody who might be interested, I'll let you know."

Corey studied the antique books on the shelves. "I'll get back to you after a little more research. You might even find something in these books that would shed light on the historical significance of this place. Does it have an official plantation name?"

Marc said, "Kennady Plantation, according to the papers I signed when I bought my land. It's been divided up many times over the years, but I guess you could still call it by the original name."

Erin smiled. "I like the sound of it, and how many people board their dogs at a legitimate plantation?"

"Su-weet." Marc always made me smile when he said sweet in two syllables.

Corey returned a book to the shelves. "We better go, but I'll be in touch."

"Thanks so much for coming by."

After they left, Marc stood by the front door. "I've got to get back to work. What are your plans?"

"Since Thomas isn't working today, I think I'll go through the books like Corey suggested. Take my Suburban, and I'll walk over later."

"I don't like leaving you here alone."

I pulled my cell phone from my denim shorts pocket. "I've got the alarm codes and will set it when you leave."

"Is it charged?"

I verified I had plenty of energy. "Yes."

Marc ran his finger over my upper arm. "How about calling me if you see Thomas or Dylan."

"Deal." I locked and dead-bolted the door after he left and turned to the living room. Music would be nice but might prevent me from hearing somebody approach. I regretted leaving Sunny at Marc's place, but I wasn't a coward.

I moved to the shelves closest to the piano and began searching from bottom to top. It didn't take long to lose myself in family Bibles, ledgers, and antique history books.

Shadows filled the room by the time I came across two crisp white papers folded in fourths stuck in an autographed copy of *Gone with the Wind*. I opened the papers. Whoa. Important papers in an important book.

The first one contained the original estimate Thomas had given Peter for the addition. There was even a pencil drawing. A few items had been crossed off the list, along with their costs. A new total had been figured at the bottom of the page. This didn't match the figure I'd seen earlier, and it didn't equal the total price Thomas had given me.

The second page contained a drawing for a guest house, along with notes to tear down one of the stables. Why would Peter build a guest house? He rarely had company spend the night, so building a guest house seemed like a waste of money. Peter had always been careful with his finances. He must've had a good reason, but what could it have been?

It still didn't make sense for Peter to hire Thomas. Had Peter chosen Margaret Mitchell's book to hide the renovation papers in because he felt like his money had gone with the wind?

A vehicle rumbled, and tires popped on the gravel driveway.

Thomas appeared in his truck. He must have contacted Mr. Farmer instead of me. Once probate was over, if the place was mine, I'd be the only person with the codes to lock or unlock the doors.

I texted Marc and ran upstairs to the office with the papers. I needed to compare dates and prices before confronting Thomas King.

Chapter Thirty-Three

UPSTAIRS WAS WARMER than the first floor. I could turn on the air conditioning, but Thomas was walking around the main rooms and I didn't want the upstairs floors to creak and tip him off. I perspired like crazy. Thomas wasn't supposed to be in any part of the house except the addition—he wasn't a complete idiot. He was up to no good.

I checked my phone. No reply from Marc, so I texted again. I sat in Peter's desk chair and listened so hard pressure filled my ears.

What was Thomas doing? From the sound of his footsteps, he was either in the living or dining room.

The sound of a squeaky drawer reached me.

I really needed to inventory this place, but I'd need another set of eyes. Regina maybe. Thomas could be stealing valuable items from the house, and I wouldn't have any idea.

I checked my phone. Still no reply from Marc. My heart pounded. What if Marc had dropped his phone in the river and nobody knew I'd run into Thomas?

I texted Juliet.

> I'm at plantation house. Thomas is here. Would you call Marc and see if he received my text? Also ask Regina if she'd help me inventory Peter's belongings. Thanks.

I sent the message.

My phone vibrated. Marc. He was heading over with both dogs.

I thanked him and let Juliet know I'd located Marc. In no time, I heard an approaching vehicle and barking dogs.

Thomas's footsteps hustled, and a door slammed.

Relief flooded through me, and my body relaxed. I hurried downstairs and surveyed the living room. Nothing seemed disturbed. In the dining room, I found a buffet drawer ajar. I opened it with my pinky finger in order not to get my prints all over it.

The drawer was lined with velvet. Silver forks, knives, spoons, and salad forks lay neatly arranged. The spoon compartment was half-full, compared to the other sections. Had Thomas stooped to stealing my silver?

The dogs clomped up the wooden front steps, and I opened the door to let them and Marc inside.

He pulled me to him and gave me what my daddy used to call a bear hug. "I was so worried. Are you okay?"

The shakes hit me, but I held on to Marc. "Fine now that you're here."

"I'm so sorry I didn't see your first message. What happened?"

The dogs circled around us.

I said, "Sit, Sunny. Sit, Chubb." My dog obeyed first, and Chubb followed her lead. "Good job."

Marc took my hand and led me to the rockers on the front porch. "Does this give us enough privacy?"

I heard the sound of some kind of electric tool whirling in the distance. "Yes, this should work. Thomas showed up, and he came inside the house. I ran upstairs and listened. Marc, he was in the main house. Not just the room he's adding on, but the dining room. I think he's stealing the silver. Do you think his situation is so dire he's pawning off items from Peter's house?"

"All I know is we need to call the sheriff."

I sighed. "You're right. I probably should tell him everything I'm finding out. I don't want to get in more trouble with him."

"I agree. Even if he's not thrilled with you interviewing your own list of suspects, he needs to know."

It took a while for Wade to arrive. My regular life on the beach was closer to law enforcement—living in the country took some getting used to.

When we had settled at the kitchen table, Wade bounced his legs. He'd always had excess energy—the reason he made such a good football player. "Running a murder investigation requires a special kind of knowledge and training. Andi Grace, you may still think you're the smartest kid in our graduating class, but this isn't high school."

Wade's words stung. My throat tightened. "I never thought I was the smartest person in our class."

His brows bobbed. "You always had high grades on exams and got all kinds of academic awards."

His words were true, but I'd never bragged about it. In fact, I'd kept quiet because it wasn't cool to be smart.

Marc cleared his throat. "I think we've gotten off track here. What are we going to do about Thomas?"

"My men are questioning him outside, and I plan to read him the riot act. To book him for trespassing is a gray area because he has access to the house."

My jumped to my feet and threw up my hands. "What about the silver he may have stolen? Can you look around for it? Maybe you could dust for fingerprints on the buffet?"

Wade crossed his arms and frowned. "I'm handling this, Andi Grace. Trust me."

I returned to my seat and dropped my head. "I do." He deserved credit for taking notes on everything I'd shared about my suspect list.

"We're going to be here for a while. Whether we release Thomas or take him in, he's going to be angry. You need to decide how you're going to handle the addition."

I took a deep breath. Thomas wasn't out of my life yet. "I don't think I can afford to hire another contractor to finish the work."

Marc said, "I don't know anything about electrical, but I can help with other aspects."

My heart softened again toward Marc. If he continued to be so nice, I'd be putty in his hands. "Thanks, Marc, but I know you've got your own business. Besides, Thomas has been paid for this job."

"It's not worth getting hurt over," Marc said.

"Marc's right. We don't know how dangerous Thomas King is. Don't go near him by yourself." Wade put his notebook away.

I looked at each man. "Do you mean don't come to the house alone?"

Wade said, "That'd be the smart thing to do."

"Right." Was the man taunting me? It didn't matter. "Okay, but I won't allow Thomas to steamroll over me. I'll be better prepared next time I come here."

Marc reached for my hand. "I think the sheriff has better things to do than talk to us. Let's go so he can do his job."

I met Wade's gaze before standing. "Will you let me know if you find the silver?"

"Yes." He stood and plopped his hat onto his head.

"Will you lock up and call me so I can set the security system?"

"Yes," Wade said, his tone clipped.

Uh oh. "Thanks."

It wouldn't do to get on Wade's bad side. After all, George Reeves had made a good point. I'd gained the most financially from Peter's death. Nobody cared I didn't want all of this. I'd give it all back in a heartbeat if it could bring Peter back. Too bad life didn't work that way.

My first goal would be to help catch the killer. Once he was caught, he couldn't kill again, and I'd be found innocent. Then I'd decide what to do about the plantation and all of the headaches involved. Some people dreamt of a big inheritance. I didn't want to appear ungrateful, but getting Peter's plantation was turning into a nightmare.

Chapter Thirty-Four

"SWEETIE, I CAN'T believe you had Thomas King arrested." Juliet used wooden spoons to toss a salad in my largest bowl. "You're asking for trouble."

I filled four glasses with ice. "I really didn't have much choice. I was minding my own business at the plantation house when Thomas showed up and pilfered some of the silver."

My phone buzzed, and I reached for it.

"Andi Grace, this is Corey. Have you got a minute?"

Surprised by his fast response, I glanced out the window. Marc and Nate stood on the deck talking while the chicken grilled. They didn't look in a hurry. "What's up?"

"The plantation definitely is part of our South Carolina history, but I see a few problems."

I grabbed a pen and notepad and sat at the kitchen table ready to take notes. "Like what?"

"Your place isn't as big as many of the other plantations, and you're off the main highway. If the past owner hadn't parceled the land off, you'd have a better shot at being a tourist attraction."

My heart sank. "What about running a B&B?"

"With the right property manager, I believe that's where you'll show a profit. I know this isn't what you hoped to hear."

I tapped the pen against the paper. "No, it isn't, but I appreciate your opinion. Thanks so much, Corey." I hung up and doodled on the pad. Rumors abounded about Corey, so why was he being nice to me?

Juliet asked, "What's going on?"

I explained my dilemma. "I don't want to run a B&B, but I feel a responsibility to do the right thing. Selling out to George Reeves wouldn't be good for the environment or the neighbors."

"Girlfriend, we need to talk." Juliet sat beside me. "First, you don't always have to do the right thing for everybody else."

"But?"

"Do you remember all those years ago when we were trying to

figure out our lives? You started your business because you could work around Nate and Lacey Jane's schedules. It wasn't your original dream to be both parents to your siblings. Becoming a hair stylist wasn't my original dream. Don't get me wrong, I enjoy helping women look their best. Attending cosmetology school was a fast way to get some kind of education. It's been a good career for me."

"What are you getting at?"

"Do you remember I took business classes before I bought the salon?"

"Yes." I was still confused but gave Juliet time to get to the point. "Did you just mention turning the plantation into a B&B?"

"Yes, it's what Corey suggested." The clouds cleared. "Do you want to run a B&B on my property?"

"I can do it, Andi Grace." She turned to a clean page on my notepad. "Start taking notes. We can boast of organic locally grown breakfast foods. We can cater to special diets. Paleo, keto, vegan, and diabetics. Are you writing this down?"

"No." I clicked my pen and scribbled the words. "Keep going."

"Do you have a boat dock?"

"It's not in as good a shape as Marc's."

"We can get it checked out. If it's up to par, we can be approached by boat or car. Maybe offer kayak or canoe rides."

"Corey mentioned we'd be a good location for weddings and other gatherings."

"I can do that. If we need any construction done, I'll ask Griffin to come up for a few days. We're not going to deal with Thomas King anymore."

I stopped writing. "I never would've hired Thomas. I guess I inherited him, along with the estate." I tapped my pen on the pad. "I can't figure out why Peter hired him. He was so much better at business than to hire someone like Thomas."

"I wonder when the cops will release him?"

"With my luck, he's already out on bail."

Juliet rubbed her hands together. "I want to go through the house and see what I've got to work with."

"Okay. Any chance you'd want to live there?"

"By myself?" Juliet's voice squeaked and her eyes went wide.

"If you run the B&B, won't you have to?"

She blinked. "I guess. Don't you want to live there?"

"I'm a simple girl, and I love my simple home. Peter's place is just too much for me. I'd already been thinking I'd live in one of the other buildings on the property." I loved the idea of Juliet taking charge of the house. "How would you feel about living in the big house?"

"I lived in filthy apartments and trailers growing up. The place I have now is clean but small. Like you said, it'll be easier to run the B&B if I lived in the plantation house."

I cocked my head and studied my best friend. "Why do you want to do this?"

"It could be a lot of fun. I'll have freedom to grow a garden and prepare food for others. I won't be stuck in a salon all day long. I'll meet new and interesting people." Excitement colored her face. "My creative juices are flowing. Some days, I do the same thing over and over. Then I wake up the next day to do the same thing. Oh, if we do weddings, the bridal party could stay at the house. I can even provide food for the bridal party and the groomsmen."

My friend's eyes sparkled, and I believed in her. "Okay. Let's do it."

Marc and Nate entered the kitchen. "The chicken's ready."

I smiled at Marc. "We're ready too."

We dished the salad into four large bowls and topped it with the grilled chicken. Our dinner conversation revolved around turning the plantation into a business.

When we finished, I rinsed the dishes and loaded the dishwasher. "Should we drive out there this evening? It won't get dark until eight-thirty or later."

Nate nodded. "May as well while we're all together. Sis, why don't you ride out with Marc. I'll drive Jules, and the three of us can ride back together."

"Sounds like a plan."

When we reached the plantation house there was no sign of Thomas. Either he was in jail or had given up working on the house for today.

"Out of respect to Wade, I'm going to text him." I alerted him we were at the plantation and in less than a minute my phone rang.

"What are you up to, Andi Grace?"

"We're not here looking for clues. I've got to figure out what to do with this place. I'm here with Marc, Nate, and Juliet Reed. She's considering running the house as a B&B."

"Okay."

"Is Thomas out of jail?"

"Not that I'm aware of. Why?"

"The lights are on in the addition."

He sighed. "Maybe one of my deputies left them on. Do you want me to come out there?"

"I'm sure we're fine, but I wanted to keep you informed. I want you to trust me and believe I'm innocent of Peter's murder."

"Thanks for the notice. Call me if you run into trouble."

I disconnected and looked at the others. "Wade seems okay with us going through the house."

Juliet pulled a sketch pad and notebook from her oversized bag. "Do you mind if I draw some of the rooms?"

"Knock yourself out. I'll sort through the books in the living room and remove the ledgers and books that won't appeal to guests. We can make one side of the room historical books and the other side can be bestsellers and such."

Marc shook his head. "It's one thing to go through the house, but until you've gone through probate, I think it's better not to change things around."

Juliet stopped sketching. "Are there any rooms I can't go in?"

"Make yourself at home."

Nate said, "I'm going outside to study the landscaping."

Juliet and Nate disappeared, and Marc turned to me. "Can I do anything?"

"Let's see what Peter's got in his library. I won't get rid of any books though. I forgot to mention I found paperwork for what I think is the original quote Thomas made Peter." I reached into my shorts pocket and pulled out the folded paper.

Marc studied the page. "Let's hold onto this and not confront Thomas right now. He's probably angry enough about the arrest."

"Then he shouldn't have stolen my silver." I took a deep breath and counted to ten in French. "It's wrong for Thomas to help himself to anything he wants."

"I agree." He set his phone on the desk and it played country music. "Do you mind?"

"It's a nice touch." I perused a shelf of South Carolina history books.

I lost track of time. Most people think I never stop moving. They see me with the dogs, and I attended my siblings' school functions. What they didn't realize was how much I loved to read. Peter's books were a treasure I'd enjoy. By the time I'd finished one section, I had a kink in my neck. I stretched my arms over my head and rolled my head back.

Marc sat in the leather wingback chair looking at a photo album.

"Did you find some interesting pictures?"

"They aren't organized, but there are some of Peter with Danny's mother."

Curious, I pulled over the desk chair and sat beside Marc. "Let me see."

"Right here. Don't you think the young woman looks like Danny's mom?"

"It's definitely her."

Marc turned the page, and Danny's mom held a baby in her arms.

I'd dreamed of marrying Danny and having his babies. It didn't hurt anymore to imagine life without him, and I had Marc to thank for my progress.

Marc turned the pages again and again. He said, "Peter seemed to enjoy owning fast cars. Will you keep his car or continue driving your Suburban?"

"I like big vehicles and will keep my SUV."

"He'd want you to enjoy it."

"My Suburban fits my life better."

"But it's a Camaro. Who doesn't want to drive a fancy sports car?"

I laughed. Spoken like the stereotypical male. "Do you have any idea how many speeding tickets I might get in a Camaro?"

"Lead foot?"

"If I'm not careful, I drive too fast. I use cruise control as much as possible to keep me a law-abiding citizen."

A tiny smile hinted at his lips. "I'm surprised you speed."

"It's really a combination of two bad habits. I'm usually running late, which causes me to drive fast."

Marc shook his head. "I'll have to add those to my list."

"List? What list? Wait, are you keeping a list of my bad habits?" My face grew warm. Surely, he was teasing.

"As a person who likes to keep lists yourself, I'd think you would appreciate my effort."

"I'd rather hear you were making a list of my good traits."

"Who says I'm not?" His smile warmed me.

I tipped my nose in the air. "Nice, but still intimidating. Some might go so far as to say creepy."

Marc chuckled. "I'm just messing with you. There's not a list."

"Good to know." He'd made a decent point, though. I loved lists— as long as I wasn't the subject.

He turned the page and whistled. "Did Peter get a new sports car every year?"

"Yeah. He liked leasing cars. He told me it was fun to drive different makes and models. It was one of the few ways he didn't mind blowing money. Why?"

"Check this out." Marc pointed to the page in the photo album. "He printed the year on each picture. It doesn't look like he ever leased the same car two years in a row."

I thought about all the years I'd known Peter. "You may be right. He didn't have a real pattern, though. I've known him to drive Beemers, Audis, Camaros, and Corvettes. Peter once told me he got more tickets the years he picked red cars. He didn't know if he drove red cars faster or if cops looked for red cars more."

Marc turned the page then went back. "Peter was forty when he died. It looks like he drove a Mustang during high school and college." Marc tapped a picture. "1967 Mustang. It's a classic."

The next picture was a BMW. "Do you think this is the first car he bought after graduating from college?"

"Maybe." Marc turned the pages back and forth. Men and their cars.

I didn't really care too much and allowed my thoughts to drift. If Juliet took over running the plantation, I could focus on my dog business and shelter. In the beginning, it'd be easier to focus only on dogs. Later, I could expand and rescue other animals.

"What year did you meet Peter?"

"Twelve years ago this month. Hard to believe." Life had turned out very different than I'd imagined, but Nate and Lacey Jane had finished growing up in a safe and loving home. Neither one seemed warped from living with me. "Why?"

"Peter had two different cars that year. I wonder why?" He pointed to two pictures. "Do you remember either one of these?"

"The Highlander seems familiar. I don't remember the BMW, though." It was a white convertible.

My body stilled. White convertible sports car. My parents had been hit by a white convertible sports car. An eyewitness had reported seeing the car, but had he named the make? The witness had told the cops the car hit my parents, sped up, and sideswiped a blue car parked on the side of the street. Chills covered my body. A whimper slipped out.

"Andi Grace, what's wrong?" Marc dropped the book.

Spots danced before my eyes.

"You're white as a sheet. Don't pass out on me. Put your head between your knees." With one hand on my back and the other on my head, Marc eased me forward.

I breathed in. And out. In. Out. My vision cleared, and I sat up. "I think I'm okay now."

"You're still pale. Don't stand yet."

The kitchen door squeaked open and banged shut. Nate called out, "It's getting too dark to see much more." As a child, he'd never hesitated to start a conversation whether he was in the same room or not. Seemed like he hadn't outgrown the habit.

I sat up, but Marc remained kneeling by my side.

Nate entered the room. "Andi Grace, you're white as a ghost crab."

Marc said, "That's what I told her. I thought she was going to pass out on me."

I stood but the room swayed. "Whoa."

"Sis, you better sit back down." Nate nudged me into the chair. "I know you ate dinner. Maybe you're dehydrated."

I shook my head. "No. We need to look through Peter's files. I think he has one labeled cars."

Nate scratched his head. "You about faint and want to look at Peter's files? Why?"

"Baby brother . . . I can't believe I'm going to say this."

Marc squeezed my hands in an encouraging way.

Nate stepped closer. "Say what?"

"I never understood why Peter took such interest in us."

Nate dropped to the edge of the coffee table. "Go on."

Juliet walked into the room, hugging her notebook and sketch pad to her chest. "Y'all look pretty serious."

Nate stood and pulled over a chair. "Have a seat. I think Andi Grace is about to drop a bomb on us."

Juliet didn't utter another word but sat in the chair Nate offered.

Three sets of eyes looked at me.

I licked my dry lips. "I think Peter was the hit-and-run driver who killed Mom and Dad."

Chapter Thirty-Five

WADE MET US AT the house. My real house. We gathered in the family room. Sunny kept her eye on the sheriff and remained at my side as I shuffled through Peter's files. My hands shook. "They aren't alphabetical. I'd been focused on reasons for murder when I sorted through them the first time."

Marc rubbed his hand along my shoulders. "Let's divide them. It'll be quicker."

I nodded. A nauseous feeling hit me, but I wouldn't vomit. I couldn't allow myself to lose focus. We each took a stack and searched. All of the manila folders were labeled in Peter's small, neat handwriting. "Nate, do you think it's possible I became friends with the man who killed our parents?"

My brother's hands stopped moving. "If so, he fooled us all."

"How could I have been so naïve? He moved to Heyward Beach at the same time Mom and Dad died. Shouldn't I have been suspicious?"

"Sis, you can't beat yourself up over Peter. Plus, we don't know anything for sure. Let's find the car folder and go from there."

My ever-practical brother returned his attention to the files in front of him.

Juliet, Marc, and Wade had remained silent during our exchange.

Worry wouldn't help, so I looked through my stack of files, with Sunny still at my side. I prayed for strength to handle the discovery.

Juliet raised a folder in the air. "I think this is it."

Wade reached out a hand. "Let me see."

We all gathered close as Wade opened the folder. He turned one page at a time until he'd glanced at every page in the folder.

Wade said, "I'll take these to the station and find the files on your parents' deaths."

I held out my hand. "Wait, I want to make a copy of what you take, and I've got some information on the wreck that killed my parents. I can make a copy for you on my printer."

"Andi Grace, let me handle this."

"They are my files. I did the right thing by contacting you, Wade. At least let me make copies."

His face relaxed. "I'm mighty thirsty."

I stilled. Was he giving me a secret message? "I've got Cokes in the fridge. Uh, Juliet, would you take Wade to the kitchen and fix him a drink. May as well fix everybody something."

I motioned for Nate to follow them and when the coast was clear, I grabbed the folder and darted into my office.

Marc entered the room. "I don't feel good about this."

"Wade practically gave me permission." I turned on my copier and made duplicates of Peter's car records and newspaper clippings about my parents and the wreck.

Marc paced.

"The files were in my possession. I'm the one who started connecting the dots between Peter and the hit-and-run driver. Not Wade and not the cops twelve years ago."

"That's true, but . . . how will you feel if you discover the truth?"

"I'm not sure." I plucked out a gray folder from between green and yellow files. Unlike Peter, I kept colorful files. All of the pet files were blue. Green for money issues. Gray for death. Yellow for inspirational stories or quotes.

"Sure." My limbs grew heavy, and the desire to sleep hit me hard. "Do you think Peter is the one?"

"I can't say at this point."

I finished the copies and put the originals into Peter's folder. "It makes sense in a way. He's at fault for the wreck that killed my parents. He panics and runs. Guilt leads him to check on my family. More guilt forces him to reach out and help us. Because he was at fault, he loaned me money to start my business and he taught me some beginning business basics. Guilty, guilty, guilty. How could I have been so blind?"

"You had a lot to deal with, and you were young and innocent. Didn't you once say some other people reached out to you? Are you going to doubt all of them?"

I shook my head. "Of course not, but those people knew me for years. Peter was a stranger." I shuffled through my duplicates and stopped when I came to the white BMW. It was a beautiful car, but what had happened to it? If Peter had gotten an estimate on repairing the vehicle, wouldn't it have been in the file? "Do you suppose there's a separate insurance file with a claim for the wreck?"

Marc shook his head. "No. Peter was too smart to file a claim if his car was involved in the hit-and-run. Money wasn't an issue. If he was smart, he would've paid off the sports car and then leased the Highlander. Everybody knows Peter was a smart man."

"So where is the BMW?"

"Very good question." Marc picked up the file for Wade. "I'm going to put this in your family room."

When Marc returned, I sighed. "Peter didn't gamble. He'd erase any trail from the car to him. How do you get rid of a car? Bury it? Drive it into a lake or down a mountain?"

Marc leaned against the doorframe. "You'd need a backhoe to bury something so big. Maybe he sold it in another town or burned it if the thing was totaled."

I crossed the room to where Marc stood. "It all seems so cold and calculating."

"I agree." He took my hands in his. "Your guests are in the family room now. Let's go."

We joined the others.

Wade picked up the folder. "Andi Grace, trust me. I'm handling Peter's murder, and I'll look into the old records of your parents' hit-and-run. I remember the summer they were killed. I'd already been considering a career in law enforcement, and I spent a lot of time wondering what kind of person could run over two people and not even stop. When the news reported a white vehicle had run them down, I looked twice at every white car. I'd love to review their case."

"Will you come to me with any questions or discoveries?"

"Yes. Give me twenty-four hours. Let's meet for breakfast Thursday morning at the BBQ Shack."

Despite its name, the BBQ Shack had an amazing low country breakfast buffet. "Okay. Marc's my attorney. Do you mind if he joins us?"

"I think it'd be a good idea. Nate and Lacey Jane may as well meet us too. See you Thursday." He walked out of my house with the papers.

I looked at the other three people. "What do y'all think?"

Nate patted my shoulder. "Give Wade a chance."

Marc pinched the bridge of his nose. "If we discover Peter was the hit-and-run driver who killed your parents, you would've had even more motive to be Peter's killer."

"I didn't suspect he was the driver until today." I gulped. How did

I keep getting deeper into trouble? What had started as a quest to prove my innocence and to make a stand for justice was quickly biting me in the backside.

Chapter Thirty-Six

LATE WEDNESDAY morning, I showed up at Marc's boat shed. "Knock, knock."

He laid his sandpaper on a workhorse and wiped his hands on his khaki shorts. His bright blue T-shirt claimed fishing was cheaper than therapy. "Hi. This is a nice surprise."

"Since trouble seems to follow me these days, I appreciate your words more than you know. I've got something for you."

"Su-weet."

He followed me to the Suburban, and I paused before opening the back. "If you don't like it, just say so."

"I'm sure I'll like it."

A sudden attack of nerves caused me to doubt his words. Too late, though. I opened the door and pulled out a circular metal sign. Butterflies swarmed in my stomach. "BJ's Wood Boats. Short and simple. What do you think?"

"I'm speechless." He blinked three times.

"I thought you could hang it on the outside of your boat shed." I handed him the sign and reached back into the vehicle. "I thought these could go on the road and your dock." I held up weather-treated signs advertising BJ's Wood Boats.

Marc nodded and disappeared into the shed.

My feet refused to move. I didn't know whether to follow Marc or skedaddle.

He came back out with a hammer in one hand. "Let's hang it."

Air whooshed out of me. I hadn't realized I'd been holding my breath. Silly to be this nervous over a gift. "So you like it?"

Marc leaned the sign against the building and approached me. He wrapped me in his arms. "This is the nicest gift I've ever gotten. It means more than you know."

A lump filled my throat. Poor Marc. How could this be the nicest gift he'd received? My heart broke for his sad childhood. "You must think I'm the biggest brat ever. At least I had my parents for eighteen years."

"Shh. My parents died in an accident. Plain and simple. Somebody needs to be held accountable for running over your parents and killing them."

"How did you get to be so amazing?"

He laughed. "I'm not, and the longer you know me, the more you'll realize it. Let's hang my new sign."

I helped Marc find the best spot so when a customer drove up they'd know they were in the right place. "It looks good."

"I agree. Do you want to hang out for a bit? Maybe we can talk while I work on the boat I'm building."

In the shed, I looked over his plans for a runabout. "You've come a long way. How many hours did this take you?"

"A bunch."

"When did you find the time?"

He shrugged. "I don't require but about five hours of sleep a night. I get up early and stay up late."

"Wow. I wonder how much work I'd accomplish if I only slept five hours." I looked at the shell of a boat. "Is this for somebody in particular?"

"A man from Georgetown."

"Do you only build one boat at a time?"

"I'm a one-man operation but can juggle three boats at once. I pay a guy to run my website, but I take care of everything else."

"There's a lot of space in here." Epoxy, bungee cords, varnish, paint, boat seats, paint brushes and squeegees filled wooden shelves along one wall.

"Yeah. Isn't it great? When I work on kayaks and canoes, I can have more than one going at a time."

"This is bigger than a garage."

Marc swiped a dry cloth along the wood structure. "Yeah, what are you thinking?"

Garages. Cars. Boat sheds. The hair on my arms popped up. "Hey, when we drove around Peter's land, we only entered one of the buildings. What if he hid his BMW right on his property?"

He stopped wiping and stared at me. "Interesting theory."

"The papers I found in the library showed Peter wanted to demolish one building to build a guest house. Hold on." I ran to my SUV, grabbed my backpack, and returned to the boat shed.

A smile coasted across his face. "You just happened to have them with you? Let's sit outside." He motioned to a bench under an old oak tree.

I sat first, and Marc filled the remaining space. "Whatcha got in there?"

"I decided to start carrying Peter's important papers and my notes about his murder with me. No more running back and forth like a chicken with its head cut off." It didn't take long to pull out my file. Red folder for Peter's murder. Soon I found the folded pages with the estimate and plan for destroying the old stable.

Marc's arm rubbed against mine as he leaned close.

The effort it took to breathe normally had nothing to do with the summer heat or distress over Peter's murder. Marc's closeness made it hard to think straight, much less inhale. "See? He wanted to demolish the stable. It'd be large enough to hide a car. Right?"

"Yes."

"Why do you suppose he didn't file this contract with the other contracts and papers on the addition?"

Marc leaned even closer to the pages in my hand. "Not sure."

It became harder to focus with Marc so near. "Here. You can hold them."

"What if I can see fine and this is just an excuse to be near you?"

My heart zoomed straight to triple-time. "Is it? We're only pretend dating."

"Maybe we should leave out the word pretend."

I gulped. "You want to date me? For real?"

"Yeah. I do." His dimple appeared and his eyes crinkled.

"Why?" The word blurted out of my mouth before I could stop myself.

He snapped his fingers and laughed. "This would be the perfect time for a list. I could read off the reasons why. Maybe we should table this discussion until Peter's killer is caught. Do you want to look through the stable?"

"I absolutely do." I also wanted to be Marc's real girlfriend. Why hadn't I kept my big mouth shut? At least he said we'd return to the conversation of dating. One thing I'd learned in the last few days was Marc Williams was a man of his word.

Chapter Thirty-Seven

I BATTED AT THE cobwebs filling the doorframe of the stable. "Oh, my gracious. This place has fallen into disrepair. Why did Peter ignore this part of his property? How long do you suppose it's been since somebody walked through these doors?"

Marc attacked the webs on his side of the entryway. "Maybe we chose the wrong place to enter."

The musty smell choked me. But if the key to my parents' death lay in this structure, I wouldn't let a few spiderwebs and the stench stop me.

Marc coughed. "I'm going to open as many doors as possible so we can see better."

"Fresh air will be good. I'll help." I turned right, and Marc swerved ed left. We opened every door and window in the building.

"Hey, you need to see this."

Expecting to find the banged-up white BMW, I hurried to Marc. When I reached him there was no sign of a car. "What?"

"Look how clean this entryway is. Every other one I opened was covered with cobwebs."

"You're right. This means somebody's been out here recently."

"My thoughts exactly."

I bent down to study the wood flooring. Nothing jumped out at me. "I can't distinguish any specific footprints."

"Let's keep exploring and see what we can find."

The first bay contained a broken-down carriage. It angled toward the left and a thick wool floral blanket was draped over the driver's seat. "It's no surrey with the fringe on top."

Marc chuckled. "True that. I wonder why it's out here and not in the carriage house?"

"Who knows? There's no car, which is all I really care about." I entered the next area. Lamps, old pictures, an oven, brooms, and more junk than I'd have dreamed. "What a pigsty. If Peter couldn't take care of his property, why did he think I could? He was one of the neatest people I knew. Neat, as in organized. Except for dog toys, he rarely had a thing out of place in his home."

"Maybe the house was so neat because he put his junk out here." Marc nudged me forward with his hand on the small of my back.

We passed two stalls with rusty and rotting horse-drawn carriages. The next area contained a large lump covered by a painter's tarp. Paint stains covered the thick off-white material, and my heart ratcheted up to warp speed.

Marc asked, "Do you want the honors?"

"Let's do it together." Each one of us lifted a corner of the tarp. I clenched the material tight. "I don't know if I'm more scared to find Peter's car or to not find it. This is a huge moment. It could answer so many questions from twelve years ago."

"We don't have to look under here, but once we do, there's no turning back."

I bit my lower lip. "I need to know the truth."

"You know we could have the sheriff do this." He paused. "So we're going to look?"

"Yes. On the count of three. *Un. Deux. Trois.*" I breathed in and tugged on the cloth. There sat an old white BMW sports car. I moved to the passenger side. A dent and a streak of blue ran along the side. I dropped my hold on the cover and leaned against the wooden wall dividing this stall from the next. "Oh, Marc. I was hoping it wasn't so."

"This doesn't prove anything for sure. We need to call Wade."

"What's the point? Peter's dead."

"Yes, but what if somebody found the car and was blackmailing Peter? It could be the motive for murder."

My legs shook so hard, I wasn't sure I could remain upright, even though I was leaning against the wall. "Who could've found it? I mean, Peter would have had to agree to let somebody in here. If he remembered he'd hidden the car in this stable, he wouldn't have allowed anybody to enter the building."

"Yes, but why didn't he have the place secured? We walked right in and even opened the other doors and windows. If this was the car that hit your parents, he should've hidden it better."

"It's not too close to the house, and nobody found it in twelve years."

"True. It's farther from the main house than some of the other outbuildings."

I lowered myself to the dirty floor and rested my back on the wall.

"It was a good hiding place for twelve years. What changed?"

Marc paced in front of the car. "Suppose Peter only wanted to add onto his house at first. Then, for some reason, he decides he needs to get rid of the car. Peter might have asked Thomas if he'd be interested in tearing down the stable and building a guest house in its place. Peter's only curious at this point. Not serious enough to get rid of the Beemer yet."

My eyes drifted from Marc to the vehicle. "Keep going."

"You remember how Thomas jumped on me about remodeling my kitchen. He didn't give me time to change my mind. He was full throttle. If Peter had even hinted about demolishing this place to build a guest house, Thomas would've come out and explored the area."

"Right. He would've come up with a fake house plan to build. Fake like the drawing he did for your kitchen remodel." I took a deep breath.

"Exactly. Sit here and catch your breath. I'm going to call Wade." Marc left me sitting next to the car that probably ended my parents' lives. I couldn't blame the car. The driver killed my parents and hadn't owned up to the truth.

The hair on the back of my neck popped up. I turned to find a gun in my face.

Thomas whispered, "Stay quiet and follow me if you don't want your boyfriend to get hurt."

My heart near about jumped out of my chest.

"Move," he hissed, and the gun glanced off my temple.

I stood and fought off a wave of dizziness. "Where are we going?"

Even in the dim light, I could see Thomas's eyes widen. He didn't have a plan.

"Thomas, you didn't mean to kill Peter. Did you?"

"Shut up and walk." He shook the gun at me.

I headed toward the door, where Marc had disappeared into the sunshine and freedom.

"Not that way. Over there."

I sighed. Thomas wanted me to leave through the door where we'd first entered. I plodded along, in hopes Marc would return soon. "Thomas, I don't think you're a murderer. What happened? Did you find the car and try to blackmail Peter?" The man was always looking to make a quick buck.

"It should've been so easy." He poked the gun against my spine, and I picked up the pace.

Through the door, I saw his truck a short distance away. Why hadn't I heard him approach? Had Marc and I been in deep conversation, or had I been lost in my thoughts? "You'll probably get a reward for solving the crime. It's a cold case, but it's still a case."

"What good is a reward if they throw me in jail for killing Peter?"

I turned and faced him. "Did you mean to kill him?"

He shook his head so hard the black strands of hair slapped his cheeks. "No."

"Tell me about it." I kept my voice as smooth as possible.

"We had an argument about the blackmail. I wanted him to get me the job at Richard Rice Plantation. It would've been so easy. The others would have listened to Peter Roth."

I caught movement in the shadows, but I didn't dare react because Thomas still pointed his gun at me. "See, I knew it. An accident is different than cold-blooded murder. How did it happen?"

"Peter refused to help me. Claimed to be a man of integrity. If that was so, he wouldn't have hidden the car. Heck, he wouldn't have left your parents to die."

My heart raced, and it became hard to breathe. "You're right. Peter should've helped my mom and dad instead of leaving. What happened after Peter refused to give you a job?"

"I told him he was a coward for leaving the scene of the accident. He kept arguing, and I got madder and madder. I don't even remember picking up one of his fancy paperweights. Next thing I knew, he was on the ground and not moving. The paperweight was in my hand, and I hightailed it out of there. When I got home and saw the paperweight in my truck, I buried it in the woods. It'll never be found. Don't waste your time trying to look for it. You know, if Peter had recommended me for the job, he'd be alive today. Too bad you kept pushing for the truth. Now I'm going to have to get rid of you."

"No. Wait, Thomas. If you kill me, it'll be harder to get off. Think about Dylan. He needs you in his life. Guys always need their dads for guidance and advice."

"He never needed me."

"You're wrong and you know it. Show him how to be a good man and turn yourself in. I know a good attorney."

"I can't afford a fancy lawyer."

Marc stepped from the shadows. "I'll represent you for a reduced fee."

Thomas whipped around and pointed the gun at Marc with a shaky hand. "Stay back."

Marc held up his hands. "I only want to talk."

Loud music blasted through the air, like the kind Dylan enjoyed. Tires rolled over the path leading to the stable. Both sounds grew louder.

I caught the flash of a black van proving my theory. "It's Dylan. Don't let him find you holding a gun on us."

Marc approached Thomas. "Give me the gun."

With two hands wrapped around the weapon, Thomas aimed at Marc. "Stay back." He swung the gun in my direction. "Or I'll kill your girlfriend."

"Whoa, whoa, whoa. Leave her out of this."

Thomas snorted. "She's the one who started snooping all over the place. She deserves to die."

"Let's handle this man to man."

He whipped around, aiming the gun at Marc.

Brakes squealed to a stop, and the music ended. "Dad!" Dylan called. "Where are you?"

I gasped. "Thomas, please, put the gun down. We'll help sort everything out."

"I already kilt one man. Another one or two won't make any difference." Like a pendulum, he aimed the shaky gun at Marc and me.

"You're wrong. It'll make a huge difference." Marc's voice quavered.

"Don't see how." Thomas stepped closer to Marc. He lowered the gun a few inches.

I wouldn't get a better opportunity. I leapt at Thomas and reached out for the gun. Thomas fought for control. The gun went off. *Boom.*

Chapter Thirty-Eight

"DAD!" DYLAN SCREAMED and fell to the ground moaning. He grabbed his arm.

"No, son." Thomas dropped the gun and fell to the ground beside Dylan.

Marc took the gun and removed the bullets before laying it on a rusty old water trough.

Tears streamed down my face. Thomas had killed Peter, and even if it was an accident, he'd tried to hide the fact.

Thomas blubbered. "I'm sorry, son. Sorry that I shot you and sorry for killing Peter."

With his good hand, Dylan reached out to his dad.

Whoop-whoop-whoop. The sound of sirens filled the air.

Thomas kissed the top of Dylan's head. "Listen to me. Clean up your life. I don't want to see you in prison. Quit gambling. Be better than your old man."

"I'll try, but how?"

My heart broke for these two messed-up men. "Maybe you can work for me with the dogs. Do you like dogs?"

"Sure." He panted.

"I plan to expand my business. We can talk about a job for you after a doctor takes care of your wound."

Thomas said, "It sounds like a decent offer. Take her up on it."

Dylan studied his dad. "You don't like Andi Grace. Never have."

"If you don't work for her, find a good job. When I get out of prison, I want a fresh start for both of us."

Woo-woo-woo. The sirens changed sound and dropped off. The brakes of multiple cars screeched to a stop.

My stomach flipped.

For over a decade, I'd always wanted to find the person who killed my parents. In the past few days, I'd wanted to find the person who killed Peter. Never had I imagined the two events would collide.

Wade and three deputies entered the stable with guns drawn.

Thomas raised his hands. "I'm turning myself in. I'm not armed. Take care of my boy. He's been shot."

Marc pointed to the antique water trough. "I laid his gun over there."

One deputy called for an ambulance, Wade retrieved the weapon, and another deputy patted down Thomas before cuffing the man. Wade knelt beside Dylan and checked his wound.

Never had I seen Thomas look so defeated. Angry, cocky, defiant, and smug, sure. Many times. Today he looked beaten. He met my gaze, and I'm not sure if I imagined it or not, but it seemed as if he looked relieved.

Chaos ensued in the carriage house.

An ambulance arrived. When medics took over caring for Dylan, Wade strode to us. "Andi Grace, we need to question Dylan as well as you and Marc. Nobody's going home anytime soon."

"What about Dylan's gunshot wound?"

"It only grazed him."

I lifted my chin. "Thomas said it was an accident that he killed Peter. They had an argument."

"We'll get everybody's story before deciding who goes home to-night."

"You can't still think I'm responsible for Peter's death. I've got witnesses. Dylan and Marc both heard Thomas confess."

Wade's nostrils flared. "Well, I haven't heard a confession yet. You may as well get comfortable until we can question you."

"There's something else you should know. We found Peter's white BMW in the stall over there. I bet it's the one that hit my parents the night they were killed."

Wade ran to that stall faster than I'd ever seen him move on a football field.

I didn't need forensic proof. It was the sports car that killed my parents.

Chapter Thirty-Nine

THE DEPUTIES questioned us for hours. By the time we left the plantation, I'd decided to refund all of my clients for the afternoon. I still managed to care for all of the animals, but it was much later than normal.

When I made it home, Sunny greeted me at the front door with a happy bark.

"Hey, girl. You need to go out? What kind of a dog walker neglects her best friend?" I let her out in the backyard, and I poured myself a Coke over lots of ice before heading outside.

I propped my feet on the deck rail and sipped my drink. What a day.

My phone vibrated with a text from Marc.

Good qualities: Kind, loyal, smart, funny, big heart, and beautiful. Determined and loves her family in a sacrificial way.

My heart melted, and it had nothing to do with the late June heat.

Sunny barked and raced around the perimeter of the yard. She was regaining her strength after the injury. I never got the chance to ask Thomas why he'd shot Sunny. I imagined he'd been scared of my German shepherd.

The runner who led all three dogs out with steaks was another story. I'd ask Thomas, but deep down, I still felt like it was Corey.

My phone vibrated again.

She even forgives those who've hurt her.

I started to reply, but another message came in from Marc.

Her life is full of family and friends.

```
I wonder if she has time to go on a
date?
```

I placed my hand over my heart. With trembling fingers, I tapped in my answer.

```
Yes, but only if you're the one asking.
```

The doorbell rang. I wanted to see Marc's reply and ignored the door.

Sunny barked and ran past me.

Keeping one eye on my phone, I opened the back door and followed Sunny inside.

The doorbell rang again.

"May as well answer it." I opened the door.

Marc stood there with a bouquet of flowers. Daisies, black-eyed Susans, and purple coneflowers.

I gasped and ran a hand over my messy hair. "Hi."

"Hi." He handed me the bouquet. "I thought we should make it official."

"They're lovely. Want to come inside?"

"Yes." He wore a turquoise polo and khaki shorts. His biceps filled the short sleeves. "Will you go on a date with me?"

"Absolutely." I stuffed the bouquet into an empty vase on the nearest table. A real date with Marc. My heart cartwheeled.

He pulled me close. "What about Danny?"

"Danny who?" I ran my fingers up his tanned arms. "Danny was my past. You're my present."

"Su-weet." He closed the small gap between us.

His lips touched mine, and fireworks exploded. When we pulled apart, I got my breathing under control. "Can you stay for dinner?"

"You cooked?"

"Ha. We can order takeout."

"Sounds like a plan." He nuzzled my neck, and I sighed. Dinner could wait a bit.

Epilogue

Six Months Later

AFTER MUCH TIME spent in prayer and reflection, I decided to keep Peter's plantation. A judge spoke to Danny and convinced him fighting me over the will would be a colossal waste of time. He wasn't happy, but Danny was smart enough to realize, as a small-town attorney, he'd present cases in front of the judge many times.

I stepped out of the plantation house with Juliet. "It's not too late to change your mind."

My best friend laughed. "Are you kidding? I sold Lovely Locks to Wendy Conn, and I moved out of my apartment this morning. I'm moving into the wonderful suite you had Griffin create."

"We're lucky he had time to change Peter's renovation into a suite for you." I wrapped my arm around her shoulder and pointed to the Waccamaw River. "You'll do an amazing job making Kennady Plantation a bed and breakfast."

"Don't forget destination wedding and the perfect setting for events." Her expression turned serious. "Have you forgiven Peter for killing your parents?"

With Peter's old BMW and the testimony provided by Thomas, the police solved the case of the hit-and-run driver who killed my parents. "I'm a work in progress. Get settled into the house. I'm going for a walk."

I made my way to the barn closest to the house where Dylan worked on converting the building into a place for me to board and train dogs. "Dylan, you in here?"

He appeared with Sunny by his side. "Hey, boss lady. Whatcha need?"

"I'm going to take Sunny for a walk. Later, I'd like to inspect the office and apartment we've constructed on the main floor."

"Sure."

Sunny and I strolled along the river trail toward Marc's place.

Instead of finding him covered in sawdust building a kayak, he drove up to his shed and hopped out of his truck. "This is a nice surprise."

"Where have you been all dressed up like that?"

He lifted a blue striped tie away from his button-down shirt. "I decided to start my own law practice in town."

"Why?" I released Sunny to explore.

"It's time for me to rejoin the human race instead of hiding out in my boat shed. I miss helping those in need and defending innocent people."

"I'm happy for you, Marc." The man amazed me every time we were together. His kindness and consideration would make him an excellent attorney in Heyward Beach. I stepped close and kissed his cheek.

He wrapped his arms around me. "Do you call that a congratulatory kiss?" I snuggled closer, touched his lips with mine, and gave him a kiss he wouldn't complain about.

Acknowledgements

I need to start by thanking my husband, Tim. He's been supportive since I first shared my dream of writing a novel. He's encouraged me with words and actions. Thank you so much, honey.

Thanks to the rest of my family who've listened to my dreams and understood my need to pursue them. Bill, Amanda, Brooke, Allie, and Cameron, thank you! Brooke deserves a special thanks for helping me come up with names for the dogs in my story. Allie also deserves a special thanks for coming to hear me speak about my writing journey. I also need to thank my youngest son Scott who still lived at home when I began writing. Between my work schedule and his tennis schedule, he sacrificed home cooked dinners for easy meals. Scott and his wife Kellianne have cheered me on every step of this journey. My parents, and Chris and Carol have also have been a good support system. I love you all.

Thanks to my critique group who have given me love and support on my writing journey, Sherrinda, Ketchersid, Connie Queen, Rhonda Herren Starnes, and Sharee Stover. Four other women who've encouraged me are Tina Radcliffe, Janet Ferguson, LeAnne Bristow, and Misty Beller. Thanks to all of you for cheering me on.

Thanks to my wonderful agent, Dawn Dowdle. I appreciate the faith you showed by signing me.

Thanks to everyone on my publishing team, and a huge thanks to Alexandra Christle and Debra Dixon.

Finally, thank you for reading *Bite the Dust*. I hope you enjoy it.

About the Author

JACKIE LAYTON spent most of her life in Kentucky working as a pharmacist and raising her family. But she always dreamed of living on a beach and writing full-time. When she and her husband finally moved to coastal South Carolina, a change of jobs allowed Jackie more time to write. She loves her life in the Low Country. Walks on the beach and collecting shells are a few of her new hobbies she enjoys when not writing.

Bite the Dust is the first book in Jackie's new Low Country Dog Walker Mystery series. Jackie also enjoys hearing from readers. Be sure to follow her on Facebook.

Made in the USA
Columbia, SC
04 June 2021